CHARLENE SANDS

THE COURTING OF WIDOW SHAW

D1324368

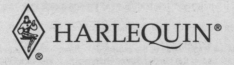

TORONTO • NEW YORK • LONDON
AMSTERDAM • PARIS • SYDNEY • HAMBURG
STOCKHOLM • ATHENS • TOKYO • MILAN • MADRID
PRAGUE • WARSAW • BUDAPEST • AUCKLAND

ISBN 0-373-29310-0

THE COURTING OF WIDOW SHAW

This edition published by arrangement with Harlequin Books S.A.

www.eHarlequin.com

Printed in U.S.A.

To my dear friend Geraldine Sparks.
Your friendship, wisdom and elegance
are a wonderful source of inspiration.

And to Carol and Joe Curesky—
dear friends through the miles, but always close in my heart.
Thank you for your love and support.

Prologue

Flames disturbed the black starless night with brilliant blinding color. Steven Harding immediately raced his horse in that direction, the red-orange blaze his beacon, guiding him to a small house outside of town. Past midnight, Steven knew most miners slept the sleep of the dead, too exhausted by a workday filled with breathless heat to allow the scent of smoke off in the distance, to wake them.

As he came to a clearing, he saw the burning house. His mare spooked, the smoke and violent flames making her jittery. "Whoa, there, Fancy." He dismounted and quickly walked her back behind a tree, shielding her from the view and tied the reins to a tree branch.

With a kerchief to his mouth, he ran to the house, squinting his eyes against the billowing cloud of smoke. Ashes flew up and swirled in the air, the scent of wood-burning destruction all around.

Dread filled his heart when he saw her.

Gloria Mae Shaw, his nemesis, the woman out to destroy his mother's livelihood, lay on the ground, just steps away from the burning building, holding a bloody knife in her hand. And just in front of her, a man who was most likely her husband, lay dead in a red pool, cut up bad from a knife wound to the chest.

The woman moaned.

Steven went down on his knees, gently lifting her up in his arms. Her beautiful face was bruised, battered brutally, and Steven instantly knew her pain had not been caused by the flames, but by the hands of a man.

Steven cursed under his breath. What kind of man could be so cruel? What fool thought to ease his hardships and frustration on a lovely young woman? Steven pushed blond strands of her hair away, mindful to keep his fingers light on her face. "Glory. Glory, can you hear me?"

She moaned again, a slight whimper of agony that slashed straight through his gut. Wood splintered, a big blast caused by the wild flames. Steven had no choice but to move her, to get her to safety. Soon the cabin would collapse, and they'd be engulfed and surrounded by fire.

He eased her up into his arms. Good God. She'd been a nuisance, a thorn in his mother's side, but Steven had always secretly admired her. He'd dreamed of one day holding the golden-haired beauty, having the right to touch her intimately, with reverence, the way she deserved. It had been a fool notion for sure, since they lived in different worlds, he being brought up in a brothel and she, the daughter of the late Reverend Caldwell. But he'd never imagined holding her like this—with pain trembling from her lips and fire ready to end her life. No, his dreams of Glory hadn't been tainted with bitter reality, they'd been mere fantasy. But now, as he gazed down at her near-breathless body, he knew he had to help her.

Dark bruises testified to the treatment she'd endured. If she'd done this, if she'd killed her husband in order to defend herself, Steven couldn't blame her. But others would, murder being a vindictive crime that warranted proper punishment.

And Steven would protect her. He'd take her away and hide her for the time being, allowing her injured body to heal until they could get at the truth.

He owed her that and probably much more.

With the utmost care, he carried her limp body to his horse and mounted quietly, his movements cautious as he adjusted her in his arms. Like a raggedy doll, she clung to him, barely.

"Just a while longer, Glory. Hold on," he whispered then eased his horse forward, back to Virginia City.

To the last place anyone would ever think to look for Gloria Mae Shaw.

Chapter One

Virginia City, Nevada
1869

Steven stared at Glory's sleeping form resting on his bed, her breaths shallow but steady. Her head moved slightly, pressing against the goose-down pillows and matting down her thick blond hair. It seemed more an involuntary movement, a struggle to find comfort under the thin cotton quilt than a sign of her awakening. He'd listened to her anguished moans in the night, a sound he hoped he'd never hear again.

The door creaked open. "Steven," Ruby whispered, popping her head inside, "you sure you don't want to call the doctor?"

Steven strode quietly to the door, giving a last quick glance at Glory before stepping out of the room. He faced Ruby. "We can't chance it." He filled his lungs, drawing air deeply. When he let down his guard, the fatigue he'd battled during the night hit him with unflinching accuracy. "No doubt they'll be looking for her in the morning."

"She killed her husband," Ruby said, shaking her head. "Can't say as I blame her none."

Steven scrubbed his jaw, wondering. "I don't know that for sure." Although he'd seen the evidence, the bloody knife in her hand, her husband's gutted body beside her, Steven just wasn't certain.

"The gal's trouble, Steven. You shouldn't have brought her here. Your mama would be the first to say so."

Steven winced and searched Ruby's light-brown eyes. She was a favorite at Rainbow House, intelligent enough to engage in conversation and pretty enough to keep the men lining up. She was one of the oldest, too, nearing thirty, and one his mother held in high regard. "My mother wouldn't want her strung up, Ruby. Don't forget Glory's father saved my mother's life."

"He took a bullet for her. I know. Everyone knows that. Reverend Caldwell saved Lorene. And we're all glad he did. It's a shame he had to die because of it, but that's what got his daughter hell-bent on closing down Rainbow House. She's out for revenge, posting those signs, writing articles on the sins of the flesh and stirring up trouble."

"Nothing's gonna close down Rainbow House, Ruby. My mother's got the finest house on C Street."

Ruby chuckled, a grin spreading wide across her face. "I know that, too. But what were you thinking, bringing a young gal like that in here? I bet that gal's never even stepped over to this side of town before, much less entered a whorehouse. Soon as she gets wind of where you brought her—"

"There'll be hell to pay. I know. But I can't take her to my place."

"''Cause it's not finished?''

"Hmmm, and the ranch doesn't have the comforts she needs to heal proper-like. She's better off here in a warm bed, with all the necessities."

His ranch house, his dream of starting a business of his own, was nearing completion. He'd worked on neighboring ranches outside of Virginia City for years, making his way as a wrangler, then as foreman, earning enough cash to build a ranch of his own. At Lorene's insistence, he'd left Rainbow House when he was fifteen. His mother had set down the rules. He wasn't to partake of the "ladies" of the house. She'd wanted a better life for her son. He understood that reasoning better now, at twenty-six, than he had at the age of fifteen.

But he'd kept a room on the third floor, alongside his mother's room, for the times when he was in town. That's where he'd brought Glory. He'd have to keep her here for the time being. It was the safest place for her to hide.

"Or maybe you're thinking it's not suitable being alone way out there with her?" Ruby asked, sidling up next to him. "Is that it, Steven? You don't trust yourself being alone with Gloria Mae Shaw?"

Steven narrowed his eyes and pressed his point. "This is the safest place for her. Nobody'd ever come looking for her here. And Emmie knows something about doctoring. She'll see that Glory heals proper."

Ruby snickered, baiting him. "She's a pretty little thing, when she's not all banged up."

Steven frowned at the reminder of the beating she'd endured. Why, Glory was just about the prettiest woman he'd ever laid eyes on, all spitfire and deter-mination, her light-blue eyes sparkling, her hair glowing gold under the sunlight. He'd seen her a time or two marching down the streets of Virginia City, with those doggone silly posters, nailing them into wood posts, straightening them up like one would tidy up a picture, as if that would make a difference.

"And who do you suppose is gonna watch over her all day? Lorene's gone on a trip to San Francisco. She's not here to mother the gal. Your mama put me in charge and I aim to do a good job with the girls. So don't you go pointing your finger at me, I've got enough to handle. And the others already said they want no part in doctoring the troublemaker."

"She's the one in trouble now, Ruby. I've got to help her. If her father hadn't died saving my mother's life, Glory wouldn't have rushed into marriage with that no-account miner. She wouldn't be lying in there, struggling to breathe."

"She made her choices, just like the rest of us."

Steven nodded, understanding the plight of Ruby and some of the other girls. Many hadn't been left with any choice but to work in a brothel. His mother had done the same when his father abandoned his family. Lorene had made do and tried her hardest to give her young son a good life. She'd done what she had to in order to survive. Steven had come to understand that. She was what she was. But Steven couldn't fault her. She was a good businesswoman and kind to her girls, taking them in and caring for them when they, too, had had nowhere else to go. "And didn't Lorene help all of you, when your choices went bad?"

A look of resignation crossed Ruby's face and she sighed. "So, you're intent on keeping her here?"

"I am," Steven said, realizing now he had no other

choice. Glory needed tending. She needed someplace to stay. As far as he knew, she had no other family in town, aside from her brother-in-law, Ned Shaw. But would he doctor and protect her if he suspected she'd killed his brother? Steven doubted that.

Glory lay injured and alone in that bed with nowhere to go and no one but Steven to rely upon. "You've got to keep this a secret, Ruby. And make sure the girls know to keep their mouths buttoned up good and tight. You tell them we're doing this for Lorene as much as for that girl in there. Lorene would want Glory to be tended properly. She'd want her protected."

"The girls won't say a word."

"I intend to keep her safe, Ruby. I owe her that much."

Ruby smiled then and lifted her red satin gown as she turned to head downstairs. "She's all yours, Steven."

Steven stood outside Glory's door, shaking his head with a frown pulling at his lips. The woman didn't know him. She wouldn't *want* to know him. But he saved her from death. And he'd protect her. That's where it would end.

Ruby had been wrong about Glory.

She wasn't all his.

Glory Mae Shaw could never be his.

Steven reentered the room. It was almost morning, but he didn't trust leaving Glory alone for too long. He stood at the foot of his large bed, noting the empty space next to Glory, the inviting sheets calling to him. A fool notion of sleeping next to Glory, just to comfort her cries in the night, crept into his brain. But he didn't dare climb in. Glory wasn't a woman who'd appreciate waking up with a strange man in her bed.

He scratched his head, watching her sleep. Her breathing seemed steadier now, and a bit stronger. Emmie had given him instructions on how to dose the laudanum. She'd said it was sure to ease the pain, allowing the patient to get some rest. And the pain-killer seemed to be working.

Steven let go a long sigh, dismissing the comfortable bed. He pulled up the cane-back chair he'd spent most the night in, and planted himself down. Folding his arms across his middle, he slouched a bit, trying for comfort but getting only more of the same, an awkward respite.

But soon, Glory's whimpers, her low muted cries woke him. He rose and went to her swiftly. She thrashed about with eyes closed, body swaying and her head tossing to and fro wildly. Coming down on the bed, he lifted her gently, taking her into his arms. "Shh. Shh, Glory," he murmured into her hair. "Shh. Go back to sleep."

She moaned softly. So pitifully softly that Steven barely heard her.

"Shh. It's okay. I've got you. You're safe now," he whispered again and again, until she calmed down, her cries quieting. "You're safe now," he said once more, lowering his head against the pillow and taking her with him. He held her loosely, her face against his chest. He waited until her ragged breathing steadied once again, then closed his eyes.

Allowing much-needed sleep to claim them both.

Morning dawned too soon and much too bright, fighting through the darkness to bathe the room in sunlight. Steven grimaced against the light, squinting his eyes open. He didn't need to turn to know that Glory's soft body curled up beside him, her rounded curves pressed against him, making his tired bones come alive in a quick flash. He had one arm wrapped around her shoulders, her head on the pillow next to him. She appeared better this morning, her restlessness from the night seeming to have faded into a peaceful sleep.

Steven inched his way off the bed, making certain not to cause a disturbance. He stood over her, as he had so often during the night, watching her sleep.

Good Lord. He'd slept with her.

And the irony seemed far too harsh to lift his spirits this morning. Because in the past, he'd had thoughts of Reverend Caldwell's daughter, of holding her, of touching her and making her his. But Steven wasn't a fool. He knew her to be a decent woman, one who'd rather be cast off than take up with the likes of him, a man who'd been raised in a whorehouse, a man who knew the "soiled doves" and considered them, friends.

Steven moved away from Glory and shed his clothes quickly, removing garments that had been layered with ash and smoke from the fire. He splashed water on his face from the gilded pitcher on his dresser, dressed in clean clothes, then combed his dark hair and brushed off his dusty boots before putting them on.

He strode down three flights of stairs, the third floor being designated for Lorene and her family, the second floor leading to the famous Rainbow rooms, each one decorated in a different color, suiting the women who entertained there. The main floor housed both the kitchen and entertaining parlors.

As he descended the stairs, Steven marveled at the contrast between the deathly still morning and the late-night goings-on at Rainbow House. At any given time during the evening, giddy laughter filled the halls and piano music poured out from the main parlor. The scent of cigar smoke flavored the rooms, along with the distinguishable pungent smell of liquor. Whiskey. Jamaican rum. French wine. Always the finest—always the best. Rainbow House had a reputation for pretty girls and the finest amenities.

As a young boy, Steven had always enjoyed the silence of the morning best. Back then, he could pretend he lived in a real house, with a mother who worked over the cookstove making crescent biscuits and sliced ham for breakfast, and a father who'd take him out for a day of regular chores. Well, he'd gotten that life, deplete of the family, when he'd taken up ranching. Only the mother had been a craggy old "cookie" named Marty who baked the best damn cornbread in ten counties and the father had been a ranch foreman who shouted tall orders from an even taller horse.

"Morning, Mattie," Steven said to the cook as he entered the large kitchen. Two cast-iron stoves banked one wall, next to a pie safe and a full-sized pantry. The cupboards held dishes and serving pieces from all around the world. A good meal was something Lorene Harding believed in. And the cook she'd chosen for the job had been her latest rescue, a sixteen-year-old girl who'd run away from an orphanage. She'd displayed culinary skills that had simply amazed Lorene.

"Morning, Mr. Harding." She cast him a shy smile and turned back to her preparations. The ladies usually didn't rise until noon or later, so Mattie always had time to fix up something mouth watering for supper.

"Mattie, how long have you worked here?"

She whirled around, wiping her hands on her apron. Her slightly freckled face held a perpetual flush of color. Steven presumed the heat of the kitchen caused it. He'd rarely seen her anyplace else but the kitchen. "I've been here six months, sir."

He smiled and kept his tone light. "And how many times have I asked you to call me Steven?"

"Oh," she said on a giggle. "I'm sorry, sir. Yes, sir. Steven." She nodded, and the rosy color in her face intensified. She turned around to stir something in a pot. "Are you here for breakfast? I've got oatmeal cooking, and I can warm some bread to have with peach preserves."

Steven poured himself a mug of coffee and sat down at a rectangular table that went nearly the length of the kitchen. "That sounds fine."

He took a sip of coffee, allowing the steamy liquid to slide down his throat and fill his empty stomach. "I'll need some broth later on, to take up to our…guest."

"Yes, sir. Is she…is she going to be all right?" Mattie continued stirring what he knew now to be oatmeal. "I heard about the fire and the…beating."

Steven's gut clenched every time he thought about Glory's injuries. "I think she'll recover just fine. At least Emmie seems to think so and she's a good judge of these things. But Mattie, it's important that you don't speak about her to anyone. I've asked Ruby to tell the girls the same. I know I can trust all of you.''

''Yes, sir. I won't tell a soul about her.''

''Good, I appreciate it. And Mattie?''

''Yes, sir?''

''Don't call me sir.'' He chuckled quietly to himself when her face flamed again.

With his belly full, Steven climbed the stairs again, anxious to see if Glory had woken up. She had had no fever last night, which he thought a good sign. But the bruises to her body had been unsightly in the dark and he could only imagine what they looked like in the light of day.

Steven entered his bedroom to find Glory taking peaceful breaths as she continued to sleep. On the bedside table, he found a jar of salve that had been deposited by Emmie, no doubt. She'd told him to wash Glory's body, then apply the salve to all the bruises. Steven had hoped Emmie would have done the deed herself, leaving him in the clear. But Emmie, like Ruby and all the others, wanted no part of the woman who'd love nothing better than to run them all out of town.

Steven sighed. He couldn't blame them. Gloria Mae Shaw had made a nuisance out of herself, but he believed she had never posed any real threat to Rainbow House. Lorene hadn't worried about it, but then his mother wouldn't find fault with the Reverend's daughter, no matter what she'd wanted to do.

Steven poured water into a bowl and set it down on the bedside table. He took a seat on the edge of the bed, carefully peeling back the covers. Glory's long hair covered most of the skin exposed by the ripped garment she wore. The dark-brown dress, tattered now, had to come off.

Perhaps it was a good thing she was in a deep drugged sleep or he doubted she'd let him come anywhere near her. But her bruises needed tending and Steven was the only one to do it.

He came around to her backside and unbuttoned the dress. With care, he lowered the dress down, exposing her shoulders, and lower yet to uncover most of her back. He slipped the dress off easily after that, deciding to leave the chemise, her cream-colored undergarment, on for her modesty and his own sanity.

Steven's hands trembled as he lifted the chemise to peer down her back. Thankfully, there were no bruises, only the sight of soft glowing skin that led down to the curve of her spine.

He took a deep swallow.

Doctoring a woman like Glory made his nerves go raw.

Sensations ripped straight through him, but he fought them off. The woman needed help, not his schoolboy gawking.

He knew, judging from the swollen purple marks on her face, that most of Glory's injuries had occurred facing her attacker. She'd taken the brunt of his abuse head-on. So Steven lifted himself off that side of the bed to come around to Glory's front. He sat down and gazed at her, noting her skin discolored in many places, the god-awful marks of aggression all over her lovely body.

He took up a cloth, dipped it into the bowl and pressed it to her face first, bathing her with coolness.

She let out a small sigh. Not a cry this time, but a whimper of slight pleasure. Steven let out a breath, relieved he hadn't caused her more pain. "Glory, can you hear me?"

She sighed quietly again but her swollen eyes remained closed.

Steven kept the cloth on her face, gently dabbing at her bruises for long minutes. Then he moved the cloth down to cover a bruise on her left shoulder. He dipped and redipped the cloth several times, cleansing and cooling the area all the while his muscles tensed at the unjust brutality the woman had suffered.

He couldn't fault her if she had killed her husband.

They'd get to the truth eventually, but for now, she needed to heal.

Steven dipped the cloth once more and noted three dark and slightly elevated bruises on her chest. He bathed those as well, allowing the water to seep down under her chemise, keeping her modesty intact, somewhat. But his plan went awry, since the chemise, when wet, lent a view that Steven couldn't tear his gaze away from. Small, round ripe breasts exposed by wet cotton held his complete attention, nearly knocking the stuffing out of him.

"Lord help me," he mumbled as he held his breath and continued to bathe her. His groin went tight. His mind rebelled. Rosy peaks pressed against the flimsy fabric outlined Glory's beautiful form, and try as he might, Steven hadn't the willpower to shift his attention. He sat there, mesmerized. How on earth was he to rub her skin with salve? Wasn't that too much to ask of an honorable man?

Steven covered her, then bounded up from the bed. Moving to the window, he glanced out, seeing nothing but the image of Glory, lying in his bed, nearly naked and needing his attention.

"God almighty," he cursed, willing his body back to normalcy. Steven wasn't a man to lose control. He wasn't a man who feared the very sight of a woman.

She made a sound. Not a moan or a cry, but words. She'd mumbled words. Steven whirled around abruptly, her low raspy voice startling him. "Glory?"

Had she spoken? Was that voice hers, or had he imagined those words only in his addled brain?

He moved to her side. "Glory?"

The woman struggled to open her eyes, but didn't quite achieve her goal. Instead, another whispered sound came forth. "Where...am...I?"

Chapter Two

Through a haze of pain, Gloria heard a man's voice. She wrestled with the sound, her mind too clouded to recognize who was calling to her. But whomever it was kept calling her Glory.

Glory.

No one ever called her Glory—except her beloved father and then only within the confines of their home. To the outside world ever-prudent Reverend Jonathan Caldwell had used her birth name of Gloria Mae.

Perhaps it was her father calling? Perhaps He was ready to take her and the good Lord saw fit to send her father as messenger.

"Glory."

The voice called to her again, but it wasn't her father. This time she was certain. How often had she dreamed of hearing his tone and tenor just once more? But his life had been taken abruptly and far too soon. Sadly she realized she'd never hear her father's voice again.

Gloria battled to open her eyes, but it was as though clay bricks weighed them down. The effort cost her too much energy so she gave up for now. It hurt to breathe. Everything ached. And she remembered nothing of what had happened to her. But she felt safe, for some odd reason. And cared for. Even though she didn't know where she was.

"Glory?"

It was the man's urgent voice again, calling to her.

Her lips were swollen, her mouth dry. "Water." She breathed out, and the weak muted sound of her voice surprised her.

A cool wet cloth was pressed to her lips. "Drink up the moisture for now," the man said. Gloria obeyed, allowing the liquid to seep through her lips. It soothed her parched mouth and slid down a throat that was sore and hoarse. She tried opening her mouth just a little wider to take in more water, but she couldn't do it, the pain nearly cracking her face in two.

She begged her mind for answers. What had happened to her? Who was this man tending to her? A doctor? Was she in a hospital? The last thing she remembered was standing over the cookstove making Boone his evening meal. He'd been unusually unsettled, discouraged with the progress of his staked claim. He'd gone outside to have a smoke, as he often did when he'd had an unproductive day. He'd all but given up on his claim.

Things hadn't gone as planned in their marriage. Boone had been unhappy with the little money he'd made on his claim. He'd been so sure, so very certain he would hit a rich strike. Ore had been plentiful in Virginia City, the Comstock Lode making many men wealthy. Boone had wanted a part of that wealth for himself.

Gloria searched her mind, hoping to recall what

had happened after that, but it was as though her mind refused to remember. Her head ached terribly. Maybe later, once the throbbing stopped, maybe then, she'd remember.

"Do you want more water?"

The man spoke softly, but she heard the rich deep tone of his voice. Again, she wondered about him. Who was he? And where had he taken her? What had occurred that had wiped all memory from her mind? Slowly, for it was the only way she could answer, she shook her head.

She felt his presence on the bed, could hear him breathing, then pausing to inhale deeply. She heard a whoosh when he let his breath rush out. "I have salve for your wounds," he said. "It will help you heal. Don't be afraid. I have to touch you."

Glory nodded slightly, the best she could do. She couldn't fight him if he had ill intentions, but somehow she didn't believe that to be the case. She only wished that he had answered her question, one that took all of her effort to ask.

Where was she?

A strong but ever-so-gentle hand came to her face as he worked foul-smelling liniment into her cheek, her lips and her chin with light fingers. Gloria's father had once used an Indian remedy on her as a child when she'd taken a terrible fall, hurting her knee. When she'd protested, he told her, the worse it smelled the faster she would heal.

Gloria decided if that were true, she'd be good as new very soon. And as the salve soaked into her skin, she did feel a bit better, its healing effects already taking hold.

"You have bruises on your chest that need tending," the man stated with quiet regard. "It has to be done."

And then, after a long pause, he added, "I won't hurt you."

Why she placed her faith in him, she couldn't fathom. Except that she'd been with only one man in her lifetime. And this man, this stranger had already displayed more tenderness toward her than Boone had, the husband who'd pledged his life to her.

Gloria wondered about Boone. Where was he? Was he hurt as well? And if not, why wasn't he here, tending to her? Fitful imaginings stirred in her brain, too many disturbing questions to deal with now. She closed off her mind, emptying it of worrisome images.

The man brought her covers down and as the air hit her chemise she realized she had been bathed. Moisture still clung to her, plastering the garment fully up against her body. The sour odor of the salve drifted up, flavoring the surrounding air.

"Try to relax," he said. "I'll be quick." And he rubbed the ointment into the skin just above her breasts.

She pressed her eyes open.

At best she saw him through swollen slits. He sat so close, his gaze focused on his task. She didn't know him. Or did she? She couldn't tell, her eyes blurred from sharp light and clouded vision.

But the tingling sensation created from his light caresses traveled clear down to her toes. His fingertips, the slight pressure on her bruised skin caused uncanny goose bumps to erupt on her arms as he continued the massage.

Gloria had never exposed herself to a man this way.

She'd never felt so vulnerable, so at a loss. She was at his mercy. Outwardly, she remained calm, for it hurt to move too much, but inwardly, Gloria panicked. His large hands worked on her tender skin, in the valley between her breasts and farther down, nearly grazing her nipples from under her chemise, bringing shame and desire, even through the pain. Surely this was sinful.

Surely, she shouldn't feel pleasure from a man other than her husband. She squeezed her eyes shut, unsure and not ready to meet his gaze.

"I've got to get to your stomach." He removed his hand from her chest and as he lifted the chemise up high on her torso a rush of air cooled her stomach. He covered her with the sheet then slipped his hand under, rubbing salve to the bruises there. A mortifying minute passed, as she laid upon the bed, completely helpless, placing ill-advised trust in the stranger.

"All through," he said with obvious relief. Perhaps the task had been as daunting to him as it had been to her. "Emmie says this will help you heal. You'll feel better soon."

One sole finger caressed her cheek, trailing down to her throat in a soft touch of encouragement. "I'll be back later. Get some rest."

Through closed eyes, Gloria gave a slow nod.

Her waking minutes had been exhausting.

And soon after he closed the door, she slept.

Steven stood at Grady's Saloon at the juncture of C Street and Union, sipping a cold beer. He'd spent the better part of the day with Glory, watching her, checking on her, hoping she'd awaken so that he could speak with her and maybe give her some of

Mattie's beef broth. But Glory hadn't woken and he needed to get out of the house for a breath of fresh air. And a drink.

Thoughts of Glory Shaw had blistered his mind. He went from thinking her a murderer, a faultless one at that, to a saintly woman, Reverend Caldwell's beloved daughter, to a lovely creature who'd sparked his mind and body with lusty images.

"Ready for another?" Grady asked, reaching for the beer pitcher.

Steven figured the whole dang pitcher wouldn't help what ailed him. He refused. "Nope. One'll do me fine."

He had to keep his wits together. If there were talk about Glory, about the death of Boone Shaw, he'd want to know. So he stood by the bar, sipping beer and listening.

As luck would have it, Sheriff Brimley entered, curling a finger around his long mustache and greeting Steven with a nod. In a town where men outnumbered women more than one hundred to one, just about every man in town knew Rainbow House, the sheriff being a patron himself.

The sheriff took up space next to him at the bar. Steven immediately tensed, but sipped his beer as he leaned against the top of the bar. "I saw Lorene leave on the stage a few days ago. She still out of town?" Sheriff Brimley asked.

"Yep. She took a business trip. She'll be back soon though. She's bringing the girls some fancy duds from San Francisco."

The sheriff ordered a whiskey. "That's a good thing, then. I got some news she won't be happy to hear, being as she feels responsible for that young gal losing her father. It seems Boone Shaw, that placer miner who married Reverend Caldwell's daughter, is dead. House burned down to the ground, but seems Boone didn't die in the fire.''

Steven took another sip of beer, keeping a calm disinterested tone. ''How do you suppose he died?''

The sheriff shrugged, a frown yanking at his mustache. ''Knife wounds. He'd been cut up some. And worse yet, a neighbor found the knife that done it. Seems Gloria Shaw is missing. It don't look good for her.''

''Why's that?'' Steven asked, looking straight ahead, trying not to appear to eager.

''Everybody in town knows that girl got a wagon-load of grief when she married Boone. He wasn't the husband she thought she was getting. Now with Boone dead and her missing, well...I'd hate to think it of her, being Jonathan Caldwell's daughter and all.''

''You said there was a fire. You sure she didn't die inside the house?''

''Nah. I just got back from checking out there with my deputies. There ain't no bodies in that house. I'm putting the word out to bring Gloria Mae Shaw in for questioning. She's got a whole lot to answer to.'' The sheriff finished off his whiskey then shook his head, sighing. ''Sometimes, my job just ain't easy.''

''I'll be sure to let Lorene know, when she gets back in town.'' Steven gulped down the last of his beer. ''Good talking to you, Sheriff.''

Sheriff Brimley nodded. ''Same here.'' Then he turned his attention to the barkeep. ''Hey, Grady. I'm asking all the saloon owners to put the word out. Gloria Mae Shaw is wanted for questioning and the possible murder of her husband. Anybody who's seen her should let me know immediately. I'd appreciate it if you asked around, and kept your eyes and ears open.''

Grady nodded, wiping dry a glass. ''Will do, Roy. I'll listen up good, but I only saw that girl once in a while coming out of church on Sunday and she don't appear to be no killer.''

Sheriff Brimley sighed again. ''Her husband's been murdered and so far, she hasn't come forth. I got neighbors who tell me they heard a ruckus earlier that night. Thought they heard the two fighting. If she killed her husband, I've got to bring her in.''

''Married people fight,'' Grady said with a shrug.

''Like I said, I've got to check it out. I'll be back in a day or two. If you hear something before that, you come get me.''

Steven waited until Roy Brimley exited the bar, then he strode out like a man who had time on his hands. But in truth, he was anxious to get back to Rainbow House to see Glory again.

He'd been right in taking her into hiding. She wouldn't stand a chance otherwise. If Sheriff Brimley thought her suspect already without having seen her bruises, then surely he would have jailed her immediately once he laid eyes on her. Not that a woman didn't have call to defend herself from an abusive husband, but the law stopped short of murder. And Roy Brimley was a hard man, trying to keep peace and justice in a town that refused both. If Brimley thought Glory guilty, he wouldn't hesitate to arrest her.

Steven ambled down the busy street.

He only half hoped Glory was awake.

Because then he'd have to question her.
And he might not like what she had to say.

Glory pushed herself up on the bed and opened her eyes, squinting against the dim light. She couldn't tell where she was. She couldn't guess the time of day. Having been shut tight from the swelling, her eyes struggled to focus. And dragging her body upright had cost her dearly.

She didn't know who had brought her here or why. She was beholden to the man who had taken care of her. He'd had a gentle touch, but it was time for Glory to put her pain aside. It was time she tried to figure out what had happened to her. It was time to get some answers.

Surprise registered as she darted quick glances around the room. The furniture was stately, made of the richest walnut and mahogany, with marble-topped dressers and gilded washstands. And the bed itself was enormous. Dark emerald curtains covered windows with ornate brass rods. A lovely oak-carved screen partially hid a porcelain bathtub. She'd never stayed anywhere nearly so elegant. Certainly, she wasn't in a hospital, which probably meant the stranger tending to her wasn't a doctor.

Even more mysterious was the fact that she'd heard female voices from time to time, but they'd never entered her room. At least, not while she'd been awake.

Only the man cared for her.

And just as she'd envisioned what the man had looked like from the tiny bit of him she'd viewed earlier, he stood at the doorway, appearing somewhat startled.

"You're awake." He closed the door behind him,

but didn't approach, his gaze taking her in, assessing her. And she was instantly reminded of earlier, when he'd had his hands on her, rubbing the salve on her skin. She pushed that mortifying picture from her mind to take a better look at him.

He was tall and broad of shoulder. He wore a hat, black in color, a shade or two darker than his hair. His eyes were brown—earth-brown her father would say, like rich soil begging to be planted. He had a strong rugged face with a jaw that right now appeared hard as granite.

"Can you speak?" he asked.

Glory closed her eyes. She didn't know if she could speak out of a mouth still swollen and bruised. She had the feeling she wouldn't want to peer into the cheval mirror on the other side of the room, for fear of how she might appear. If she looked anything like she felt, seeing her image might just set her healing back for days.

She tested her lips, opening them slightly and wincing at the pain. "I...think...so."

Her voice drifted, sounding ever so faint.

The man approached slowly, never taking his eyes from her. He removed his hat and hung it on a peg. "Good. But don't tire yourself out."

He pulled up a chair and sat down. "You've been hurt bad and it's going to take time to heal proper-like."

Gloria nodded. "Where...am...I?" she managed to ask.

"In a safe place."

His ominous answer didn't quell her curiosity, but she knew she only had minutes before she'd fall into a deep sleep again, the effort to sit up, to try to talk, draining her energy.

"I found you," he said. "There was a fire at your house."

"Fire?" She got that one word out, but it didn't mean anything to her. She couldn't remember anything of that night. Last she'd seen of Boone, he'd gone outside to have a smoke. She'd stayed in the kitchen, cooking his evening meal.

"Your husband is dead."

"Boone." Gloria's mind flashed an image of her husband, his sharp temper and sour moods. She'd tried to be a good wife to him, but early on she'd discovered she'd made a terrible mistake in marrying him. She didn't want to see him dead. But the love she'd had for him had died long ago. Yet, a single tear trickled down her cheek. He must have died in the fire.

"He'd been stabbed to death. Murdered."

Gloria blinked her eyes, her heart racing as fast as her mind. Someone had killed Boone.

The man touched her cheek, wiping away the tear. Gloria didn't flinch and she didn't turn away from him. Perhaps she was too weary or perhaps a slow tentative trust had developed while he'd cared for her. Either way, Gloria was too stunned at this horrible news to worry about the stranger right now.

Once again, she searched her mind for answers, but came away with nothing. She couldn't recall a thing.

"Did he do this to you? Did he beat you?" He spoke with compassion, but the usual soft edge of his tone had vanished.

Gloria swallowed. She struggled to take in a lungful of air. She had no answers. "I...don't know."

The man tried to hide his frustration, but she saw it in the twist of his mouth, the narrowing of his eyes. "You don't know?"

"I...can't...remember."

He leaned back in his chair and stared at her.

"You'd better rest," he said, after a time. "Now that you're awake, I'll bring you broth. You must be half-starved. Close your eyes until I come back."

Gloria's stomach seemed to be working fine. It grumbled aloud and there was no need to answer. The man smiled and got up to leave.

After all he'd told her, Gloria's mind had clouded with one thought after another, until they lay atop each other in her mind. It would take time for her to sort them all out, but she had one question for him. Something she would muster the energy to ask. "Wait," she called out quietly.

He turned just as his hand reached the doorknob.

"Who...are...you?" she asked.

He paused, as if making up his mind how to answer. All she wanted was his name. And after a long moment, he responded.

"My name is Steven."

Chapter Three

As the days went by, Gloria became stronger. She'd spent the better part of those days sleeping, her body needing the rest. And each one of those days, the man called Steven had come to wash her, to apply more salve on her bruises and to feed her light meals. Even in her sleep, she'd felt his presence, knew instinctively he'd been there, watching her, perhaps worrying over her.

She'd tried many times to get more answers from him, but he had a knack for being evasive, promising her that once she was strong enough, he would answer all of her questions. She estimated she'd been here five days.

And today she felt strong enough to hear his answers.

Gloria lifted up from the bed and placed both feet on the carpeted floor. With determination, she stood up, taking a moment to gain her balance. The room spun. Gloria paused, letting that sensation pass. Then once again, she moved, taking a step forward on weakened legs. She almost stumbled, then righted herself.

Then Steven walked in.

Gloria immediately tied the silk wrapper that had magically appeared one day on the edge of her bed, tighter around her waist.

"What are you doing, Glory?" he asked in a stern voice. He came forward, curving an arm around her shoulders.

"I'm getting up," she said, trying to hide her frustration. "And my name is Gloria Mae, not Glory."

He ignored her comment regarding her name. She still didn't know how he knew her, which baffled her because she couldn't recall ever meeting him. He'd refused her that information each time she'd asked.

"It's too soon to get up," he stated.

He stood close, held her tight and with tender care. The scent of him, fresh, clean and perfectly groomed struck her with clarity. She liked the way he smelled. She liked him. He was kind and good to her, but anger boiled up inside regardless. She couldn't tamp it down no matter how hard she tried.

He held all the answers, but denied her that privilege. "It's not too soon. I'm ready. I can walk."

He huffed out a breath. "Okay," he countered, raising his voice.

She moved slightly, her knees buckling. He caught her, gripping her arms gently—always so gently. "You don't need to do this today."

"I'll tell you what I need, Steven. I need to stay out of that bed. I need to move. I need to walk. But most of all, I need a bath!"

Steven's lips curved up in a smile he tried to hide. "A bath?"

Then he laughed, a full-out flagrant laugh that caught her completely off guard.

She chuckled, too, the sound so distant, so foreign as though it was coming from someone else. How long had it been since she'd laughed? She couldn't remember. And she discovered something else as her chuckles died down, the laughter erupting in her chest had caused her no pain. She was truly healing, thanks to this man. Thanks to Steven.

"Okay, a bath it is," he said, in that compromising way he had. "I'll make you a deal. If you go back to bed, I'll bring up hot water so you can take a bath."

Gloria twisted her mouth. She wanted to bathe so badly she could almost feel the water droplets caressing her skin, cleansing her body and warming her unsettled bones. "Deal."

Steven helped her back to bed. "I'll be up in a few minutes."

Gloria rested back against her bed pillows, once again wondering about Steven. Today, without compromise, she'd find out where she was. Today, she'd find out about Steven and why he was so determined to help her.

Today. Sometime.

Definitely *after* her bath.

Steven entered the kitchen to find all of Lorene's girls seated around the table, eating their afternoon meal. He was somewhat annoyed at them for not being willing to help with Glory and her needs, leaving him to do the most inappropriate, yet necessary things to the woman.

"Mattie, when you get time, heat up several pots of water, please."

"Yes, sir, Steven." Her face flamed at using his

given name, but she smiled this time. Maybe the shy girl was coming around.

"Do you take an afternoon bath, Señor Steven?" Carmen asked in her heavy Mexican accent.

"I bet it's the girl who wants the bath," Julia chimed in, after forking a chunk of beef stew.

"Ah, and Steven's going to *help* her, right?" Merry asked.

Steven glanced at their smiling faces, all bright and eager to hear about Glory. "No," he said adamantly. "I'm not going to *help* her," then added, "exactly." He scratched his head, definitely thinking he shouldn't go anywhere near Glory Shaw, in her natural form—unless of course, she needed his help. Damn, but he'd have to stay close by, just in case. "I was hoping one of you ladies might volunteer, out of the goodness in your heart."

"We are good," Carmen said, grinning and glancing at her friends at the table. "We are told all the time."

The rest of the girls chuckled at her joke.

"But we said straight away, we want no part of that...that—"

"That...woman," Steven finished Julia's sentence, giving her a stern glance. Of all women, Julia should understand Glory's predicament. After all, Lorene had found her penniless, after she'd been robbed of all her funds, beaten and left for dead. Lorene had taken her in and given her a job, cleaning house. It had been Julia's choice to enter into the life at Rainbow House. That had always been Lorene's policy. No innocent inexperienced girls would "work" here. She'd always gotten them back on their feet and allowed them to decide. They could go, as many had, or they could stay. Lorene never compromised the girls. They were here by their own choice.

"She's wanted for murder," Ruby reminded.

"Sheriff Brimley wants to question her," Steven explained. "He has no proof one way or the other." He didn't mention the bloody knife that had been found by a neighbor, the one he too had found, right in Glory's hand.

"What does the girl say?" Eva asked, her dark eyes cold and unforgiving. She wasn't much older than Glory's eighteen years, yet there was a hard edge to her, one that aged her considerably. She'd had a rough life also before coming here. "Does she claim her innocence as they all do?"

Steven drew in a deep breath. "She has no memory of that night. She doesn't even know she's wanted for questioning."

"Steven," Ruby warned, "the girl should be told. Last night, I heard something from Big Joe Strowleski. He said Boone Shaw's brother Ned is making accusations. He's claiming his sister-in-law killed his brother. He's been shooting off his mouth in town about Gloria Mae Shaw getting away with murder. He went to the sheriff, demanding justice."

Steven's gut clenched. The last thing Glory needed was her brother-in-law stirring up trouble. She was already a suspect and if Ned Shaw knew anything about her guilt, he'd be sure to tell the sheriff.

"She needs to know what kind of trouble she's in," Ruby said with a firm nod of her head.

"She wasn't up to hearing it before." Steven spoke defiantly, defending his actions.

"But she is now," Emmie offered gently. She'd been the only one who had remotely helped Glory, by giving him advice as to how to tend her. Emmie's father had been a doctor and she had assisted him, learning all that she could as a young girl, until a renegade Sioux attack had destroyed her family and sealed her fate. She'd moved on, leaving the plains and the life she'd known to live with a relation here in Virginia City. Lorene had taken her in when she'd heard her aunt had passed on and Emmie had nowhere else to go. "I'm glad she is recovering."

The girls all peered at her with suspicion.

"Well, I am. She didn't deserve getting beaten up like that. No one does." Emmie looked around the room, casting each girl a somber look.

Steven knew many of the women had had bad experiences before coming here. That's why Lorene had hired Marcus, the watchman. He stood by the door and made sure none of the girls would be subject to any cruel behavior by the men. If Marcus didn't like a man's appearance, he wouldn't let him into Rainbow House, no matter how much gold he waved in front of him. Marcus was loyal to Lorene. They went way back. "And," Emmie added, "the sooner she heals, the sooner she can leave."

Steven had heard just about enough of this. He understood the girls' attitude about Glory, but didn't agree with it. She hadn't done anything but write some articles and post some signs. Whatever else she'd done to close down the brothels in Virginia City hadn't worked, either.

The fact remained that there were thousands of lonely miners in town who had need of female companionship. Rainbow House and the other bordellos provided the men a place to unwind, have drinks and conversation and satisfy all of their other male needs without guilt or recrimination. Nothing Glory could possibly do would change that.

Steven planted his fists on his hips and spoke with quiet determination. "She's staying as long as she has to. I don't want any of you thinking any different. And not a word to anyone about this."

"We won't say anything," Ruby announced. "We all owe Lorene. We're not going to do anything to upset her. She already feels responsible for getting Reverend Caldwell killed. The last thing she'd want is for his daughter to get strung up. Right?" Ruby glanced at all the girls.

They all nodded in agreement. At least, Steven could bank on their loyalty. They might be "soiled doves," ladies who weren't held in high regard by normal standards, but they were loyal to Lorene.

"Okay," Steven said, "fair enough. And one more thing, if Ned Shaw comes in here, I want you to be especially nice to him. Get him talking, then let me know what you find out."

The ladies agreed and Steven took up the large pots of steaming water. He gritted his teeth, realizing now he had two obstacles to overcome.

Telling Glory the truth.

And giving her a bath.

Both made his nerves go raw.

Gloria sat patiently on her bed, waiting for Steven to finish filling the tub. The steam rising up from that hot tub made her toes curl in anticipation. She knew she'd feel so much better after a long relaxing soak.

"Okay, all ready," Steven said, coming out from behind the partition that hid the tub. He glanced at her with those wonderful eyes and she nearly melted into a silly puddle. When she wasn't spitting mad at him for keeping her in the dark about so many things, she found herself drawn to him in ways she'd never been drawn to Boone.

That fact in itself baffled her.

Gloria had been raised by a pious man, one who believed wholeheartedly in the sanctity of marriage, of living a clean wholesome life, of holding the Lord and all his teachings with the utmost regard. He'd taught her the value of honesty, of truth and morals. He brought her up believing that good shall always prevail against evil, although, the Lord in his wisdom often tests us.

So now, with her husband Boone not gone from this earth five days, Gloria found herself attracted to the man who had clearly saved her life. Perhaps it wasn't unusual for a victim to feel *something* for her savior. Perhaps what she felt for Steven was only profound gratitude for saving her life.

She'd like nothing more, but to think so.

"The water's hot. Be careful." He reached for her hand. Without pause, Gloria placed her hand in his. He helped her toward the tub. She found herself stronger, more balanced. The thought brought forth a measure of joy. She'd been incapacitated long enough.

Once they reached the tub, she glanced at him. "Thank you."

"You'll be all right on your own?"

Rapid heat flamed her face. "I guess I have to be, don't I?"

"I could—"

"No." She shook her head. "No, you couldn't possibly."

Steven nodded. "There's rose soap for you by the tub. And I'll hang a gown for you on the back of the door."

Again, another puzzle. Was this man a widower? Was he sharing his wife's belongings with her? How was he privy to so many female things? "Where do you get—"

"Later, Glory. I'll tell you later. Enjoy your bath. I'll be just outside the door. Call if you need me."

"That's not necessary. I'll be fine."

"Still, I'll wait outside."

Once he was gone, Glory removed her robe and the chemise that had clung to her body for the past five days, glad to peel it off.

She tested the water with her toe. "Oh, so nice," she said with a sigh, then climbed in with both feet and lowered her body down. Immediately tension oozed from her body and she relished the distinct soothing effect hot water and rose soap had on her.

She scrubbed her body for a long while, the sweet scent of roses wafting up in such a way that ought to be deemed sinful from the delight and pleasure it created.

Gloria hummed a tune, a gospel hymn that she'd sung many times while in church, silently, in her head, not wanting to cause any disrespect toward her dead husband.

But, oh, she felt marvelous.

She washed her hair, scouring it until it squeaked clean. And then, as the water grew tepid, she knew her bathtime was over. She lingered another minute, until goose bumps rose up on her arms.

"Time to get out," she thought to herself. She sighed with contentment.

And proceeded to get out of the tub.

* * *

Steven stood behind the bedroom door, waiting, listening. He'd be forever grateful he hadn't had to help Glory with her bath, but as he leaned heavily against the door frame, he heard her sighs of pleasure, the sound of her sweet voice torturing him with images he should not entertain.

He heard the water lapping and swishing and imagined her washing her body, the soap caressing her skin, making it glow. He envisioned her scrubbing her honey-blond hair, fingering the long tresses, dipping her head back...

And thankfully, after more than half an hour behind that door, he no longer heard any splashing sounds.

She'd gotten out of the tub.

He wouldn't think of her drying off with the large fluffy towel he'd brought in earlier. But he still had to listen, in case she called for him. In case, she needed him.

"Ohhhhh!" She screamed, the panicked shriek ripping into his gut. He shoved open her door and found her standing before the mirror with a horrified expression.

"What..." And he couldn't get the words out. He swallowed, taking all of her in. He'd given her one of Emmie's gowns, thinking they were the closest in size. But Glory surely filled this dress out more fully, the bodice tight about her torso, the low cut of the blue silk gown lifting her small breasts up, pushing them out in a way that made his heart nearly stop. The gown accentuated her lovely form to perfection, and brought out the sky-blue in her eyes, completely overshadowing the light bruises left on her face. He'd never known temptation like this, the strong desire to reach out and touch her cheek, to trail a hand along the bodice of that dress and to run his fingers through honey-gold hair that flowed freely in long waves past her shoulders.

He sucked in a breath. "What's wrong?" he managed to ask.

She turned to him with a plea in her voice. "I can't wear this."

She could and did, beautifully.

"It's not proper. Why, it's…it's…" she began then lowered her voice. "It's sinful."

Steven scratched his head and rubbed his nose.

Then blinked.

"Steven?"

"Sorry, it was the best I could do."

"Whose dress is this?" she asked, lifting the silk up as though it were diseased.

"It's Emmie's. I thought you and she…well, you looked like the same size, but maybe one of the other girls' gowns would do you better. I mean to say, *I* like it. You look beautiful."

She narrowed her eyes, casting him a look of suspicion. "What other girls?"

"How do you feel, Glory? Tired? Want to sit down?" He gestured toward the chair.

Glory shook her head, a fierce and fearful look crossing her features. "What other girls? Where am I? And who in heaven's name are you?"

"My name is Steven."

"I know that."

Steven couldn't put it off any longer. It was time to tell her the truth. She needed to know. Steven had never been ashamed of his name or who he was, but to tell her could spell disaster. Yet, she had a right to know what had happened that night. She had a right to know where he'd taken her. "Harding. Steven Harding." He shot her a long look, waiting for his name to register.

She repeated his name silently, mouthing it until her eyes went wide and round as an owl. "You're Steven Harding? You're…you're Lorene Harding's son. And your mother is that madam who caused my father's death. The madam of…of that *whore*house?" She spoke the word quietly, almost inaudibly as though she couldn't believe any of this.

"That's right. I'm Steven Harding. And I brought you here because—"

"Here? Where?" She had a hand to her chest now, as if warding off the worst possible evil. Then she glanced at the drawn curtain and walked to the window, parting the thick fabric. She peered down at the street and gasped, taking a step back in shock. "I'm on C Street, the Barbary Coast of Virginia City. I've heard talk about it, but I've never come here. Father would never allow it."

And then she turned to him with sharp glaring eyes, marking him as a traitor, the betrayal she felt written all over her face. "You brought me to Rainbow House."

She spoke quietly and calmly, her voice distant as if she just now realized the truth. "You took care of me, nursed me back to health. Is this some sort of a cruel joke? A way to get back at me? I trusted you to help me, but now I see what you've done."

"You think you know the truth, Glory. But you don't. Let me explain."

"No. I won't hear your lies." She shook her head and brushed past him, grabbing the knob at the door.

"You're wanted for the murder of your husband," Steven stated so dispassionately that she turned to him in disbelief.

"W-What?"

"When I found you, you had a bloody knife in your hand. Your husband was inches away, stabbed to death. The fire was raging, ready to crumble the house, so I took you away quickly. You were hurt and it was plain to see that you had suffered your injuries at the hands of a man. I don't blame you, Glory. He had no right hurting you that way."

Her lips quivered when she spoke. "You think I killed Boone?"

"I wouldn't blame you if you did, but Sheriff Brimley believes he was murdered. And now Ned Shaw's got people out looking for you. He wants to avenge his brother's death."

"Why did you bring me here? Why, Steven? Why didn't you just take me to the sheriff if you thought I killed my husband?"

Steven moved toward her slowly, keeping his gaze locked to hers. "You know why. Your father saved my mother's life. It's something I'll never forget. I know you hate my mother and me for it, but the fact is, I owe him something. And I'm gonna protect you for as long as I have to."

Glory's lips twitched. Anger lit her face, bringing color and pain, her disgust obvious. "I don't need your protection. You owe me nothing."

She yanked the door open and lifted her gown as she raced down the stairs.

Steven cursed up to high heaven. He'd known she

wouldn't take this well. What had he expected, for her to fall into his arms? Had he expected her to thank him graciously for bringing her to the one place she abhorred? The one establishment no decent woman should enter?

And then common sense knocked him in the head.

He couldn't let her leave.

She wouldn't last five minutes before she'd be arrested.

"Dammit, Glory," he called after her.

He raced down the stairs, chasing after a woman he had no call knowing, much less wanting. But right now, all that mattered was getting her back before she landed herself in even more trouble.

She wasn't ten feet out the door before Steven caught up to her, pulling her aside, plastering her to the wall of the building. He spread out across her, covering her with the breadth of his own body. "Don't fight me, Glory," he whispered through tight lips. "Here comes Ed Hurley. He's sure to recognize you."

Steven crushed his mouth to hers, one hand firmly holding both of hers behind her back, not allowing her struggle to show. He took claim to her lips, hating that he might be hurting her, but having no choice. He felt her movements, her will fighting his, but he was too strong for her, too powerful. He knew the exact moment when she'd given up, her body relaxing against his, her muted cries no longer pleas, but moans of pleasure. Steven cursed silently at this turn of events, even as her sweet taste made an indelible mark on his soul.

Gloria could barely breathe. Her heart raced furiously, the kiss making her head spin. Steven had no right. He had taken her so quickly, catching her unaware. She'd never dreamed of being kissed so passionately before. As indecent as it was, Gloria had to admit, once she'd given up the fight, the kiss had been wonderful.

But then the reality of her situation had struck her. She came to realize the trouble she might be in. Everything Steven had told her upstairs had finally registered. She might be arrested for murder. She might be tried and convicted. She had no defense. She couldn't recall anything about that night. And now someone she knew might recognize her and tell the sheriff. Breathless, she asked, "Are you sure it's Mr. Hurley, the banker?"

"Shh." He dipped his head and kissed her again, sending her mind in a tizzy. This time, she didn't fight him. Trembling, Gloria understood Steven was once again protecting her. She felt his tension, the rigid set of his jaw, the tender tough way he held her, almost desperately. "He's going into the house."

Steven turned his body to hide her completely from view, the press of his clothes rustling against hers, his breath hot on her skin, his lips surprisingly gentle for a man Gloria knew to be furious.

"Evening, Steven," Mr. Hurley said with a chuckle.

Steven waved a hand in his direction. She figured it was enough of a greeting for a man wrapped up in a kiss, busy concentrating on seducing a woman on the street.

Once they heard the door to Rainbow House close, Steven looked her dead in the eyes, his tone far from kind. "You try my patience, woman. Don't you know staying at Rainbow House is the safest place for you right now? How many beautiful young women do you think live in this town? Hardly enough to count. And with the sheriff and your brother-in-law putting the word out, you wouldn't get halfway down the street without being recognized. You'd get arrested for sure. What kind of a hearing do you think you'd have, when all the odds are stacked against you?''

Gloria swallowed hard. She knew Steven was right. She had no place to hide. She didn't know whom she could trust. She didn't even know if she was innocent, having no recollection of that night. Maybe she had killed Boone.

Yet, how could she possibly stay here? She had ill feelings toward Lorene Harding. She hated how senselessly her father had died because of her. She had come to loathe anything about the woman, the brothel she ran and her son, the man she now knew to be Steven. Gloria's heart raged with dread and fear. She had no choice in the matter. Bravely, she held back tears, staring down at her bare feet. In her haste to run out, she'd failed to put on her shoes.

Steven glanced down, too. ''Ah, hell, Glory.''

He hoisted her up, settling her in his arms, and carried her toward the back of the house. She didn't fight him. She couldn't, but the irony was almost too much to bear. She couldn't believe she was agreeing to this. She would hide out in the very whorehouse that she meant to close down.

At least she still had her pride. And there was one thing left she could control in her life. One thing she could correct, at the moment. ''My name is Gloria. That's what I'd like to be called.''

Steven didn't miss a step. He pinned her with a thunderous gaze. "Glory suits you better."

"But—"

"Or maybe I'll just call you Trouble."

Chapter Four

"So I'm to be a prisoner here, in this room?" Gloria asked, gesturing about the room with a wide sweep of her arms.

With fury in his eyes and a frown on his lips, Steven had deposited her in this room and was ready to take his leave. Surely this was not the same man who had carefully tended her for the past five days.

"Better here than in Sheriff Brimley's jailhouse, wouldn't you say?"

Gloria took in a deep breath, still fighting her loss of control, still rebelling against her situation. For the entire time she'd been married to Boone, she'd been a dutiful wife. It was the Lord's way and what was expected. And she'd tried her best to make a good marriage, although Boone hadn't made it easy. Now, she no longer had a husband. She no longer had to submit to a man. Especially not to Steven Harding. She knew she was on her own—with no choice but to hide away here for the time being. "No, I wouldn't say. I'm in a whorehouse, a bordello, living among prostitutes." She squeezed her eyes shut momentarily. Saying those words aloud made her cringe with disbelief.

"Rainbow House serves a purpose. This is a business establishment. Don't make it sound like a living hell."

"Hah." An unfeminine snort escaped. "That's exactly what it is. It's the devil's doing, so don't defend it. Or your mother."

"My mother is who she is, Glory. I make no apologies for her."

Suddenly, Gloria's legs wobbled. The stress of the day had fatigued her. She sat down on the bed, too prideful to lie down and rest her head against the pillow while Steven was watching her.

"You need to rest. Running out in the street like that was a fool thing to do. And now you're tuckered out."

"I'm not tuckered out," she said as a yawn pulled open her mouth. She lifted her arms to stretch, noting Steven hadn't taken his eyes off her. She remembered his kiss, that one single moment of passion that Gloria would never forget.

Even if it had come from the last man in town she should ever allow to kiss her. Was he remembering, too? Was that dark gleam in his eyes anger or was it something more forbidden, something more daunting?

Steven shrugged then and headed for the door.

"Where are you going?"

"You need to rest. You don't need me anymore."

Oh, but she did. She hated to admit that she had come to rely on Steven. He'd been caring, seeing to her needs and comfort. But that's not what she needed from him now. He'd been her only link to the outside world. And now that Gloria knew what awaited her beyond the confines of Steven's room, fear entered her heart. "What will I do now? Do I stay here all night and day?"

Steven stared into her eyes. "No. You can come downstairs in the mornings. You'll have the house to yourself. Mattie, the cook, will make you a meal. The girls don't wake until after noon. They start taking gentleman callers at four o'clock, so you'd best be upstairs well before that."

Gloria bit her lip. Then nodded. What could she say? She was privy to the prostitutes' living arrangements. She now knew their schedule, when they entertained men. She slid her palm across the comfortable smooth sheets and wondered whose bed she'd taken since she'd been here. "Is this one of their rooms?"

"No."

She lifted her face to meet his eyes. "No? Whose room is this, then?"

"Mine."

Gloria blinked back her surprise. "Y-yours?"

She'd never considered that notion. She'd slept in Steven's room, in his bed, for five entire days. She made a sweep of the size of the bed, its breadth and length. There was room enough for more than one person. "Where did you...I mean, did we—?"

He pointed out a single cane-backed chair that didn't appear comfortable in the least. "I slept there, for the most part."

"Oh." Gloria didn't want to owe him her gratitude, but the fact remained, he had saved her life. He'd hidden her away and brought her to safety. He'd tended to her through the nights, she presumed. And he'd given her his bed. "Thank you."

She owed him her thanks, but she didn't have to like it. Not one bit. Yet, he'd been the one to find her. He'd been the one to hide her here. He'd been the one who chose to nurse her back to health. And heaven only knew why it had to be Steven Harding to do all those things. Now she found herself in an impossible situation that only seemed to intensify with each new truth that she learned. Lately, Gloria's faith in the Lord had been truly and sorely tested.

A quick nod was his only response to her offer of thanks. "I won't be back until tomorrow evening. I'm gonna trust you not to run out again. And make darn sure you're up in this room before the four o'clock hour. You can't be seen."

She nodded, understanding her plight. This room, elegant as it as, wasn't much better than a prison and her jailer, a handsome man who was her savior and her enemy, all at the same time. "Where, uh, where will you sleep?"

A crooked smile lifted the corner of his mouth. "Don't you worry about me, I have a few options."

Gloria's gut clenched involuntarily. Where he slept was none of her business. But it wasn't the *where* that had her feathers ruffled. And again, she berated herself for caring. Frustrated, she had the uncanny need to toss something. As soon as he closed the door, she gave in to that childish impulse. She lifted her pillow and flung it across the room. The goose-down sack plopped unceremoniously near the door, without making a sound.

Darn him anyway.

She didn't care where the man slept.

As long as he left her alone.

* * *

Steven strode down the stairs, banking his temper. He hoped he'd gotten through to Glory that staying here was her only option right now. She didn't like it. He knew that she'd fight him. He'd expected her wrath, a fury created by the injustice of her father's death. But what he hadn't expected was her disgust, the telling look on her face when she'd found out who he was—Lorene Harding's son. The son of a famous Virginia City madam, the woman she felt had been responsible for the Reverend's death.

Steven had lived his life making excuses to no one, yet in that one moment while facing Glory, he'd found himself wishing he'd been someone different, someone she could respect and admire.

Kissing her had been a necessity, he thought. He'd done it deliberately to hide her from view of the men wandering about the street, especially Ed Hurley. Most people knew the town's most prominent banker and he would have surely recognized Reverend Caldwell's daughter. Glory Shaw, blue-eyed, blond and beautiful, was hard to miss. But he hadn't expected that kiss to knock the air from his lungs the way that it had. And he hadn't expected the woman to give in and partake in the kiss with warmth and passion.

Steven shook free lusty thoughts of Glory Shaw. He owed her for the sacrifice her father had made. And he planned to pay up by keeping her safe. He had to forget about that kiss. Forget that he had any sort of feelings for the young determined woman. She was an obligation and nothing more. Besides, she had made it very clear what she thought of him. Glory had no use for him as a man.

And now, the woman who scorned him was his sole responsibility.

Hell, he didn't like any of this. He was too damn drawn to a woman he hardly knew. But deep down, Steven did know her. He'd watched her, admired her from a distance. He'd seen her smile sweetly to townsfolk on the street, seen her play with children on the church grounds. He'd witnessed her riding in the buggy with her father, as they headed out of town, no doubt visiting the sick and downtrodden.

He'd been there with his mother, standing in the background as Reverend Caldwell's entire congregation, it seemed, had come out for his burial. He'd seen Glory stand tall and brave, graciously receiving well wishes and sympathy from friends and neighbors. He'd seen such sadness in her eyes, such dismay, the love she had for her father so evident on a lovely face stricken by grief. She'd been only seventeen at the time, too young to be orphaned, and too unworldly to recognize Boone Shaw for the man he truly was.

Boone had been somewhat of a regular at Rainbow House before his marriage to Glory. And Marcus had escorted him out on more than one occasion for his unruly behavior. Steven had hoped Boone would have treated Glory with the respect she deserved, new bride that she was, but he'd heard rumors about the marriage that didn't set well. In a town full of men, surely young Glory Caldwell could have chosen more wisely.

Steven sighed with resignation. He'd been gone too long from the ranch. He had work to do or his place would never get finished. And a day away from Glory Shaw would do him a world of good. Five days watching her mend, seeing the beauty come back to her face, the shine come back in her hair and the body he'd carefully tended glow again with life, had his insides gnarled up with emotions he didn't care to name.

He stopped when he reached the foot of the stairs. Gentlemen callers were beginning to filter into the house and soon the quiet of the day would give way to a noisy animated night. Steven headed for the foyer and waited for the watchman to turn away from the front door. "Afternoon, Marcus."

The big burly Scot greeted him with a nod. "Steven."

"I need to speak with you in private."

Taking one last look around, Marcus closed and locked the front door. Anybody outside would have to wait to come in.

Marcus followed Steven into a hallway that led to the back of the house, and out of view of any of the patrons. "You know we have a guest living here now, right?"

Marcus, a man of few words, once again nodded.

"She's in trouble and I'm seeing to her safety. It's important that no one knows she is here. Watch out for anyone snooping around and asking too many questions. No one is allowed on the third floor. I'm asking you as a special favor to make sure no one wanders up there. Be even more careful about who you let into the house. Our guest is, well, she might not always cooperate, so if you spot her coming downstairs during business time, for any reason, escort her back to her room. No matter how you have to do it."

"Aye. I can do that." Marcus smiled.

Steven only hoped Glory wouldn't confront Marcus. The man wouldn't think twice about tossing her over his shoulder like a sack of flour to get the job done.

"Good." Steven took in a sharp breath. "I'm leaving tonight. Hope to be back after sundown tomorrow. I appreciate your help."

Steven headed for the livery stables. He had an hour's ride tonight to get to his ranch. Maybe then he could get Glory Shaw off his mind for a time. Maybe then, he could get much-needed sleep.

He had a ranch house to finish building.

Grumbling in her stomach woke Gloria from a sound sleep. She sat up, once again surprised by her surroundings. At times she forgot her plight, the situation that landed her at Rainbow House. But now as a slice of sunlight streamed through the heavy curtains, Gloria recalled everything with brutal clarity. She was hiding out here, devoid of all memory of the night her husband died. She was wanted for murder. And probably worst of all, she had to live in a house of prostitution, the proprietor being the very woman who had caused her father's death.

Gloria lifted up from the bed. The sigh that escaped had less to do with body soreness, and more to do with facing the new day. Without Steven's help.

She had to fend for herself now. Her stomach growled again, reminding her she needed nourishment. With her injuries healing and her body recovering, she found that her appetite had come back full force. Although she loathed the idea of going downstairs, Gloria knew she had little choice if she wanted to have a meal.

She slipped on the gown she'd worn last night—the one that made her feel like an overstuffed Christmas goose. She'd hoped Steven would have placed something more fitting on the hook behind the door as he had in the past, perhaps something from her own wardrobe. But she put that notion aside. If the fire at her house had been as severe as he'd said, then nothing would have been salvaged. All of her belongings, everything she owned, would have been destroyed.

Glory shut her mind off to those disturbing thoughts.

She'd have to do something about her attire later, but for now she had no other option but to wear this dress. She recited her father's favorite mantra. "If it's to be, make the best of it."

Gloria prayed for guidance to see her out of this predicament, counting on her father's teachings and the wisdom he had so readily shared with her.

She was ready to make the best of it.

Gloria ambled slowly down the stairs. She stopped at the second-floor landing, gazing at the doors painted in different colors.

Rainbow House.

Now she understood, the dawning knowledge grasping her with complete surprise. She'd never known why the house had such a charming, winsome name. Rainbows made you think of hope, of a higher being, of something quite miraculous.

But as she peered at the red door, the purple, the blue, the green and the yellow one, she understood the clever idea behind the house. And she wondered what the inside of those rooms looked like. Were they, too, part of the colorful rainbow?

Gloria stopped gawking and continued down the stairs. With any amount of luck, she'd be out of this house long before she discovered the answers to her questions.

Once on the main floor, she moved through a few rooms decorated with the finest furniture she'd ever seen, highly polished and arranged in a way that lent for large groups to converse and be entertained. A Dresden piano graced the back of the room and a small Cornish and Company pump organ anchored the adjacent wall. And as she strode past with quiet determination, the stale scent of cigars and tobacco layered the air.

When Gloria finally reached the kitchen area, she breathed a sigh of relief. True to Steven's word, only the cook was present. She was busy turning a long row of dough onto a floured tabletop. She glanced up with a flour-stained face and Gloria was taken by how young the cook appeared. Why, she looked young enough to still attend school.

"Hello," she said with a welcoming smile.

Gloria smiled back. She hadn't expected to be greeted with warmth, not even from the cook. "Hello."

"You must be Glory. Mr. Har— uh, Steven told us about you."

Rapid heat rose up her neck, shaking Gloria's resolve. She wondered just what Steven had told everyone about her. "Yes, I'm Gloria Mae Shaw. Steven seems to think my name is Glory."

"Glory is a pretty name. I'm Mattie. Don't like my name much." The girl put her head down.

"Mattie is a fine name. What are you baking?"

"Strawberry pie. The last of the season. Got the dough almost ready." She pressed out the dough with her hands and set the pie plates over it, ready to make the shape. "The girls like pie."

Gloria nodded and her stomach grumbled. She set her hand there when Mattie looked up knowingly. "Sorry, I should have realized you'd be hungry. I can cook you up anything you'd like."

"Oh, no. Don't go to any trouble. Anything will do. All of a sudden I have an appetite again."

Mattie nodded and wiped her face with her sleeve, getting most of the flour off her face. "That's good." She eyed Gloria with an honest, searching expression. "I'm glad to see you're healing. Can't really tell you had bruises except for a little yellow discolor on your chest and some scrapes still left on your face. Emmie's remedy did you good."

"Y-yes. I'm feeling better."

The girl turned around and began filling a plate from the cookstove. Without ceremony, she set down a dish of thin-sliced potatoes, bacon and corn biscuits. "I also have fried chicken and dumplings leftover from yesterday, if you'd like. Have a seat. Would you like tea or coffee?"

"Oh, you don't have to serve me. I'll get it myself."

"No, please. You just sit put. You're the guest here."

"But—"

"Coffee or tea?" The girl had already set a napkin down with utensils and pulled out a seat for her. Gloria didn't want to be rude. It seemed this young girl took pride in serving up her food.

"Coffee is just fine and thank you." She took the offered seat. "This looks wonderful." But Gloria hadn't eaten solid food for nearly a week. Hungry or not, she knew her stomach wouldn't abide such a large meal. She wouldn't be able to get too much of it down.

"Dear Lord," she began, putting her head down. "Thank you for this bountiful meal before me. And…and thank you for seeing to my care these last few days. Amen."

It was the shortest prayer she'd ever offered up. Though Gloria had much to be thankful for, right now, her heart wasn't in her prayers. She struggled with her faith, the night Boone died weighing heavily on her mind.

When Gloria looked up, she found Mattie staring at her. "That sounds real nice. Haven't heard a prayer since I left the orphanage. We used to say our prayers mornings and nights, just before bed."

"You were in an orphanage?"

Mattie nodded, intent on shaping dough into the pie plates. "For as long as I can remember."

Gloria took a bite of her potatoes, not wanting to pry into Mattie's life. But she couldn't help wondering how a girl so young had gone from living in an orphanage to being employed in a brothel.

"I, uh—"

"Go on?" Gloria encouraged her with a nod. "I'd really like to hear what you have to say."

Mattie shrugged and stopped her work to look at her. "It's just that, in the beginning I had hope of being adopted. But as time went on and I got older, there was less and less chance of that ever happening. Most people picked the young boys. Sister Marie said it's because boys are extra help on the ranches and farms. Saint Catherine's isn't a bad place really. It's where I learned to cook." She beamed a big smile.

"Sounds as though you were happy there."

"Yes, for a time. I was beginning to understand that I might never leave. Until one day when the sisters came for me. They said they had a family who wanted me and just days later I was living at the Clemons' homestead in Stockton. One week later, I ran away."

"What happened?"

Mattie closed her eyes as if shutting her mind off to a terrible memory. She shook her head. "Mrs. Clemons was more ill than she let on to the sisters. She had taken to her bed, the consumption pretty much keeping her down all the time. And Mr. Clemons...uh, he was always looking at me funny. He came to me wanting—"

"Wanting?"

Mattie took a big swallow.

"He wanted...favors?" Gloria asked, knowing it for truth.

Mattie nodded, biting her lip. "But I ran away. I left Stockton and headed to San Francisco. That's where I met Lorene. She took me in and hired me as a cook."

"You can cook anywhere, Mattie. You didn't have to come here."

"I tried to find employment, but nobody wanted to give me a chance. I guess I don't look sixteen to most folks. But I am. I swear it. And Lorene is paying me to do what I love. There's no harm in that."

Gloria understood that a young girl, desperate and feeling beholden to the madam of the house, wouldn't find fault in that. But Gloria certainly did. The problem was, she wasn't in any position to help Mattie right now. If she could, she'd convince her not to stay on here.

Gloria finished what she could of the food, her stomach satisfied for the moment. "Thank you. That was delicious."

Mattie flashed her another smile and reached for her plate. "You're welcome. I'll have this cleaned up straight away."

Gloria waved her away, "No, please. Let me do it. I want to help."

The girl blushed. "Heavens, I can't have you washing up the dishes."

"But I'd like to help. There's nothing for me to do up in that room. And I'm feeling much better. At least let me help with the pies."

Mattie glanced at the eight pies she had yet to finish. "Well—"

"Please."

Mattie cast her a wide grin. "Okay." She handed Gloria a white cotton apron.

"Let's get to baking," Gloria said, anxious to do something. She stood behind the worktable, glancing at the large tins ready for filling. "How many girls does that woman employ?"

"Eight."

"Eight? You make one pie for each girl?"

Mattie chuckled. "Oh no, no. But we always have dessert ready for, um, the male guests."

"Oh." The reminder made Gloria's stomach knot with tension. She stared down at the pies she'd pretty much begged Mattie to help with, suddenly unsure what she should do.

Make the best of it, dear girl.

Her father's words rattled in her head and Gloria

recognized her fate once again. She didn't have to like it, but the fact remained, she was living at Rainbow House for the time being so she might as well make herself useful.

"If you'll fill up the pies with strawberries, I'll cut the dough to make the topping," Mattie said, taking command of her kitchen and making Gloria smile.

They worked together for twenty minutes, filling the tins, criss-crossing the strips of dough on top and setting them in the cookstove. Then ignoring Mattie's admonishments, Gloria helped her clean the worktable.

"Something smells awfully good in here, Mattie."

"What is baking to make my stomach talk?"

"I'm starving, Mattie, honey. Sure hope you have our meal ready."

Gloria turned abruptly to see three "ladies" saunter into the kitchen dressed in flowing silk robes, varying in colors from sapphire-blue to cherry-red to meadow-green.

"Look who we have here. If it ain't our new houseguest." The woman in red spoke in a polite enough tone, but there was no welcome in her eyes.

"Dio," the woman in green declared.

The woman dressed in soft blue smiled. "Hello. I'm Emmie." She came forward and searched Gloria's face. "You're healing real good."

Gloria stood rooted to the spot. "Y-yes. Th-thank you. Steven told me what you've done."

"All I did was give him salve for your injuries. He did the rest. I see he also gave you one of my gowns."

"Oh! I, uh…" Gloria put a hand to her chest. "My clothes burned in the fire."

A dark-haired woman stepped up. "Steven is very clever, is he not? He knows what dress to fit you. Steven understands about women, no? And now you wear the clothes of a *soiled* woman." The full-bodied woman with a heavy Mexican accent glanced at the others, nodding.

Mortified, Gloria wanted to dash from the room.

"Oh, hush, Carmen." The woman in red turned to her. "Don't you pay attention to Carmen. She has a mouth on her. I'm Ruby and I'm in charge while Lorene is away."

Ruby eyed her up and down, then let go a pained sigh. "I suppose you don't want to be here any more than we want you here."

Gloria nodded her agreement. "I…don't."

"But you are, so we're just going to have to deal with it."

"She is one who thinks she is better than us. The murderer," Carmen announced coolly, "should not be so eager to judge us."

Gloria's ire sparked, lit like a candle on a moonless night. "You're right. I don't want to be here. If I could, I'd shut down this place, along with all the other brothels. What you do is—"

"Is by choice," Ruby cut in. "We do what we do. You don't have to like it. But Carmen is right. You should not judge us. You killed your husband defending yourself. You did what you had to do…to survive. We're not all that different."

"Lorene is good to us. We have a good life. Much better than if we hadn't come here," Emmie offered with softness in her tone. "And now, you're here, among us. Steven is bent on protecting you."

"I didn't ask for his help," Gloria responded irrationally. She knew if Steven hadn't rescued her, she would have died alongside Boone that night.

Carmen snorted, a most unladylike gesture.

The others scowled.

"But I'm grateful to him," she added quickly. "He saved my life."

And that's all she'd allow herself to feel for the man whose life was worlds apart from hers. She couldn't condone who and what he was any more than she could these ladies, who stood tall and proud defending themselves. "I'd better go. Thank you for the meal, Mattie."

A sad smile lifted Mattie's mouth up slightly. She, too, thought she judged the "ladies" too harshly. "I appreciate the help with the pies."

Gloria raised her chin and walked out of the kitchen as regally as she could manage. She'd confronted the prostitutes on their own ground, and hadn't cowered. She held firm her resolve. The brothels had no place in Virginia City or any other town. They brought in rowdies, people like Denny Pratt, a drunken drifter who had quarrelled with Lorene Harding and had pulled a gun on her. Gloria's unsuspecting father had gotten caught in the turmoil and lost his life over a mindless squabble with a whorehouse madam.

Gloria would never find forgiveness with these women. She'd never understand the choices they made. If the good Lord wanted that, then He asked far too much from her. She climbed the stairs slowly contemplating her life and headed back to Steven's bedroom.

Her prison.

Chapter Five

Alone in her room, Gloria peeked out the heavy curtain to the street below. Situated on the corner of Union and C, Rainbow House sat in the heart of the rowdiest part of town, a place where saloons, music halls and brothels attracted miners by the hundreds. Tonight was no different. Drunken men swaggered with women on their arm and from her third-floor perch, faint sounds of music from the street below drifted up, rivaling the lively piano playing coming from just three flights down in this very house.

Gloria shuddered involuntarily. The notion of where she was living still came as quite a shock. "Lord, what am I to do?" she muttered, closing the curtains and lowering her head. Even though her faith had been tested at times, Gloria still believed in the Almighty, His power and wisdom. There must be a reason for all this, she mused. He must have a grand plan, a motive for placing her here now, amid the kind of life she so adamantly and wholeheartedly denounced.

A beautifully ornate grandfather clock made of brass and carved walnut struck the eleventh hour.

Gloria had left the kitchen earlier in the day in a huff, grateful to be away from the fallen women who defended their profession with all the dignity of heroic soldiers. With nothing to do and not a soul around, she'd fallen into a deep, mindless sleep. She'd woken up an hour ago well rested and completely bored.

"Well, Glory," she said, trying out the name on her lips, debating whether she preferred it, as her father had...and Steven. "What now?"

"What now?" The door creaked open and she whirled around. Her traitorous heart rejoiced at seeing Steven, somewhat weather-beaten, standing in her doorway. He stepped inside quickly, shutting out the boisterous music and laughter from downstairs, as he closed the door.

She was lonely and he represented company, someone to quell her boredom tonight for a moment or two, she rationalized. She tamped down the joy she felt watching his beautiful eyes move over her softly, in an assessing way, as if checking on her well-being. She could never have warm feelings for this man, despite the fact that he'd saved her life.

"Are you talking to yourself?" he asked, a quick grin flashing across his face.

She gestured with a swipe of her arms. "Do you see anybody else here for me to speak with?"

"Yeah. I'm here now."

She bounced her bottom on the bed, much like a child who hadn't gotten her way. "Why are you?"

Steven moved closer and his scent, the smell of earth and fresh air and leather, assailed her instantly. It was a brutal reminder of her plight. She was a prisoner in this house, this very room. She longed to go outside, to be free again. To have that right would be the grandest gift she'd ever receive.

"I came to see you."

She glanced at him, his rugged, handsome face appearing road-weary. "You look tired."

"I worked all day at the ranch. Building the house with my own hands, and setting up the corrals for my horses."

"And you came all this way to check on me? To make sure I hadn't escaped?"

Steven walked over to the window, pulled the drapes apart and leaned heavily on the window frame. With his back to her, he spoke in an edgy tone. "You're not a prisoner here, dammit. If you want to get your hide thrown in jail, walk down those stairs and out the door." He turned to face her. "I guarantee you'd find Sheriff Brimley's jail cell a lot less accommodating than this room."

Gloria bounded up from the bed to face him evenly. "I'm sorry. I do apologize. I suppose that wasn't at all gracious of me. I, uh...I don't know exactly how to handle this."

The hardness in his eyes softened a bit. "Did you go downstairs today?"

"For a short time. I met Mattie." She smiled, remembering how good it felt to make those pies. "We baked strawberry pies."

He raised a brow and nodded, apparently in approval.

"But then some of the...the ladies came into the kitchen."

Steven scratched his chin and sighed. "They give you a bad time of it?"

Gloria winced. "I think we gave each other a bad time."

"They'll come around," he declared, as if that would heal the situation.

"I'm not sure I want them to." She lifted her chin defiantly. "I'm…we aren't…"

"Doesn't your God believe in forgiveness, Glory? Doesn't He believe we can all live in the world, differences and all?"

Gloria put her head down. "I used to believe that. I don't know anymore."

And then, Steven was there, placing a finger under her chin and lifting it up so that their eyes met. He searched her face for a moment, then smiled. That smile, a brief glimpse into the tender man who had nursed her injuries, created a stirring once again in her heart.

"I'll let you rest. You must be tired."

"I'm not a bit tired," she stated, stepping away from his touch, his soft scrutiny. If she sounded the shrew, she couldn't help it. A moment's visit with Steven wasn't enough. How would she endure the long torturous night without benefit of something to do? "I came up here early in the afternoon and slept away the entire day and most of the evening. I'm awake now, in the middle of the night, with nothing to do."

Steven took a step closer. The gleam in his earth-brown eyes caused her heart to flutter momentarily. "Whatever you'd like to do, in the middle of the night," he said in low whisper. "I'll try to accommodate."

"Really, Steven? You'd get me some material and sewing implements? I need different clothes. I can't go around wearing gowns of this sort.'' The thought of sewing up new garments took hold with thrilling excitement. She'd have something to concentrate on and the result of her endeavors meant more appropriate attire.

He glanced at her gown, his gaze flowing over the dress with interest, until finally, he settled on her chest. "You don't, uh…that gown looks perfect on you."

Her hand flew up to the skin exposed by the low bodice of the gown, the very area that held Steven's direct attention. "It's unsuitable."

He nodded, his gaze staying on her chest. Heat stirred her insides from his direct, unflinching perusal and the glow of appreciation she witnessed in his eyes. He liked the way she looked in a prostitute's gown. That didn't surprise her and his admission only marked the distinct differences between them.

"Right. Well, I can't go out and get you sewing materials in the dead of night. Fact is, I can't ever get those things for you. It'd look real suspicious if I purchased female things like that. And the girls here have all their dresses made for them by fancy dressmakers, so it wouldn't do to have them buy the material you need."

"But—"

"No, Glory. I'm sorry. I'll think of something tomorrow." He glanced at her chest once more, lifted his gaze to her throat, her mouth, then looked into her eyes before turning away.

"It's more important to keep you safe then worry over your clothes," he said, parting the heavy curtains again and glancing out the window.

"So I'm left with nothing to do?" Dejected, Gloria

sat down on the bed once again, her voice a pitiful croak of disappointment.

Steven whirled around to meet her eyes. He twisted his mouth, obviously in a deep struggle with something on his mind. "Ah, hell, Glory." He strode to the door, reaching for the knob before turning to her. "Wait right here. I have an idea."

He was out the door instantly, but Gloria still called out, "What kind of idea?"

Silence.

"And where would I possibly go?"

Less than an hour later, Steven stood outside his bedroom door cursing under his breath and calling himself every kind of fool for taking this chance. He knew the safest place for Glory was right here inside Rainbow House, yet the look in her eyes and her softly spoken misery shattered his good sense. Glory had that effect on him. She shattered him. He'd be better off not dealing with her tonight. He'd be better off allowing her boredom to coax her to sleep. But the image of Glory, sitting upon that bed looking lost and lonely, almost undid him.

He knocked then entered.

"You're back," she said, her voice giving away her surprise and her blue eyes lighting up upon his return. Steven held back the frown that threatened to ruin her joy. He almost wished he hadn't thought up this lamebrained idea, but he had and he meant to see it through.

"I told you I'd be back. I never go back on my word. You can count on that."

She nodded, but her attention focused solely on what he held in his hand. "What's that?"

"It's a cloak."

She peered at the ink-black woolen cloak and shook her head. "Oh Steven. You really can't expect me to wear that over this gown. Why, it's hotter than a cookstove in here during the day."

"It's not for the day. It's for tonight. How'd you like to get out of here for a while? I've got my horse saddled up behind the house. We can sneak down the back stairs. I figure with you wearing this black cloak and me taking the back trails nobody would notice our midnight run."

Hope sparked in her eyes. "It is midnight, isn't it?"

He nodded. "And the streets are emptying. Most men have a hard day in the mines ahead of them. We won't be seen."

Glory reached for the cloak, putting the hood over her head. Strands of her glorious blond hair peeked through. Steven took a step closer to tuck the loose hair under the hood. Then she smiled at him and, a flash of joy cut right through his gut.

"I'm ready," she said without hesitation.

Steven wondered if he was ready. Traveling alone on a midnight ride with the woman he vowed to protect, the woman he owed a great debt, the one and only woman he'd ever really wanted, gave him cause to turn tail and run.

Ah, hell, Glory. I'm ready, too. I just hope this isn't a big mistake.

"Steven," she said again softly, putting a hand to his arm, "I'm ready." She searched his eyes.

"Let's go." He took her hand and led her out the door toward the back of the house. There, they descended the stairs quickly and faced Fancy, his steadfast horse.

The mare snorted and sidestepped a bit. Steven calmed her with soothing words and a stroke to her nose. "It's okay, girl." The horse was used to only one rider, one man. But she'd be fine once Glory was atop the saddle. Fancy was one the finest horses in Virginia City.

Every instinct Steven possessed told him this was not a good idea, but not because Glory wouldn't be safe from the sheriff or Ned Shaw. No, he could almost assure her safety tonight from the likes of those men.

The hell of it was that she was probably in more danger being alone with him.

Sure, he'd displayed a world of willpower when she'd been injured and bedridden. But this new Glory, healing now, spirited and beautiful could undoubtedly melt his resolve with just one sweet smile.

Steven spanned his hands around Glory's tiny waist, pulling her in close first so that their bodies brushed. "Trust me, Glory," he whispered into her ear, "but not too much."

He let her go briskly and mounted, shutting off her protests by reaching down to hoist her up. "Shhh. No talking until we get out of town. Stay close and hide your face against my back. With luck if anyone spots us, they'll think it's just one rider."

He settled her behind him, wrapping both her arms around his middle. "Don't let go."

She mumbled something he couldn't quite make out, but he was more than certain from her tone, he didn't want to know what she'd said. He grinned and took off at a fast pace.

The reverend's daughter was no docile female.

Though it would make his life easier if she was, that fact didn't bother him in the least.

But what did bother him was the feminine press of her body up against his, the soft crush of two perfectly formed breasts nestled to his back and her delicate hands splayed around his stomach. He willed his breaths to remain even, willed his body not to respond, willed his heart and mind not to take heed. He would not dally with Gloria Mae Shaw, he promised himself.

He slowed Fancy to a pace more suitable for two riders, hoping to give Glory a smooth ride. They traveled along a narrow trail, up through hills taking them away from Virginia City, Gold Hill and Silver City. They climbed their way through a cropping of tall pines until they came upon a small running stream. Steven had been here before, many times. It was one of his favorite places and as far as he knew, no one else around these parts knew of this particular, secluded spot.

"We're here." He turned to find Glory's blue eyes taking in the scenery—as much as light from the half moon would allow. A tall rocky-peaked mountain was their shield on one side and lofty Nevada sugar pines protected them from the other. The stream, a tributary from the Truckee River, cut the balance of the land in two.

"Do you want to get down?" he asked, fully aware of Glory's arms still wrapped around him.

"Oh, yes. Please."

Tentatively, with a shyness he'd not witnessed before, Glory removed her arms from his waist. He helped her down first, before dismounting.

He watched her run toward the rushing stream and thrust her arms out wide, breathing deeply, taking in fresh mountain air.

She'd been cooped up for a week and it was plain to see how much she enjoyed being free of her confinement.

She giggled like a small child and twirled around, her hood dropping down and allowing her blond hair to escape. She was a vision in the moonlight, a free, uninhibited spirit spinning around with joy in her heart. "Thank you. Thank you for bringing me here."

Steven tied Fancy's reins around a tree and leaned against it, folding his arms, keeping his distance. It would be too easy to go to her. It would be too easy to take full advantage of her happiness. It would be too doggone easy.

And wrong.

Steven unrolled a gray blanket and laid it out on the ground. He undid the strap of his saddlebag and brought out a jar of apple cider and some leftover treats that Mattie had packed for him.

The blanket looked too inviting for a man pretty much dead on his feet. He'd worked at his ranch all day, rode more than an hour late tonight to check on Glory, and now, when he should be sleeping, he found himself entertaining her, like some smitten boy courting his girl.

Glory walked up and down the streambed balancing herself on rocks, bending to put a hand into the water and splash around. Steven put a hand to his gun, making sure he'd be ready if an intruder came upon them. One never knew when a hungry bear or wolf might approach. This was an isolated area, and though he'd been up here as a young boy and never had a problem, no sense being reckless. They might be disturbing some wild creature's habitat without knowing it.

He lowered himself down on the blanket, keeping a watchful eye on Glory. As he leaned his head back against the tree, Glory came forward. She glanced at the food and drink. With eyes that simply danced, she asked, "Are we having a picnic?"

A midnight picnic?

Now if that didn't beat all. Steven hadn't thought of it that way. And it'd be best if she didn't, either.

"Mattie sent along some food."

"That was real sweet of her."

Glory sat down on the blanket. Her face, cast in the glow of moonlight, was beaming.

"Is it all right if I take this off?"

"Huh?" He lifted his head. "Oh, yeah." She meant the cape. "For now."

"It's a warm night."

"Uh-huh."

She unfastened the tie at her throat. The cape slipped off her shoulders, exposing creamy skin underneath and a surge of heat threatened to do him in. As she leaned forward to fold the cape, her small breasts pressed tight against the fabric of her gown in such a way that she nearly spilled out of the darn thing.

He had to remember that tonight she was grateful to him for bringing her here. But in the morning, she'd remember her hatred of him, his mother and Rainbow House.

"This is a beautiful place. How do you know about it?"

Steven leaned back, putting his hat on, and slanting

it down across his forehead. He couldn't be lusting after Glory all night. Keeping his eyes averted would help.

"I used to come here, when I was a boy."

"By yourself?"

He nodded. "I guess it was a way to get out of the house for a time." With a finger, he raised his hat enough to look her in the eye. "At night."

Glory blinked. "Oh."

"My mother never knew."

"But you felt you had to get away from…from—"

"Yeah." That's all he would say. He wouldn't allow Glory any more ammunition to use against his mother or her way of life.

Glory smoothed the blanket out with her palm, making circles, her mind probably spinning just the same way. "What did you mean before—when you said not to trust you?"

Steven slumped back against the tree trunk and yanked his hat farther down. That subject was risky as well, and he didn't feel the need to explain. "Nothing."

"It was something, Steven," she said on a whisper.

"Forget I said anything."

"Why?"

"Because knowing won't make life any easier for either of us."

"Are you sorry you saved my life?"

"No."

"Are you sorry you're hiding me out?"

"It has to be done."

"Then why can't I trust you?"

Steven raised himself up to stare into her studious, innocent eyes. She didn't know how he felt about her.

That was a good thing. She probably thought he disliked her as much as she disliked him. That was another good thing. Best to keep it that way.

"Here," he said, handing her his gun. "I haven't had any sleep for nearly a day. Watch out for preying animals. Eat something. And wake me well before dawn."

"What kind of animals?" she asked in a shaky voice, holding his gun with her fingertips as if to touch it completely would scorch her hand.

He grabbed the gun from her, thinking better of giving her a weapon. "All kinds. Just wake me if you see something. And don't go far."

"F-far?" She glanced around. "I'm not going anywhere."

She scooted closer to him and the scent of roses struck him like a thunderbolt.

He groaned and slammed his eyes shut, hoping sleep would claim him. He needed rest. He needed willpower. He needed to get the woman off his mind.

Because one thing was certain.

Midnight and Glory were a dangerous combination.

A creature's howl off in the distance woke Gloria with a start. She opened her eyes and gasped her surprise when she realized her late-night surroundings. Tall pines and rushing waters reminded her of the hours before. She'd been whisked off on a midnight ride, escaping the boredom that came hand-in-hand with healing and recovery. And now as she cuddled up against Steven, his arms cradling her shoulders and his chest her pillow, she recalled just how she'd come to rest in the safety of his arms.

It was entirely that darn raccoon's fault! She'd been

left to herself, Steven falling into an immediate and deep sleep. His warning about wild creatures kept her from venturing out, yet nature had called and Gloria had no choice but to leave the safety of the blanket. She dashed to the nearest cropping of trees and when she returned, eyes as black as pitch met her in the darkness. She shrieked. Her loud crude dismay brought Steven out of his slumber. He went for his gun and nearly shot the famished animal. The raccoon had sought nourishment from the foodstuffs left out near the blanket. Steven shooed him away and grabbed for Gloria, bringing her down on the blanket with him.

''Keep quiet and let me sleep,'' he'd said as grumpy as an old bear.

Gloria made no struggle when he'd taken her in his arms, throwing the cape over both of them. She knew it hadn't been a lusty move on his part, but more a way to keep her contained and quiet. She'd calmed her rapid heartbeats and soon found the sleep she needed.

But now, it was nearing dawn. She lifted her head to peer at Steven. He still slept peacefully. She breathed in the scent of leather and earth, of lye soap and raw man.

On a deep silent sigh, she wondered how she'd feel about Steven Harding if he hadn't been who he was, and if the entire situation had been different. Would she find him fascinating, handsome and surly, wearing that gun on his hip as if it was part of his body? Would he somehow find a way into her heart? Or would he have fooled her with empty promises of a happy life filled with children, the way Boone had?

She glanced at him again. How very safe she felt

in his arms. The thought of waking him again made her cringe, yet it had to be done. Carefully, without making a sound, Gloria removed herself from his arms. She rose in silence and took a moment for herself. Walking to the stream, she stared out, admiring the way everything God put on this earth blended beautifully, working together with quiet ease.

If only people could come together as successfully.

"It's time to go," Steven whispered in her ear. Startled, she made a move to whirl around, but he braced her, wrapping his arms around her waist.

She settled against him, leaning back, his breaths warming her throat, his scent enveloping her. Since meeting Steven Harding, all sense of propriety had fairly vanished. To lie with him on that blanket then to stand here, cradled in his protective arms, made no sense at all. He was, by all means, the enemy. He was a man she should despise. But at the moment, that was the last thing on her mind. "I hate to leave."

"Wild creatures and all?"

There was mirth in his tone.

"Did you frighten me on purpose?"

In a somber tone, he replied, "No. I'd never do that. There is a real danger out here, Glory. From the elements, the creatures and…"

"And?"

"Me," he added, his voice a soft caress.

"Y-you?"

His hand came up to her neck. He held her softly, gently, stroking the underside of her face. Then his lips brushed the base of her throat, the kiss a whisper in the night. But Gloria couldn't miss his rigid stance, solid against her back, reminding her he was very much a man, with needs. Needs she would never entertain. Yet she trembled from his touch and the warm protection of his body.

His lips moved higher up on her throat, another kiss, then another, soft and exquisitely tender. Insides quaking, Gloria realized it wasn't Steven that made her shudder, but the tender way he touched her. She'd never been treated with such gentle regard before. Boone had been callous and cold, an unyielding hard man.

This sensation was new. And it startled her. It couldn't be Steven Harding making her toes curl. No, it had to be the revelation that a man could be so gentle and that a woman could respond in kind, with breathless awe.

Her senses reeling, Gloria relished each of his kisses now, because she knew the reason. She made a tiny moan, a whimper of delight, that both amused and embarrassed her.

''We'd better go,'' Steven rasped out, stepping away quickly.

She turned around to glance at him. Anger burned deep in his eyes, a fiery gaze she couldn't mistake. What had she done to irritate him?

''Steven?''

''It's almost dawn.''

He shoved the cape at her. His tone was sharp and quick, in complete contrast to the man who'd just held her moments ago. He busied himself with rolling the blanket and filling his saddlebags with the food that they hadn't eaten. Then he led Fancy to her. With finesse, he mounted then reached down to help her up. She settled her bottom onto the saddle.

''Remember to keep the hood over your head. Ready?''

"Yes, I'm ready."

"Dammit, Glory. You'd better hold on to me."

Gloria hated putting her hands anywhere on the man. One minute he was warm and sweet like a candied apple, the next he behaved as sourly as a pickle left too long in the jar. But her good instincts took hold. It wouldn't bode well if she fell from the horse. She wrapped her arms loosely around his middle, garnering a distinct stubborn grunt from him.

"You need more sleep, Steven."

"That's not what I need, Glory." Then he urged Fancy forward, breaking into a fast trot.

And they rode back to Rainbow House in silence.

Chapter Six

When Gloria woke the next morning and glanced at the brass-and-oak carved grandfather clock, she hustled out of bed in a flurry. She couldn't believe the time. Why, it was after noon. Her stomach also, recalled the time and that she hadn't eaten.

She'd missed her quiet morning time with Mattie.

And unless she wanted to starve to death in this room, she'd have to face the ladies of the house once again. Gloria poured water from a pitcher into the delicate gilded bowl and washed her face. She combed her hair and fashioned a chignon, pinning the strands up and out of her way. Then she donned the gown.

She had just finished fastening the last button when she heard a knock at the door. Surprised, she wondered if Steven had come with a tray of food, taking on the role of savior again. Or perhaps, Mattie saw fit to bring her a meal, but Gloria realized with remorse, she'd be mortified if that were the case. Goodness, she wasn't helpless. Surely she could fend for herself, even if it meant joining the women downstairs to share a noontime meal.

"Just a second," she called out, taking a quick look into the cheval mirror to make sure she was properly dressed.

When she opened the door, her mouth gaped open. "Oh, um, hello."

"Good afternoon," Emmie said in greeting. The woman who always dressed in blue, smiled warmly. She held a small carpetbag in her hand. "May I come in?"

Gloria hesitated only a second. She had no cause to refuse the woman entrance. She had no claim to the room, or anything else at Rainbow House. She was here because of Steven, due to his hospitality. It was his room.

She nodded and opened the door wider, stepping back to allow her to enter.

"Steven said you weren't comfortable wearing my gown."

"Oh! No, I didn't mean that. It's just that," she began, and her hand immediately, involuntarily, went to her chest, covering up the skin exposed there. "It's just that it's a bit tight on me and well, quite frankly, I'm used to more material in, uh, certain places."

Emmie chuckled, not in a disparaging way, but sweetly, with understanding in her eyes. "Of course you're not accustomed to wearing such gowns. That's understandable. When I was younger, I never had such clothes, either."

She set the carpetbag down on the bed and opened it. "We don't have much in the way of sewing implements, but at times, we have to make a quick repair."

Gloria didn't want to think about why that was. "I see."

Emmie brought out a yard of Belgian lace, cream in color and an inch wide. "I thought this might help. You can sew it all around the bodice, maybe twice over. It will save your modesty."

A wealth of gratitude played heavy in her heart. She wanted so much to accept. But Gloria knew a moment of indecision. "Oh, it's lovely and...and very kind of you. But I couldn't possibly accept it. The lace must be expensive. I couldn't possibly pay you back."

With a knowing smile, Emmie sat on the bed. "Consider it a gift. From Steven."

"Steven?" she croaked out.

"Yes, it was his idea."

"Oh, but don't you see, now that's more reason why I can't accept it."

"You must. Steven insisted."

"He *insisted?*" Stunned, Gloria sank down on the bed.

Emmie grinned. "I promised not to repeat what he said. But, he was quite certain. He wants you to cover up."

Cover up? Gloria mouthed those two words, hardly believing any of this. The nerve of that man! All the while Gloria had declared the dress inappropriate, Steven had complimented her, speaking kind words, telling her she looked lovely in the gown. Now, suddenly, after last night, he'd had a change of heart. Gloria put her face in her hands and lowered her head.

Emmie rested a hand on her shoulder. "No need to cry about it. It's just a bit of lace."

When Gloria lifted up, laughter spilled out, silly, giddy, ridiculous laughter. She met Emmie's puzzled gaze. Then with a start, Emmie too began to laugh.

The room filled with merriment, finally dying down to a giggle or two.

"Oh, this is just too impossible," Gloria declared, settling down from her bout of amusement. The release had been wonderful, a cleansing of sorts, of tension and pain created first by the death of her father and then by her ill-fated marriage. Oh, she'd cried and cried, until she hadn't a tear left to shed, but the laughter today had been more liberating and freeing than the weeping she had done in the past.

Perhaps Steven was also responsible for her gaiety, but at the same time, he perplexed her with his unpredictable ways. "That man doesn't make a bit of sense."

Emmie grinned. "Men usually don't. But what do you mean?"

"First he tells me I look beautiful. He kisses me. Then he behaves as though I have the plague or something far worse, hardly speaking a word to me. And now this—*insisting* I cover up as if it was all his idea."

"It's what you want, isn't it? I mean about the lace."

"Yes, of course." She lifted the lace and fingered the delicate edges. She did want to save her modesty. "It's lovely."

Gloria didn't know what else to say. Steven had a way of confusing her. She didn't know if she should commend his gesture, or be spitting mad at him.

"Steven *kissed* you?" Emmie asked with a great deal of interest.

"Oh!" She hadn't meant to divulge that bit of information. "Well, the first time, it was only to hide me. I'd dashed out of the house and Mr. Hurley was…'' Gloria stopped when Emmie's eyes grew wide with astonishment.

"It really wasn't anything," Gloria offered, the explanation a lie on her lips. The kiss had been remarkable, more passionate than she could ever imagine. She didn't know a man could initiate such passion. Or that she would take part in such a kiss from a near-stranger.

"How many times has he kissed you?"

"Just that one time. Last night doesn't count. I mean, we had just woken up and he…really… only…kissed my…uh—"

Gloria couldn't go on. She couldn't explain about last night. How wonderful she'd felt being out of the house for a time, enjoying the night air, the mountains and warm breezes. Steven had done that for her. Though exhausted, he'd taken her out to keep her from boredom. But, she wasn't a fool and she wasn't all that innocent. She *had* been married, after all, and the telling gleam in Emmie's eyes left no room for doubt what she'd been thinking.

"You *slept* with him?" Emmie asked, fully intrigued now.

Gloria concealed her dismay. Truth be told, she had, in a sense, slept with Steven. Yet, she couldn't very well lead Emmie to believe anything indecent had happened. The irony was almost too much to bear. Gloria worried over her reputation with a woman who quite obviously made her living in an ill-reputed profession. "No, of course not. Not in that way."

Emmie sighed, a dramatic, heavy sound escaping her lips. "Steven has grown into a wonderful man. And he's obviously smitten. Many of the girls are infatuated with him, and he likes us all fine, but he's nothing more than our friend.''

"A friend? I thought that he…um—" Gloria couldn't voice what she'd been thinking all the while. She was more than certain that Steven sought solace with the ''ladies'' at night, when he hadn't been nursing her injuries.

"No.'' Emmie smiled knowingly. "Besides, Lorene strictly forbids it. I don't think that would matter much to Steven though. He pretty much goes after what he wants. And it seems he wants—''

"What? What does he want?''

Emmie hesitated. She appeared to be a woman who spoke her mind, but Gloria sensed she held something back. Her voice softened, mellowing her words. "Steven wants to keep you safe.''

Because of the sacrifice her father had made. Because her beloved father had intervened, hoping to stop an altercation on the streets of the town he loved. Steven's mother had lived, while Jonathan Caldwell had died. He'd been gunned down brutally, the bullet piercing two hearts, his and that of his daughter. Gloria hadn't recovered from her father's death. She'd spent the next year trying to change the immoral ways of this town. But her father hadn't cared that he risked his life for a mere harlot. That was the kind of man he was. To him, all were equal in the eyes of the Lord.

Gloria didn't have the same kind of charity in her heart.

Emmie stood and reached into her bag again. "I almost forgot. I brought you some undergarments as well. I have plenty and I'm willing to share. Here's a chemise and petticoat for you. Oh, and here's a pair of stockings. They're all new.'' She laid each one of the garments out on the bed. ''You're welcome to them.''

Gloria stared at a pair of fine silk stockings, a pure white muslin chemise and a frilly petticoat, completely taken by the generous gesture. Emotion overwhelmed her and she struggled to take hold of the situation. ''I d-don't know what to say.'' She swallowed down, fighting back tears.

Softly, Emmie said, ''Say you'll wear them.''

Gloria looked into Emmie's eyes. The girl couldn't be much older than her. She wondered how Emmie had come to live here at Rainbow House. She was pretty and she obviously knew something about doctoring. Surely, she wouldn't have to work in such a place. Surely, Emmie could have found suitable employment or a husband in a town swarming with miners and businessmen.

''Thank you.''

''You're welcome.'' Emmie headed for the door. ''I'm starved. No doubt Mattie has cooked up something delicious by now. Are you coming down?''

Most likely Gloria was even more famished than Emmie. She hadn't eaten a thing since yesterday afternoon. But the thought of facing all those women again knotted her growling stomach. ''Oh, uh, yes. I suppose.''

''I'll wait. We'll go down together.''

Emmie stood patiently waiting. Relieved, Gloria nodded, somewhat dismayed at finding the girl who always wore blue to have a generous and kind nature. The images of these ladies painted inside Gloria's head had been dark and filled with gloom, but as she peered at Emmie as they made their way down the stairs, Gloria only saw bright, unfettered light.

Mattie smiled a quick greeting and continued cooking when they entered the kitchen. Ruby ignored her. Carmen turned her back. All the others put their heads down and stopped their gay chattering, all but one.

"Hello." A young freckle-faced woman grinned, her red hair a burst of color against the pale yellow gown she wore. "Oh, I don't rightly care," she said to all the others. "Today, I'm just too blessed happy. It's Thursday. And my sweet Bud McKenzie is coming to call."

"You make it sound like he's courting you, Merry," Ruby admonished. "You know there's trouble in that thinking."

The one called Merry didn't flinch. "My Bud is different. He only comes to see me and you all know it."

Carmen, the black-eyed Mexican woman grunted, but then spoke softly, almost motherly. "We all have regulars, *amiga*."

"He's bringing me another gift tonight. He said so. The others don't do that."

Gloria noted how the girl caressed a lovely brooch on her gown designed in silver and gold. Two perfect pearl fasteners stayed her thick red hair and on her right hand she wore a gemstone ring made of sapphire.

"Some of them do and some of them don't. It don't mean a whole lot," another woman stated.

Gloria felt ill-at-ease, listening in on this conversation. She made a move to exit the room. Emmie took her arm and guided her farther into the kitchen.

"This is Gloria, everyone," Emmie said. "She's staying here as Lorene's guest."

The women shifted their focus from Merry to her, their gaze resting on her gown. She must look like one of them, she thought, mortified.

"We know who she is," declared a woman wearing soft lavender taffeta.

"Glory, this is Julia," Emmie said. "And Merry is the one all fancied up who's been doing all the talking. Eva is sitting at the far end of the table. I believe you've met the rest."

"Yes, um, we've met."

Carmen made a noise.

The others became quiet.

"Mattie, we're both starved. Set us up some plates, please," Emmie said, taking a seat.

Mattie busied herself, filling dishes up with curried rice, long string beans, and some sort of fancy chicken dish. The food smelled mouthwatering. Gloria was nearly faint from hunger now.

Gloria took a seat next to Emmie and ignored the looks she received from the women. She bowed her head, clasped her hands together and began, "Heavenly Father, we thank you for this abundant meal. We thank you for today, the health you have bestowed upon all of us and for your ever-present kindness. As we sit before this meal, we praise you, Dear Lord, and hope that your wisdom will help the many who have turned to an unrighteous path. Amen."

When Glory lifted her head, Carmen had hers still bent in prayer, Julia and Eva stared at each other with curious regard, and the others, as if not knowing how else to respond, finally complied with a hushed "Amen."

They ate in silence for a time. Gloria hadn't realized how her daily prayer, something she'd done since she was a tot, had affected the women.

"That was nice, Glory. It's been too long since we've said our prayers." Emmie cut her piece of chicken into small bites.

"It's something I've done since I was able to form a complete sentence."

Carmen glared at her. "Yes, the woman reminds us all that we are not good Christians."

"You're not Christian, Carmen," Ruby piped in. "You're Catholic. And you used to go to mass at Saint Mary's in the Mountains."

"*Si*, yes. I did go before the winds tore it down."

"It's been rebuilt, Carmen. About a year now," Mattie interjected. "You should come with me on Sunday."

"They do not want me in their 'bonanza' church."

"God wants you in His church," Gloria stated, glancing at Carmen to gauge her reaction. "That's all that matters."

Carmen stared deeply into her eyes, probing, searching, until finally, she nodded. "Maybe."

"And maybe tomorrow, you'd like to lead our supper prayers," Gloria suggested.

Carmen stiffened, her shoulders rigid, but her heart was in her eyes. She softened her tone and with a bob of her head, she replied, "Maybe."

The rest of the meal was eaten in unusual silence, perhaps the others as deep in thought as Gloria. She ate up heartily, filling her stomach until she didn't think it could possibly hold another bite.

Mattie placed hot dishes of peach cobbler on the table. "Dessert, ladies."

Gloria now understood why young Mattie had won over all the ladies at Rainbow House so quickly. They commended her meals, but nothing compared to the silly noises they made when she showered them with such rich and delicious desserts.

Gloria took her plate and stood. "Thank you, Mattie. I'll save mine for later. Good afternoon, ladies."

And to her amazement, some of the women looked up, meeting with her gaze and smiled. Others offered the same farewell. Gloria climbed the stairs with a plate of peach cobbler in one hand and a heavy dose of conscience in the other.

She'd have to pray long and hard tonight to find her balance. Because right now, disturbing thoughts rushed in, upsetting her rigid code of principles.

It was just before midnight when Steven knocked on Glory's door. He half hoped she wouldn't answer. If she'd had a full day, maybe she'd been tired and gone to bed. Then he wouldn't have to spend half the night with her, keeping her company and looking into those sky-blue eyes. Of course, he could have stayed at the ranch, leaving Glory to her own devices tonight. But Steven had a compelling need to see her, and if he was honest with himself, it wasn't completely because he needed to check on her safety.

He'd worked on his corrals all day, then after fixing himself a plate of bacon and beans at sundown, he'd slept for a few hours, needing the rest to keep his wits about him. With his obligation to Glory firmly in his mind, Steven couldn't afford any slip-ups.

Glory appeared in the doorway and Steven sucked in a breath. How the woman managed to look more beautiful each day, he couldn't figure, but there she stood, blond hair pinned up in a fashionable do, eyes sparkling and her mouth just as tempting as ever. "Steven."

"Evening, Glory."

She stared at him with uncertainty in her eyes.

"You gonna let me in?"

Piano music drifted up, a song he'd been accustomed to hearing about "Calico Women." The lively tune mixed with laughter and voices, some coming from just one floor below. "Make up your mind quick, Glory." He glanced down the hallway toward the stairs.

Her pretty mouth twisted and she stepped aside.

He entered, wondering what kind of bug she had in her bonnet this time. "Something got you perplexed?"

He closed the door and waited, none too patiently.

She fairly ignored him, walking to the far side of the room, peeking out the window, striding about the room and finding interest in the most inconsequential objects on the dresser.

"Glory." The warning came out more harshly than he intended.

She turned to him, those blue eyes blazing with fire. "Am I covered up to your satisfaction, Steven?"

He blinked. Then noticed her gown. She'd sewn lace around the edges of her dress, helping to hide her female assets. "It was the best I could do. What's got your feathers ruffled, anyway?"

"You told Emmie you wanted me to cover up. You insisted on it."

"Yeah, that's right. You're forever saying how indecent you look in that dress."

"And you finally agreed?"

Steven scratched his neck. He'd been around women most of his life, but he'd be damned if he could figure a single one of them out. "Hell, no, you don't look indecent. You don't really want to know what I think now, honey. So just drop it. I'm too tired to figure out your puzzles tonight."

Glory sank down on the bed apparently dejected. "But I do want to know what you think."

"Why?" He stood a distance away, with boots rooted to the floor and hands planted on hips, unnerved by the softness in her tone.

"I'm...not really certain." She lifted soft eyes his way, the blue not ablaze anymore, but a bright beckoning gleam.

The woman made his gut twist with emotion. At times, just looking at her stirred his heart and made his head throb. The effect she had on him was potent.

She had power over him.

He hated the thought. If he hadn't saved her from that fire, she'd never once look in his direction, but he had, and now they were stuck with each other. Wanting her had nothing to do with it. He wouldn't compromise her or take advantage of her situation. She would never be his.

For all he knew, she was beholden to him for saving her life, but secretly detested him. She blamed him and his mother for the loss of her father. Clearly, he'd gotten her point. She had no use for the son of a brothel owner. He wasn't held high in her regard. That notion didn't set well.

"Ah, hell, Glory. You want the truth? You're a temptation I can't afford. You asked if I was satisfied that you covered up. Well, dammit, no, I'm not nearly satisfied. I'd like nothing better than to *uncover* all of you and take you to my bed. Then I'd be satisfied.''

''Steven!''

Red color crawled up her throat, scorching her face. Now he'd done it. He'd angered and humiliated her. He was ready for her wrath. He needed it. He had to drive a wedge between them to stop the tender feelings he had for her. He had to stop wanting her. And what better way than to ensure her hatred of him and confirm his suspicions?

But Glory didn't lash out. Her spirit hadn't taken hold as he'd planned. Instead of blasting him with her fury, she laid her head down on her pillow and shed deep, soulful tears.

Steven cursed. Glory cried louder.

Causing her even a single moment of pain hadn't been his intent. Against his better judgment, he went to her. Kneeling down beside her bed, he took her hands in his.

''Don't,'' she said, pulling back. ''I hate you, Steven Harding.''

Well, he'd gotten what he'd wanted. But the means surely didn't justify the end in this case. ''I know.''

He took her hands again and because she'd gone limp, he was able to lift her up. They stood close, Steven caught by the look of hurt in her eyes, the stream of tears flowing down her face.

''Y-you're no different than Boone.''

The words cut straight through his heart. She compared him to her abusive husband.

Her sobbing ebbed a bit and she stuttered her confession. ''H-he never c-cared about my f-feelings. He was hurtful and cruel and when he wanted me,'' she said, lowering her voice to a whisper, "he was b-brutal."

Steven swallowed hard, fully realizing what Glory had gone through at the hands of a merciless man. He was glad the man was dead. And if she had killed him with that knife, he knew he would never hold that against her.

Steven took her into his arms. Surprised that she allowed it, he hugged her close. She rested her head on his shoulders, her body ragged, falling into him for support. Her tears soaked through his shirt, the moisture searing his skin like a hot torch of pain. He held her with all the tenderness he had inside. Gently, he stroked her hair and spoke soft soothing words of comfort. She settled in a pattern of regular breathing, her tears all shed.

"You don't really think I'm like Boone, do you?" he asked quietly.

She hesitated then slowly shook her head. "I don't want to think so."

"I'm not, Glory. Trust me."

She gazed up, her eyes filled with confusion. "I don't know if I can. Ever."

"I'd never hurt you."

"But you have," she said. And he knew she hadn't meant tonight.

"I know. And I know you hate me."

Glory sighed and lay her head back on his shoulders. "Yes, I hate you very much," she whispered in the dark.

Steven held her close, relishing the feel of her supple body, the crush of her breasts against him. His body grew tight and desire assailed him like a traitorous enemy.

He pulled away from her roughly, disengaging her from his clutches. "Look, I came up here to see if you wanted to get out again. For a ride. But you probably don't want—"

Hope filled her lovely eyes, vanquishing all remnants of her tears. "A ride? Oh, I'd love a ride tonight."

"Well, get your cape," he said hastily and before thinking better of it, he added, "Let's go."

Chapter Seven

He hadn't planned on a windstorm. He hadn't planned on dust biting at his eyes, making it hard to see the ground, much less the trail. He hadn't planned on shrieking sounds and the sheer terror of nature spooking Fancy so much that he'd had to hightail it toward the mountainside just to make certain his mare wouldn't throw them.

Hell, he hadn't planned on being shoved into close quarters in an abandoned mine with Glory all dog-gone night. He'd been lucky to find shelter amid the swirling gusts and dim moonlight, but that's where his luck had ended. Because he was alone again with Glory, probably for the entire night. He hoped the winds would let up before dawn. He had to get her back to Rainbow House before daybreak.

He'd offered Glory a midnight ride, something to calm her, to soothe her feelings and get her some fresh air. Instead, she stood by the east wall of the mine next to Fancy, shivering, with fear in her eyes as the wind howled like a pack of wild animals outside. They couldn't go any farther into the mine for fear of a collapse. No telling the stability of these walls. "I'll light a fire."

There was enough dry wood around from broken-down shafts to build a blazing fire. Soon, warmth spread out, lighting up the small alcove and he beckoned Glory to come close. "Sit down on the blanket where it's warm."

She took a seat and he reached for her hands, rubbing warmth into them. "Sorry about the windstorm. I'd never have brought you out if I'd known."

"You can't predict the weather, Steven. Only God knows when to unleash His fury." She stared at their entwined hands.

"Is that what it is, fury?" Satisfied once he'd brought her warmth, he released her. She placed her hands under the cape and cast him a timid smile.

Her hood had fallen to her shoulders, exposing her hair, the golden mass catching the glow of the fire. Steven had to glance away briefly, the impact of firelight and Glory too much to take.

"That's what Father would say. He'd say the Lord knew when to unleash his fury. He knew what he was doing, even if we couldn't quite figure it out. Father had so much faith. He never questioned it." Glory put her head down. "Sometimes I wish I had his faith."

Steven touched her cheek, and she lifted her head. "I think you do. But you've been through a lot lately. And just because your father didn't voice his questions, doesn't mean he didn't have them. We all have doubts, Glory."

"But Father was so...settled, in his mind. He taught me so much."

"I'm sorry for your loss."

Glory closed her eyes. Her light-blond lashes rested on her cheek like a butterfly settling on a flower. "How can you be? My father's death meant your mother's life."

"Glory, look at me."

He waited patiently, watching her struggle to open her eyes, look at his face and hear what he had to say.

Finally, when she did, he began. "Yes, your father's death meant my mother's life, but that doesn't mean that I'm not sorry for the events of that day. I wish your father hadn't died. And my mother is sorry over it as well. She's dealt with the guilt every day since."

"But don't you see, if she wasn't who she was, if the brothel hadn't existed, then that drifter wouldn't have call to seek your mother out. He had quarrel with her, for heaven only knows what reason."

"Mother refused him entry into Rainbow House. Marcus had tossed him out. He'd been falling-down drunk and abusive at the door. My mother protects her girls and didn't want him causing trouble inside. The drifter probably wouldn't have done anything about it, except he spotted my mother coming out of church the next day."

"Church?" Glory's eyes rounded with disbelief.

"Mother went whenever she could. She'd go in late, sit in the back pew and leave early. She never wanted to cause a ruckus."

"I never saw her."

"And I bet you never saw me, either?"

"No, no." She studied his face, her eyes searching for something, perhaps the truth. "The church was always packed to overflowing. I never noticed you."

But Steven had noticed her. He'd admired her from a distance and soon, attending church with Lorene held new meaning. He'd catch a glimpse of the beautiful young daughter of Reverend Caldwell, smiling to the members of the congregation, sitting up front, sometimes right next to her father, wearing a sweet smile, with pride in her eyes. Steven often hadn't heard the words of the sermon being offered, being too smitten with the young girl with the blue eyes and honey-gold hair.

During those times, Steven had wished he'd been someone different—someone worthy of Miss Gloria Mae Caldwell.

Steven poked at the fire, causing a big blast of heat to swell up. "Maybe we should try to rest up a bit. Why don't you lie down?"

Glory stared at the fire. "You think it's sinful for us…to sleep together like this?"

Steven lowered down onto his back, bringing his arms up to pillow his head. "There's nothing sinful in what we're doing, Glory. We haven't done one…sinful…thing."

"Some might say because we're alone, unchaperoned, well, it's compromising."

"Nah. Not a soul will know, so your reputation won't get harmed. Besides, you hate me, remember."

Glory turned her head from the fire to peer down at him. She nodded slowly, looking at him with remorse. She lowered her body down and snuggled into the blanket. "Yes, I hate you," she whispered, her voice a light caress.

And Steven wondered if her admission was meant to convince him.

Or herself.

*   *   *

The earth was cold and hard. Aged timber and distressed walls were all around, giving off a musty scent that nearly swallowed her up. Yet, she was tucked safely away in the foyer of this mine, shielded from the billowing gusts that threatened to down trees. Gloria opened her eyes to find Steven asleep just inches away. Somehow during the night, they'd come together on the blanket, his arm protectively covering her shoulder.

She stared at him in the firelight, thinking him a handsome man, with a strong jaw, strong body and even stronger mind. They both had a stubborn streak, she admitted honestly and without pause. They both felt righteous in their beliefs. Steven didn't find fault in how he'd been raised. He didn't hold his mother accountable to the way she chose to live. He considered the prostitutes his friends and lived his life accordingly.

Her questionable faith aside, Gloria had been raised with morals. She'd been taught about duty and honor and charity. She believed in those things and held them close at hand, for to do so also meant to keep her father's dear memory in her heart.

But the one thing she hadn't the courage to do was to forgive. She'd listened to countless sermons on the power of forgiveness, the Lord asking that of his fellow man without qualm. But for Gloria, forgiveness didn't come easy. And now, looking at Steven Harding, perhaps *not* hating him in the way she'd declared earlier when she'd been distraught, but she found no way to forgive him—or his mother. She found no way to pardon the crimes that had occurred in the past or the crimes that are bound to happen in the future.

Steven stirred and Gloria pretended sleep, closing her eyes, keeping still but for her deep breathing.

A finger touched her cheek, and a whisper touched her ear. "You smell like roses." Then his lips were on her, a tender brushing and the gentle slide of his mouth greeted hers. Gloria kissed him back timidly, with hesitation because she knew it to be wrong, yet she'd been overwhelmed with the tenderness he displayed almost as if she were a delicate flower and he feared injuring even one velvety petal.

Hazy with sleep, Steven peered at her through heavy lids. "I dreamt of you. And when I woke, you were here."

"You dreamt of me?"

"You were in a garden. And you picked a pretty rose."

"And what did I do with my rose?" she asked, breathless from the image, the thought of being free to enjoy a garden of flowers once again.

"You gave it to me."

He bent his head and kissed her again. Her heart did a small flip, the exquisite emotion far too overwhelming to deny.

When he pulled away slightly, she shook her head. "We shouldn't."

"Because I'm your enemy?" he asked.

"Because we're not married." And we never will be. Of that, Gloria was certain. To entertain romantic notions of Steven Harding would simply be foolish. "It's sinful."

Steven splayed his hand through her hair, his fingers weaving through to stroke her head softly. She nearly purred aloud from his ministrations. "Tell me, what could be more sinful than a man's cruelty to his wife, to hurt her in unimaginable ways? No sin is greater than that."

The argument she was ready to voice died on her lips. Steven was right and Gloria wouldn't deny him that. "Yes, that's true."

Steven slid the palm of his hand along her throat, coaxing a little whimper from her. Then he moved his hands along her shoulders, touching her skin, and the movement released the fabric. Cool air assailed her as the material fell off her shoulders, baring her skin. "You're beautiful and young, Glory. You deserve to know tenderness from a man."

His words warmed her and made her wish for impossible things. His eyes warmed her as well, with an admiring look, as if she were more precious than a gold strike. It was a look she'd never once received from her husband.

His hand came up to graze her chest, his fingertips spreading out, caressing her skin, sliding down until his fingers slipped under the barrier of lace Steven insisted she wear.

Hot tingles of delight swarmed her senses as he found the slope of her breasts. And then one finger traveled over the tip of her breast. She inhaled sharply as he flicked the crest gently. Stirring heat shot up and down her body. "Steven."

He kissed her. "You're perfect, Glory."

He rubbed her again and again, his finger working magic, the heat and intense pleasure causing her great anguish. She'd never known these sensations before. She'd never had these powerful urges. Surely this was sinful.

"Don't think, honey," he whispered, as if he could read her thoughts. He brushed his mouth over hers again "Just feel. For once, enjoy the pleasure."

Pleasure? She had never known anything but harshness and impatience from her husband. And whether sinful or not, Gloria wanted to know what tenderness could bring. She'd been curious before, but now it was more. Her body responded to Steven in newfound ways. She couldn't deny him and the incredible desire he created within her. She was at his mercy, too wrapped up with passion to think clearly.

He parted the lace with his hand and brought his head down, planting tiny kisses along her breasts, causing the ache inside to grow hot and heavy. Her female parts throbbed. And when he thrust his tongue over one hardened peak, laving, moistening, licking, she jolted, her body lifting and falling again in rhythm with his movements. His lips and tongue did mysteriously wonderful things to her. Again and again, until she could barely breathe. She responded to him in ways that thrilled and confused her. She had little room for rational thought, the lusty stroking making her head swim deliciously. "Oh, Steven," she pleaded, her breathing labored, "if you were to take me now, I'd not have the will to stop you."

Steven stopped as if cold water had been dumped on his head. He stared into her eyes, then took her hand and placed it below his waist. She felt the rigid length of his desire through his trousers. Her heartbeats sped up and she believed the quick thumping pounded inside her head as well.

"I have willpower, Glory. I'm not like Boone. I would never hurt you. I would never take what is not offered freely. But you and I both know that will never happen. We will never be together in that way. You have nothing to fear from me.''

Gloria bit down on her lip, nodding her head and removing her hand. Emotions raged and she tried to sort them out. She knew what she felt could not be shame. There was no shame in something so wonderful. Surely there couldn't be. But she had remorse and it ran deep to her very core. What Steven said was true. They could never be together in that way. Sadly, she had to agree.

Steven Harding had no place in her life.

And she had no place in his.

''The wind's died down some,'' he said. ''I think we can make it back now. We'd best get going.''

Gloria mounted on Fancy behind Steven, her disguise intact. And as they traveled through the backwoods to town, regrets filled her head. Steven had dreamed of her in a garden. He'd dreamed of her picking a flower.

But tonight he'd made her remember something that she'd almost forgotten—that the rose she picked from that garden could never be given to him.

As Gloria headed down the stairs for the noon meal, Emmie leaned over the railing on the second floor when she spotted her. ''Glory, come quick. You have to see Merry's gift this time.''

Gloria hesitated. She'd never been on the second floor. That's where the women, uh, entertained the clientele. Those were their bedrooms. The Rainbow Rooms. Curiosity won out as well as fear of being rude to Emmie, the woman who'd clothed her and helped save her life.

Gloria came to stand just outside the painted yellow

door and noted many of the women all huddled around Merry. She couldn't see anything of the girl from her standpoint, but the room itself held her interest. The entire room was done in yellow—cheery bright yellow from flowery curtains and bright wallpaper to pitchers and vases filled with tall sunflowers. The room hardly looked like what she'd expected from a brothel, but Glory had come to realize that Rainbow House was the exception, not the rule when it came down to comparisons. Small wonder Lorene Harding had done so well in this business. She kept her girls and the clients happy and wound up making a prosperous living selling all of their souls.

Gloria prayed for guidance. She prayed to be free of her predicament. She had no place here among the prostitutes.

"Come in," Emmie said, gesturing for Glory to enter the room. "Isn't he precious?"

"He?"

The women parted, allowing Glory full view of what Merry held in her arms. "Oh, my. I've never seen a puppy so, so unique."

"Bud says he comes all the way from France. Isn't he the sweetest thing?"

Glory had to agree. With a coat of curly apricot fur and the most adorable face, the animal's dark round eyes stared up at her. "Yes. He's sweet."

"I'm naming him Buddy. After my Bud."

Ruby, who'd been quiet up until this time, spoke up. "Where are you planning to keep him?"

"In here, of course," Merry answered. And it was fitting, Gloria thought, the animal would blend in perfectly in this room of soft golden hues.

"And what if he gets in your way when you've got a man in here?"

"Oh, I'm not worried about that. Bud says he won't grow much bigger than he is right now." She hugged the dog close, kissing the top of his little head. "Besides, I don't plan on being here much longer." Merry looked at each one of her friends with glowing hopeful eyes. "I think Bud's going to ask me to marry him."

Ruby sighed heavily.

The other girls chattered noisily, asking questions, all of them with equal amounts of promise and cheerfulness in their expressions.

But it was Carmen who spoke up this time. "Merry, do not be fooled by gifts. Has this man, this Bud spokcn to you of marriage?"

Merry stroked the puppy's head, already spoiling the animal with lavish attention. "Well, no. But he's forever talking about how he plans on building a place of his own. He's doing real good in the mines."

Carmen's expression hardened. "He will not want a whore for his wife, Merry. You must not get your hopes up."

"You don't know my Bud. He's different. Besides, it ain't all that unusual. Lorene once said she's let a girl or two go to get married to their customers."

"That's right, I remember one of the gals. She'd only been here three months when a miner struck it rich and asked her to marry him," Emmie offered. "They moved up to Oregon to start a new life."

"You see," Merry said with determination, "it does happen."

Carmen looked at Ruby and both twisted their mouths in disapproval, but their eyes held certain hopeful warmth, as though they too wished it so for Merry.

"Well, if we all don't get downstairs, Mattie's gonna toss our supper out. You know how she gets when she's cooked up something special and we don't go down," Ruby said. "You coming, Merry?"

"Oh, uh, no." She stroked the puppy's head again, then laid down on her bed, smiling. "I think I'll just keep Buddy company for now. I hate the thought of leaving him alone."

Ruby ushered the girls out, including Gloria. "Fine. I'll tell Mattie to save you something. But I can't guarantee dessert, if one of the girls wants your piece of pie."

"Oh, that's all right. I have everything I need right here."

And Gloria ambled downstairs with the rest of the women, hungry for food and praying for Merry. Perhaps, one soul might get saved from this place.

"Dear Jesus, thank you for the meal before us. We ask you to keep us safely in our house. And we ask you for the justice. To find the bastard who killed Trudy Tremaine and slit his throat."

"Carmen!" Mattie and Gloria both chorused.

The news at supper had not been good. Toby, who'd delivered provisions to Mattie from the mercantile, had relayed a terrible story. Trudy Tremaine, a local prostitute who'd fallen on hard times, had been murdered in the street late last night. Some of the Rainbow House women had known her. But even the ones who hadn't known her still reeled in shock and despair.

The mood at the table was somber now, in direct

contrast to minutes ago when all were taken by the little curly-haired dog that had brought Merry so much joy. With heads down in contemplation, some ate their meal in silence. Others had lost their appetite. Gloria had suggested that Carmen offer up the afternoon prayer.

After a brief pause and stern looks from Gloria and Mattie, Carmen continued, "We pray, dear Jesus, that You find mercy for Trudy Tremaine. It is not right that Trudy is dead. God rest her soul. Amen."

"Amen," all of the ladies repeated.

"It ain't fair," Julia said. "Trudy never hurt anybody."

"I hope the sheriff finds the bastard that done it," Eva said firmly, glancing in defiance at Gloria.

"She should have took a knife to him the way Glory did," another one suggested.

Mortified, Gloria sucked in a lungful of air. "I'm not sure what happened the night Boone died."

"It's okay, Glory. We all know how you suffered that night. You had good reason to kill him, if you did," Emmie said, and Glory found the other ladies nodding. "We only wished Trudy would've had the same opportunity."

"But don't you see? You can't compare me to her," Glory began, wondering if she should try to make her point with these women. "Your very livelihood puts you all in danger every day. You don't know these men or what they are capable of. Many are strangers from another land. You expose yourself to trouble every day."

"Are you saying Trudy asked to be killed?" Ruby asked, her brows raised, her expression grim.

"No, of course not. No one deserves that sort of

treatment. But she chose a dangerous way of life. Look what happened to my poor father, a beloved sweet man, just because he got in the way.''

"It's not Lorene's fault your father got killed, Glory,'' Emmie said softly.

Even Emmie didn't understand.

"Because of Lorene Harding. Because of Rainbow House. That drifter was mad over getting thrown out of here. And my father paid the price.''

"What's this got to do with Trudy, anyhow?'' Eva asked, puzzled.

"Yeah, and we have Marcus to protect us,'' Julia added.

Gloria tried to explain. "I'm glad that you're safe, but not all women are. They don't have Marcus around. Don't you see, if you all found different professions, you wouldn't have call to worry about your life every time you walk down the street.''

Carmen grunted. Gloria was getting used to the unfeminine sound. "We do not worry. It is you who worry. You have to hide here in the house, while the rest of us are free to go anywhere we like, no?''

"Yes, but that's different,'' Gloria argued. "My profession didn't cause my trouble.''

"No, you only married the wrong man,'' Emmie said gently.

Gloria squeezed her eyes shut. "Yes, yes…I did. I made a mistake.''

"The girls are happy here, Glory. And Lorene makes sure we are safe,'' Ruby said, taking charge of the conversation. "We understand your grief about your father, but don't come in here and try to change things.''

"Even if it's for your own good?'' Gloria asked.

"We're all grown women. We know what's right for us," Ruby said. "Now, this conversation is over. It's getting late and the girls need to get ready for tonight. Finish up your meal, everyone, and no more distressing talk about Trudy."

Gloria waited until all the women left the room, then stood to help Mattie with the clean-up. "No, you don't have to help." Mattie's voice was sweet, but firm. "It's my job."

"Mattie, if I don't *do* something, I'm going to pull all my hair out. I have to do something useful around here. And it may shock you to learn that I used to clean my father's house and my husband's house. Every day."

Mattie chuckled.

Gloria grinned, grateful for the release of tension. Her conversation earlier hadn't gone well. She hadn't made her point with the women here. She couldn't make them see that life had more to offer them. They just needed to believe. They needed more faith. "So hand over that cloth and let me help clean up."

Mattie relented and Gloria spent the next hour cleaning the kitchen, dusting the main rooms downstairs and beating the carpets. She needed to tire herself out. She didn't want boredom to set in again this evening, because she'd decided that she couldn't spend any more time with Steven. Last night, he'd made her feel things she shouldn't feel. He'd made her come alive in a way she never had before. She had no regrets, but she also didn't want to encourage him in any way.

She'd spent the afternoon preaching her morals to the ladies here at Rainbow House. She couldn't very well fall from grace. She couldn't give Steven liberty to her body, while trying to keep her faith and soul intact.

Her decision made, great relief washed over her. It was the first positive thing she'd done for herself. She would stay away from Steven Harding tonight and for the rest of the nights to come.

For as long as she had to hide out here.

Chapter Eight

Steven slipped into Rainbow House right behind Sheriff Brimley and followed him into the main parlor. After the night he'd spent with Glory, Steven had debated about whether to show up here tonight at all. He told himself to stay away, steer clear of Glory for a while, to keep his concentration sharp and focus solely on her safety. She had a way of distracting him. He needed to stay on track to keep her from falling into the hands of the law.

But he'd come to town earlier today to make some purchases for his ranch and found out that Sheriff Brimley and his deputies were on the lookout for Trudy Tremaine's murderer. The sheriff and his men planned on visiting all the brothels nearby to investigate.

And if the sheriff decided he needed to search the rooms at Rainbow House, Steven couldn't stop him.

"Evening, Sheriff," Steven said matter-of-factly. "What brings you to the house tonight?" He walked over to the bar and poured whiskey into two glasses.

"Investigating a murder. Another murder. Still haven't found out a dang thing regarding the whereabouts of Mrs. Shaw. She sort of disappeared, mysteriously."

Steven nodded and handed the sheriff the drink. They spoke in one corner of the room, while the women all floated about entertaining their customers. Every so often, one of them would catch Steven's eye. Business as usual, he told them with a quick look. No need to worry. He couldn't afford to have any of the ladies behave suspiciously.

"Thanks," Brimley said, lifting his glass. "I sorta wondered if Lorene knew anything about the girl. Seems to me, she left town about the time of Boone Shaw's death."

Shocked, Steven's gut clenched. "You don't think my mother had anything to do with it, do you?"

The sheriff sipped his whiskey. "Well now, I don't rightly know what to think. We've had two murders in Storey County this month, and both seem to relate back to the whorehouses."

"How so?"

"You got a woman missing who was hell bent on shutting them down. And you got a prostitute dead on the back streets."

"Yes, and neither had anything to do with Rainbow House."

"Well, Mrs. Shaw wasn't exactly a disinterested party. Seems she aimed most of her wrath at Rainbow House. Makes me think that maybe someone wanted to shut her up."

"You know Lorene. Glory Shaw is the last person my mother would want to see hurt, regardless of her attempts to shut this place down."

"Glory, huh?"

Steven's slip of the tongue had the sheriff eyeing him warily. He'd have to be more careful.

"Don't most folks call her Gloria?"

Steven shrugged, sipping his drink. "Hell, I don't know. I don't even know the woman."

"Well, I'm going to have to check this place out. I want to question the girls here about Trudy. Who knows, maybe her killer is right here in this room tonight."

The sheriff made a quick cursory glance around, then focused his attention on him again. "How's the new place coming? What's the ranch called again?"

"I haven't named it yet. It's nearly done. Working hard to finish up. Gonna get my horses soon."

"That's why I'm surprised you've been spending so much time here, with Lorene gone and all. One of my deputies says he sees you coming into town late at night." There was no mistaking the suspicion laced in his tone or the doubt in his eyes.

Emmie drifted by their corner of the room with perfect timing. She was the same height as Glory and had the same light coloring. Emmie had even loaned her one of her signature blue gowns. If anyone had seen Steven with a woman, he'd make sure they'd think it was Emmie.

"Come here, honey," Steven said, grabbing Emmie's hand. She flowed into him without hesitation. He wrapped his arm around her waist and pulled her up close and tight. Kissing her throat and running his hand just under her breast, he glanced at the sheriff. "The sheriff's been wondering why I come around so much while Lorene's gone. You want me to tell him?"

Emmie caught on immediately and played her part

well. "Oh, dear. Sheriff, you won't tell Lorene, will you? I mean, she'd be furious if she found out about Steven and me. She might even send me away from here. Lorene's got her strict rules."

The sheriff cleared his throat and glanced at Steven, this time with a bit of apology in his eyes, before turning back to Emmie. "Uh, no. Don't you worry. I won't tell Lorene about this."

"Well, seeing as my mother is coming back in a few days, I might as well make the best of it. You ready to go upstairs, darlin'?"

Emmie splayed her hand across his chest lovingly. "You bet I am."

Steven grinned. "See you around, Roy."

He left the sheriff to his task of questioning the clientele and escorted Emmie up to the second floor. He turned to her once they reached her room. "Thanks. You did great," he said, swamped with relief. "You mind staying up in your room for a few hours? I've got to get Glory out of here before the sheriff comes nosing around."

"Don't worry about me, Steven. I'll keep Buddy company up here. Sorta falling for that sweet little pup, myself. You go on and take care of Glory."

Steven kissed Emmie's cheek, thanking her again, before heading up the last flight of stairs to Glory.

Gloria didn't want to answer the soft knock at her door, knowing it was most likely Steven. It was earlier than he usually came for her and though she'd worked herself into a frenzy today, hoping to tire by cleaning, dusting and doing all manner of chores, she simply couldn't sleep. She lay restless in bed, trying to get her mind to shut down some so she could claim fatigue but in truth, she simply wasn't tired.

"Let me in," Steven demanded quietly.

Gloria tied the robe tight and walked to the door. "I'm trying to sleep," she whispered.

"Sheriff Brimley is downstairs, nosing around," he whispered back. "So your sleep is most likely going to get disturbed if you don't open this door now."

Gloria opened the door and quickly closed it after Steven rushed in.

"Sheriff Brimley is here?" Gloria asked, her throat tight.

"Yeah, he's here. Claims he's investigating Trudy's murder, but he sure had a whole lot of questions about you."

Gloria swallowed. There was still a part of her that wanted to turn herself in, to be done with all this hiding and deception. The only thing stopping her entirely was the thought of a tight noose around her neck.

And the fact that she had no real defense. She couldn't recall anything from the night Boone had died.

"What did you tell him?"

"He's seen me riding into town every night. It's getting more dangerous for me to come here. But I think I covered okay."

"How?"

"By pretending I'm coming here for one of the women. Emmie happened to be close at hand and it makes good sense, with my mother out of town, that I'd want to, uh…well, I think Sheriff Brimley got the idea."

Gloria swallowed again, wondering about Steven's

real relationship with the women here. Emmie was young and so pretty. Something painful jabbed at her insides, creating turmoil in her heart and mind. "What do we do now?"

"Well, we can't stay here. He might decide he needs to examine all the rooms."

"Another night ride?" Gloria didn't want to be alone with Steven again, but if it meant keeping one step ahead of the sheriff, she'd have to submit.

"No, I have a better idea. Get dressed."

Steven opened his armoire and brought out a clean shirt and trousers. He began unbuttoning his shirt.

"Steven?" she asked, watching in awe as he removed his shirt entirely, exposing a strong chest stretching a thin undershirt to its limit. She glanced at his powerful arms and the breath just whooshed out of her.

"Glory, we don't have much time. You'd best get your clothes on behind that screen."

Gloria grabbed her dress and petticoat off a peg and went behind the screen, her mind spinning. "Where are you taking me?"

"We're going to the opera house."

"Are you sure nobody will know it's me?" Gloria whispered as Steven ushered her into the back door of the opera house. They'd deliberately arrived late so that all the other patrons would be seated already. Glory kept her head down, her hood covering up her blond hair.

"I think I fixed that with the sheriff. If anyone reports back to him, he'll think I'm with Emmie," Steven said, keeping his voice low. "And we have a special private box upstairs."

"What kind of special box?"

"It's a place where our ladies go with their escorts." He shuffled her up a staircase and they moved briskly down the hallway of the upper balcony floor. Entering the curtained box, Gloria found four seats facing the stage, two in front and two directly behind them. She had to look down considerably and at an angle, but the view was remarkable.

Steven made quick work of securing the curtains to the back and in front, he parted the curtains only partway.

He offered her one of the seats in the back. "If we sit here, no one will be able to see us, but you'll still have a good view of the stage."

"I don't understand. Why are we here?"

Gloria glanced around, seeing lanterns light the stage. All else was dark.

"I told you. Sheriff Brimley was nosing around the house. And I'd been spotted too often coming and going out of town. I couldn't chance taking you out of town again tonight. Staying in town is the safest for us. So sit back and enjoy the show."

"Steven, I don't know if I can." Gloria fidgeted in her seat, her pulse racing. If Steven was wrong about this, she'd be the one with a noose around her neck.

He took hold of her hand and squeezed gently. "Trust me. I'm not going to let anyone hurt you."

He reassured her with a solid look, but Gloria still had doubts. This was the first time she was out in public, if one could call it that, since before Boone was killed. "What if someone comes in here?"

Steven grinned. "They won't."

Again, Gloria had doubts, even when Steven seemed so sure. "How can you be so certain?"

Steven leaned over and whispered in her ear, his breath warm and inviting. "Because they know what goes on up here."

Gloria's shoulders went stiff. She blinked and turned to find Steven smiling. "What does go on up here?"

Steven leaned back in his seat and stretched his body out. He'd dressed for the occasion, wearing black trousers, a white linen shirt, and a string tie under a dark suede vest. Gloria had never seen him look so handsome. He actually appeared civilized, except of course, for the gun he toted on his hip, no matter what. She should be grateful to him for all he'd done to protect her, but bringing her here, where she would be mistaken for a prostitute, even if she were in disguise, didn't quite set well.

"The ladies entertain men, up here."

"Oh!" She gasped and all sorts of images swirled through her head as his meaning came through with clarity. "And how many times have you been entertained here?" The words slipped from her lips before she had the mind to stop them. She didn't have reason to question Steven. What he did with the "ladies" was his own private affair.

Steven peered at her with somber honest eyes. "Just this once, Glory." He leaned over, cupped her head in his hand and brushed a soft kiss to her lips. "Now try to relax."

Relax? His kisses made her heart thunder in her chest. But after a time, she did calm down and took note of the performance in progress. Mandrel's troupe of dancers paraded around on stage in colorful dresses, their wild dances like nothing Gloria had ever seen before. Women lifted their legs up high in the air in unison and others did tumbles that streaked across the width of the floor.

The opera house was packed solid, some men standing in the aisles and others against the back walls. Miners in need of a little distraction applauded with gusto, the room exploding with hoots and calls when the music stopped. Tied-up sacks of ore were thrown onto the stage, the women grabbing for their share of silver or gold.

Gloria stretched her neck, peering down in concentration. "It appears the stage is moving."

Steven took her hand in his and laughed quietly. "You've never been here before?"

"Oh, why yes, years ago, when Mr. Maguire owned it. Father took me here for a prayer recital one afternoon. But I never noticed the stage bouncing up and down."

"One of the things Piper did when he took over the opera house was to put railroad springs underneath the stage," Steven offered. "That ore weighs heavily. And some of the performances can get kinda…rambunctious."

Gloria nodded, thinking she had a better word to describe tonight's performance. She didn't bother to voice her thoughts.

"Are you enjoying yourself tonight, Glory?"

Gloria had feared coming here. She thought it a risky move on Steven's part, but she'd placed her faith in him and he'd been true to his word. So far, not a soul had come to disturb them. She felt confident they were hidden successfully up in their private curtained box. And though the performance hadn't been what she'd expected, this was far better than pining away all alone in her room at Rainbow House.

"It's certainly a different kind of entertainment, Steven. But yes, it's a nice diversion."

Steven seemed satisfied with her answer and when the performance resumed, a female singer came forth. She entertained the house with a variety of tunes and ballads, her voice amazingly clear and beautiful. Gloria sat back in her seat and closed her eyes, absorbing the melodious sound, finding a measure of peace and joy as the lyrics and music resonated in her mind.

When the performance ended, Steven stood to close the curtains fully. "No sense tempting fate," he said and soon they were encased in total darkness. "We'll wait here until everyone's gone. Might be a while."

Gloria stood also, to stretch her legs. She'd been sitting for what seemed like four hours, though it couldn't possibly have been that long. When she scooted over a bit, she nearly toppled over one of the chairs. "Oh, mercy!"

Steven grabbed her instantly, his hands latching onto her arms to steady her. "You okay?"

"I just can't see a thing in here," she whispered quietly.

"Come stand with me against the side wall."

Steven took her hand and guided her over to the wall. The opera house had begun to quiet down as the patrons exited the theater. But all Gloria heard was the sound of Steven's breathing, his warmth cocooning her with his nearness, and his fresh soapy scent permeating the very air she took in.

"How long do we have to wait here?" she asked, quite breathless now.

"We'll be the very last ones to leave, Glory. Are you impatient?"

Steven shifted his body. He faced her and all she

could see was the dark earthy brown of his eyes. "I-impatient, uh, no. I'm not impatient."

"Good," he whispered, "because we can't take any chances with your safety."

He stroked his finger across her cheek with utmost tenderness. His touch created shivers that spiraled down her spine. At times, Gloria forgot why Steven was doing this. She forgot that he felt obligated to help her. At times, she forgot that Steven Harding wasn't the man for her. "Steven," she said, the soft warning falling from her lips.

"Are you scared, Glory?"

Her pulse sped up as she gazed into his eyes. "Very."

"Of me?"

Yes, she feared him, but not because he wore a gun. And not because he made her feel things way down to her toes. She feared him because irrationally she blamed him partly for her father's death. Gloria couldn't draw the line of distinction. He was a Harding—Lorene Harding's son. "Yes, of you."

Steven bent his head and brushed a kiss to her lips. "I'd never hurt you, Glory. Don't fear me," he said quietly, taking her into his arms. Her dress rustled against his thighs, his solid strength reassuring her, while the wild beating of her heart put every sort of doubt in her head.

"You're beautiful." He kissed her again and all of her well-thought-out resistance vanished. Heat shot through her like a hot summer wind. She had no will of her own when she was in Steven's arms. She returned his kiss and he pressed her closer, their bodies touching intimately.

In a bold move, Steven leaned heavily against the

wall and brought her up, cupping her bottom and gently tugging her into him. There was no mistaking his desire as he kissed her urgently. His velvet hands brought her pleasure as she gave him free rein of her body.

Her cape fell from her shoulders, and Steven was there, with his palms smoothing over her skin and his lips planting thrilling kisses on her throat.

A loud crashing noise from down below startled her, bringing her out of this pleasurable fantasy. It was just a theater worker closing down the stage area, she presumed, but the sound helped put clarity on the interlude. "Steven, don't." She shoved at him delicately, her clouded mind clearing. "I'm not a trollop to dally with."

Her pronouncement surprised him. He blew out a sharp breath.

"You brought me up here and treat me no better than a whore. Was that your intent? To see what it's like to seduce a woman up in this private box?"

The muscles in his arms tensed before they dropped to his side. With a dark heated gleam in his eyes, he answered. "No."

She wanted to believe him. "Then why?"

He moved away from her. She watched him steal a peek out of the curtains, before turning back to her. "Maybe I don't know how to stay away."

"But you must. Certainly you know there's no future for us."

He snorted, a graceless sound. "I know that for a fact, Glory."

Gloria heard the regret in his voice and wondered at her own bouts of regret. "So, you'll treat me with respect from now on?"

Steven strode briskly forward. "Dammit, Glory," he hissed. "I have nothing but respect for you. Don't confuse desire with respect. If anything, I've put you high above all women."

"You think I killed my husband."

"I—" he began then hesitated. "That man deserved to die."

"No one should die like that."

"Glory, it doesn't matter to me whether you killed your husband or not."

"It matters to me," she said. She didn't want to think of herself as a brazen woman. And she surely didn't want to think of herself as a murderer. Two things she'd been certain Steven thought about her just minutes ago.

"I didn't bring you up here to seduce you," he stated plainly.

"I hope that's true because there could never be anything between us. I am nothing to you."

Steven shot his head up and she witnessed the flash in his eyes. "You're wrong about that, Glory. You are something to me."

"What could I possibly be to you?"

Steven peered out the curtain one last time. He faced her again and spoke with purpose. "You're my…responsibility."

Chapter Nine

Gloria sat on her bed in Rainbow house, too restless to sleep. It had been two nights since Steven had taken her to Piper's Opera House. Two nights since he'd carefully escorted her home, leaving her at the bedroom threshold, his farewell a polite tip of his hat. She'd endured two lonely nights without Steven, so when the knock resounded this evening, Gloria bounded up and moved toward the door with unwelcome eagerness. She shouldn't want to see him. She shouldn't anticipate his company. It was best that Gloria keep her distance, but gladness filled her heart thinking of Steven on the other side of the door. She opened the door and stared into the somber face of Lorene Harding.

She swallowed hard and stood like a statue in her nightclothes at the bedroom door. Seeing Steven's mother this evening was the last thing she had expected. Although she knew the woman would arrive home soon, Gloria had banished their eventual meeting from her thoughts.

And now, Mrs. Harding faced her with a Bible in her hand. She stood with stately grace, wearing an elegant gown, her once-blond hair silvering at the temples. Her dark eyes were rich with color, so much like her son's. "Hello, Gloria Mae."

Gloria flinched at the familiar tone the woman took with her. Her shoulders stiff, she didn't know how to respond. She was living here in her house, eating her food and taking refuge in Steven's bedroom, although she hadn't seen him since their time at Piper's Opera House. "Mrs. Harding."

"I want you to know that I'm glad Steven took you in. He did the right thing. I know all about your troubles, the girls filled me in. But that's not why I'm here now."

Gloria swallowed. Mrs. Harding, the woman whom she'd scorned since the day her father died, spoke to her with softness in her tone, a generosity Gloria couldn't return. "Why are you here?"

"It's Merry. I'm afraid she took a heavy dose of drugs. She's in a bad way."

"Oh! Dear Lord." Gloria pressed her hand to her heart. "What happened?"

"I suppose she got her heart set on this young fella, Bud McKenzie. And the man came here tonight, telling her he couldn't see her anymore. He's marrying one of those picture brides he sent for."

"Oh, mercy. Merry was so sure he'd marry her."

"Ruby told me she'd warned her over and over not to get her hopes up. I've done the same myself."

"Well, how is she? Is she going to live?"

"We had the doctor come out. He purged her stomach, but she's weak. I'm afraid she's lost the will to live."

"Dear Lord, that poor girl." Gloria's heart ached at the thought of the rejection and terrible disappointment that young red-haired girl must have endured tonight. Gloria shook her head, distressed at this turn of events.

Lorene peered down at the Bible she held. "The girls said you're good with prayers, just like your father." She glanced up to meet her eyes. "Would you sit with Merry and say a prayer?"

"Of course. Just let me get dressed."

"Here, please take this. You'll need it." She handed her the Bible. "Ruby, Emmie and Carmen are sitting with her now, but I think you'll have the words to help her."

"I'll do my best," Gloria said before closing the door. A tear dripped from her eye, then another. Gloria couldn't weep now. She had to be strong for Merry's sake. She wiped away her tears quickly then dressed. Lifting the Bible again, she noted a marked page. She opened to a verse of Matthew, finding the marker that held the page of interest.

It was funny, but she was sure her father had one just like it, Gloria thought, glancing at a thin strip of white lace with an embroidered red rose in the center. He used to mark all of his pages with it.

But that marker had been set inside his Bible on his favorite verse and placed in her father's hand when he'd been buried.

Gloria shook off that thought for the moment. She dashed out of her room and raced down the stairs to Merry's room with the light yellow door.

When she opened the door, all eyes shifted to her and then to the Bible in her hand. Carmen walked over to her and squeezed her hand tenderly. "It is good that you came. Sit with Merry. She is in need of your prayers."

Gloria nodded and took the seat closest to the bed. She glanced at the ladies surrounding her. All of them were there now, waiting with hope-filled eyes. "Merry needs all of our prayers."

Gloria peered down at the fragile young woman in the bed. Seeing her freckles fading into the paleness of her wan skin, Gloria ached deep inside. She took hold of Merry's cold hand. "Merry, it's me...Glory."

She didn't mind using the name everyone at Rainbow House insisted on calling her, since she was beginning to think of herself that way as well. Besides, Merry knew her as Glory and that was fine with her at the moment.

Merry opened her eyes. She spoke slowly, like a child just learning how to formulate sentences. "Bud...isn't...coming...back." She closed her eyes. "Ever."

"I know. I'm sorry. We're all sorry. All of your friends are here. And Lorene, she's here, too. And the Lord is with you. The Lord wants you to live. He wants you to get better."

"I am not...the Lord's child."

"Yes, yes you are. All of us are. He loves you."

"Nobody...loves...me."

"Oh, yes, many love you. The Lord loves all of his children. But we love you, too. All of the girls are here, praying for you. Will you listen to my prayers?"

Merry opened eyes devoid of life.

It was the best answer she would get, so Glory opened the Bible and went to Psalm 116. She began reading quietly, "I love the Lord, because he hears my voice and my supplications. Because he has inclined his ear to me, therefore I shall call upon him as long as I live. The cords of death encompassed me

And the terrors of Sheol came upon me; I found distress and sorrow. Then I called upon the name of the LORD: 'O Lord, I beseech You, save my life!' Gracious is the Lord, and righteous; Yes, our God is compassionate…''

Glory read until well after Merry's face grew peaceful and she fell into a deep sleep.

Ruby rested a hand on her shoulder. ''Thank you, Glory.''

The other women as well, took turns to speak to her with kindness, thanking her for her prayers.

When the room emptied, Glory turned to find Lorene watching her. They stared at each other for a time. Glory's heart and mind filled with such sorrow and regret, and it appeared, Lorene Harding, too, mirrored her feelings.

''I'll sit with her through the night,'' Glory said, shifting back to face a sleeping Merry.

''I know how you feel about me and the girls here. But as you can see, we aren't such a bad lot. We all have feelings, just like those you consider decent folk.''

Glory lowered her head, her thoughts swirling around like a threatening thunderstorm, moving far too fast to make much sense of them.

''Merry ran away from the farmlands in Kansas when she was fifteen,'' Lorene explained. ''She wanted to live a different life, to see something of the world, but things didn't go as she'd hoped. If I hadn't taken her in, she'd be on the streets now, or in one of the awful cribs barely making enough money to feed or clothe herself.''

Glory's insides quaked. She still couldn't fathom what manner of desperation would bring a girl down so far that she'd take her own life. "Shouldn't there be more than that?"

"Yes, for some. But Merry had no skills and no means of support."

"You could have sent her home," Glory said firmly.

"I tried. She didn't want to go home."

Glory turned to Lorene. "I'll never understand that." She waved her arm in the air and spoke with quiet resolve. "Or what goes on here."

"I know." Lorene put her hand on the doorknob. Before exiting the room she added, "But don't judge the girls too harshly. They all have their reasons. And so did I."

Glory sat with Merry that night and into the morning. She'd asked Mattie to bring some supper up, and she managed to spoon-feed Merry a portion of broth. And when Merry was up to it, Glory got her talking, willing her to hang on to the life she was so eager to discard. They talked for hours about anything and everything, important matters and frivolous things. By the end of the third day, Merry had improved considerably.

"Want some more soup?" Glory asked.

Merry shook her head. "My stomach's still acting up."

Glory grasped Merry's hand and a sad smile played on her lips. "Morphine and laudanum will do that to a stomach."

Merry sighed heavily. "I guess that was a pretty stupid thing to do."

"As long as you don't ever do that again."

Merry looked away, toward the window, but night

had fallen so she stared blankly into the hollow darkness. "I might have if it wasn't for you."

"I'm glad I could help."

"It's just that…I loved Bud McKenzie. He hurt me real bad."

Glory sat in deep concentration, recalling so many of her father's teachings. She'd been her father's pupil, learning the scriptures well and remembering how truly wise her father had been. "My father once told me that the only true and pure love is with the Lord. That sometimes earthly love fails you. My mama died giving birth to me. I think that's what he meant. And for me, well, my marriage to Boone failed me. So maybe Father was right. Although, sometimes I question my own faith and the Lord's wisdom."

"You?" Merry asked, snapping her head around, her eyes sparking with great surprise.

"Yes, Merry. I'm afraid I'm not entirely like my father. I couldn't devote my life to my faith, not after the way he died," she confessed solemnly.

"You blamed us for his death and tried to shut us down."

"Yes, I did."

"And yet you helped me. If it wasn't for you," Merry began, tears welling up in her eyes, her face flushed now with rosy color. "If it wasn't for what you did…I would have surely given up."

"The others care, too, Merry."

"But you…you hate Lorene and everything about Rainbow House."

The words cut straight through her. Glory leaned back in her chair, allowing the thoughts she'd so heartily refused before to finally come through. She knew now that the women at Rainbow House had souls. They hurt. They bled. They cared. For the first time since Steven had brought her here, Glory could look upon the women who sold their bodies for a price with a little more clarity. She couldn't condone their actions or their profession and she probably never would. But now, as she'd gotten to know them, she saw them differently.

It put her at great unease. The tight cord of morality that she'd been raised to believe in, virtue and principle, decency and integrity, was beginning to unravel in her mind.

"And that's what makes what you did for me more remarkable," Merry said softly.

"I don't hate you. Or the others." Glory found truth in that revelation. And the dawning knowledge left her a little bewildered. She didn't hate Ruby, who had given her such a hard time when she'd arrived, or Carmen, who had a rash tongue, but who sang the supper prayers like a melodious songstress. And how could she hate Emmie, who had helped her heal, given her clothes and befriended her? "I don't hate anyone."

The tiny curly-haired animal that had been sleeping by the foot of the bed decided it was time enough to join his mistress. He jumped up, wiggled his rump and plopped himself down beside Merry.

"Buddy has missed you, Merry."

Merry lifted her mouth in a small smile. The very first she'd seen on the girl in days. Then she raised her arm to stroke his head tenderly and Glory felt relief at the strength her patient exhibited.

"I think I want to change his name."

Glory chuckled softly. "I think that's a grand idea.

But let's do that tomorrow. It's late and you need to rest some more.''

Glory said good-night to Merry then donned her black cloak, making sure to cover her head with the hood. Rainbow House had reopened last night and by all appearances it seemed business as usual. She'd been sitting with Merry in her room on the Rainbow floor. Leaving would be tricky. She had to be sure not to be noticed.

She opened the door slightly and peeked out. When she determined the hallway was clear, she exited the room and took a step up the stairs, heading for the third floor.

''Hey, w-what've we got us 'ere,'' a slurred voice from behind called out. Glory felt a tug on the back of her cape. The strong scent of whiskey assailed her. She froze on the step, fearful her movements might cause her cloak to fall, but even more afraid of turning around to face the drunken man standing just inches behind her. ''Lorene's h-holding out on us, eh? Gots a new gal she ain't allowed us to m-meet.''

''Hands off, O'Malley. This one's mine tonight.'' Steven stepped onto the landing and faced the man. Stunned, Glory stood motionless until Steven grabbed her hand. With a tug, he guided her up the step and whispered in her ear. ''Just don't turn around.''

''Aw, that's j-just plain ain't f-fair.''

''Better get yourself down these stairs. Marcus is heading up here and he doesn't look too happy.''

With that, Steven lifted her into his arms and carried her up the rest of the stairs. Heart pounding hard against her chest, Glory had trouble taking her breaths. Mercy, she'd almost been caught. And she'd tried to be so careful.

Steven nearly kicked the door down, getting her inside. He set her on the bed and cursed up and down until Glory thought her ears would burn right off her head. He paced in front of her for a time giving her a chance to calm down. But his next words jolted her into shock.

"You can't stay here any more."

Chapter Ten

"When I brought Glory here, I really thought I could keep her safe," Steven said to his mother.

He'd left Glory last night in his room wearing a surprised expression. He'd told her to get some sleep and they'd talk in the morning. Problem was, Steven didn't have any easy solutions to the problem, but he didn't want to frighten Glory anymore than she'd already been last night when Floyd O'Malley had almost spotted her. Good thing the man was too falling-down drunk to recall the incident. And Marcus had escorted him out before the town merchant could ask any questions.

Lorene sat on a crimson velvet settee in her bedroom and patted the chair, willing him to sit beside her as he had so often when he'd been a youngster. "We need to talk about Gloria Mae."

"Time for talk is over, Mother. I have to do something. With the sheriff nosing around, Ned Shaw making accusations about her murdering his brother and Glory almost getting caught last night, it's getting too dangerous for her to stay here."

"Sit down, Steven," his mother repeated. "And calm down."

Steven plopped onto the settee and spread his legs wide, sinking his head down, searching for a solution.

"You did the right thing in protecting her, Steven. From what you've told me, she had cause to kill her husband. But my heart tells me she didn't do it. Jonathan Caldwell didn't raise his daughter to murder."

"Even if it was in self-defense?"

His mother shook her head, not even an iota of doubt creeping into her expression. Steven wished he could be as sure. "She didn't do it."

"You didn't see her injuries. She'd been badly beaten. Any woman would take a knife to protect herself from that kind of treatment."

"Steven, no matter if she did or didn't kill her husband, she's wanted for his murder. And now you say it's too dangerous for her to stay here."

"It is, Mother."

"You saved her life when you rescued her from that fire. You brought her here. Why, Steven? And I want the truth."

"I told you why once already."

"Yes, I know you said you felt we owed her that much. And we both do. But is it more than that, Steven? Are you—"

"I'm not. I never could be." Steven bounded up from the seat and avoided his mother's knowing eyes. "She has no use for me, you or Rainbow House. She'd still shut you down if she had the chance."

"I'm not worried about that. But I want to know about you and...her."

"Like I said, there's nothing to know. Nothing to say."

Lorene stood and walked over to him. She put her hand on his arm and held on to him. "You know why I started this business. You know how I wanted you to have a better life than anything I could offer you. I had little choice when I was younger, much like many of the girls here now. But you're a fine man, Steven. You've got nothing to be ashamed of."

"I'm not ashamed, Mother. But I can't change the way other people see me."

"Can't you?"

"If you're speaking of Glory, the answer is no. She's dead set against who and what I am."

"Steven, are you saying there's no feelings between the two of you?"

Steven frowned, realizing that he'd held out hope for Glory to see him differently. But he knew in his heart she'd never accept him. She deserved more than he could give her, anyway. He only hoped once all this was resolved, that he'd have the will to let her go, so that she could live a happy life. "That's what I'm saying, Mother."

Lorene smiled and Steven wasn't sure he liked the reason behind her smile. "Okay, then. The answer is simple. If there's nothing between you, no way you'd compromise her, then you can hide her away at your ranch."

"What?"

"Steven, I know you're not hard of hearing."

"I heard you, Mother. I just can't believe you think that's a good idea."

Lorene stepped away from him to pour herself a cup of coffee from the corner table. She lowered the coffeepot and turned to him. "It's a wonderful idea. Your ranch is an hour's ride from here. You'd be taking Gloria Mae away from all suspicion. You'd still have to be very careful, but chances are you won't get a whole lot of callers way out on your ranch. Hiding her here was a good idea, but there's too much chance of someone getting suspicious.''

''I haven't finished the house yet.''

''She's a bright gal. She'll find ways to help you.''

''Mother, I can't *live* with Glory.''

His mother walked over to him and searched his eyes, looking deep, and seeking his truth. ''Steven, ask yourself this, can you live *without* her?''

Steven closed his eyes. Damn his mother for knowing more than she had a right to know.

''She won't want to go.''

Lorene sat down on her settee again, and sipped her coffee. ''Convince her.''

Steven's gut clenched. Taking Glory out to his ranch might be the smart move, but he didn't know how he'd endure the torment of having her there.

''It won't be easy,'' he said. She'd be hard to convince and he'd rather face a pack of wild wolves than look into Glory's light-blue eyes and see the disdain she held for him.

''Then tell her I don't want her here. You found her. You take care of her. She doesn't belong at Rainbow House.''

Steven filled his lungs and let his breath out slowly. ''She'll hate you even more.''

Lorene sipped her coffee. ''Yes, but she'll be safe. Jonathan Caldwell would want it that way. And I'd do anything to save his daughter.''

Later that morning, Steven stood behind Merry's door, ready to knock, but cackles of female laughter stopped him. As he listened to their giggles, his curiosity got the better of him and he slipped inside the room. No one noticed. All of the girls stood huddled around the bed where Merry and Glory were seated.

"And the next thing we see is big Floyd O'Malley being escorted out by Marcus," Ruby said with merriment. "Marcus tugged big old Floyd out by his ear!"

"It was a sight to see, all right," Emmie joined in. "But Glory held up okay, didn't you?"

"I suppose. I couldn't move. He just about scared all the hair off my head," Glory said. "I don't know what would have happened if Steven hadn't come when he did."

"Not to worry, Glory," Eva announced.

"That is right. O'Malley, he was drunk," Carmen added.

Julia nodded with a glow in her eyes. "And when Floyd O'Malley drinks—"

"He can do *nothing!*" Carmen, Eva and Ruby chorused simultaneously.

"Oh!" Glory put her hand to her mouth. Then she darted glances at all the girls, and it seemed she couldn't contain her own laughter. Her mirth poured out sweetly, a hearty sound of true joy that brought a rosy flush of color to her face. They laughed together for a long while, until only a chuckle here or a chortle there could be heard.

Steven watched a scene he thought he'd never witness and realized he'd have to take Glory away from her new friends.

Steven cleared his throat and strode farther into the room. All eyes turned toward him. He walked over to Merry and smiled. "Glad to see you're feeling better, Merry."

"I'm feeling fine, thanks to Glory. She wouldn't let me give up." Merry glanced at Glory and the two exchanged a look. "All of the girls have helped me. They've been wonderful friends."

"Merry is thinking of going back home to Kansas," Glory said, keeping her concentration on the recovering girl. "She hasn't seen her ma and pa for five years."

Merry nodded slightly. "I'm thinking about going home...for a visit. Maybe."

"I bet your folks will be happy to see you...for a visit," Steven said, his eyes meeting with Glory's.

"If I had folks, I'd like to visit them," Julia offered.

The others agreed.

Steven pursed his lips. Now that the gaiety was over, he had to speak with Glory. "Glory, we have some talking to do."

He reached for her hand.

She turned the shade of blood-red roses and glanced at the girls. They watched her with eagle-like precision and he knew that she'd confided in them, telling the girls what he'd said to her last night. She couldn't stay here any longer. It was getting too dangerous. No matter how she pleaded with those silent blue eyes, she'd still have to leave.

"Go on," Emmie urged. "Talk to him."

Glory appeared doubtful.

"A handsome man wants to do some talking, I wouldn't hesitate," Julia teased.

"You would not hesitate no matter what the man looked like," Carmen said, her dark eyes glittering.

Glory didn't smile at the jest and he couldn't blame her. Hell, Steven had nothing to smile about either. He didn't like what he was about to tell her, yet he had no other choice.

Finally and with a slow nod, Glory put her hand in his and she stood. "I'll see you all later," she said to the girls before exiting the room.

When they reached Steven's bedroom, he opened the door for her and followed her in. Glory turned to him with those piercing blue eyes. Steven sucked in a breath. He couldn't let her sway him. "I've got something to say and nothing is going to change my mind."

"Nothing's going to change Steven's mind," Glory said, unable to keep disappointment from her voice, or a full-out pout from puckering her lips. She slumped into the kitchen chair, too distraught to help Mattie with preparing the afternoon meal.

"Honey, there are more than a dozen ways to change a man's mind," Julia said. "All you have to do use the assets given you."

Glory had her doubts. She'd never been able to sway Boone one way or another. He'd been stubborn and set in his ways and all the reasoning and encouragement in the world wouldn't lift his sour moods. Glory had tried being a good wife, but toward the last months of their marriage, it seemed nothing she did pleased him. "I'm afraid I'm not very good at that."

Mattie chuckled, taking a large pan of biscuits from the cookstove. "I don't think she knows what you mean, Julia."

Julia stared at Glory as though she was as hopeless

as a young doe facing down the barrel of a gun. "No, I guess she doesn't."

"Julia's not speaking of *reasoning* with a man," Mattie explained softly.

"Oh!" Glory finally understood her meaning. Foolishly, she'd thought Julia had meant using the powers of wisdom and logic to bend a man's notions. "You're talking about seduction?"

Julia smiled. "Let me give you a quick lesson. Whenever you want to catch a man's eye, every blink of the eye or wiggle of the hips should be aimed solely at him with slow deliberate calculation."

Julia walked to the wall and turned. She focused on Glory, slowly running a hand through her long wavy hair then skimming her throat until her hand followed the path down the curves of the rest of her body. She walked forward, her hips swaying, her lips parted and her eyes wide. "Every move you make has a purpose. Every flutter of the eyes or touch of the hair, tells the man what you want."

Glory watched in awe at how quickly Julia had transformed herself into a seductress. Since living here, she hadn't been exposed to the professional side of the business, though she knew it existed. Every night, she'd heard the sounds, the telltale giggles and laughter of men enjoying themselves with the women she had come to know. "I couldn't ever do that," Glory said, believing it with her whole heart. There were too many obstacles; her ingrained morals and cursed self-doubt prevented Glory from ever behaving in such a way.

Especially with Steven.

"You have what it takes, Glory. Every woman does, whether you believe it or not. You're just afraid to use it." Julia took a seat next to her. "So, I guess you'll be leaving us after all."

"Yes. I guess so."

Carmen, Emmie and Ruby walked into the kitchen and the room became a colorful mingling of satin gowns, in all colors of the rainbow and chattering female voices.

Carmen approached her first, her hands behind her back. "We know you must leave. Lorene has told us what you must do. This is for the best. Steven will keep you safe."

Glory nodded, keeping her head up, not showing the fear she experienced at being thrown into another ominous situation—one that would once again tempt fate.

"I would like very much to give you this Bible. It is from the Church of Saint Mary's."

"You've gone?" Glory asked, secretly elated that Carmen had found her way back to her religion.

"Yes, to pray for Merry, and myself."

Carmen set the leather-bound Bible in her hand. "This will keep you safe."

Glory stared into Carmen's dark eyes, no longer seeing hostility, but the warmth one would relay to a friend. "Thank you, Carmen."

When Carmen stepped away, Ruby stepped up placing a beautiful crimson shawl around her shoulders. "This is from me. It will keep you warm out there on the range."

"Oh! This is lovely." Tears misted in Glory's eyes as she slid her hand over the thick crocheted covering. Gratitude swelled in her heart. For the past year, she'd been fighting an unknown force, her wrath for Rainbow House and the women here hardening her heart and mind. But Glory had seen into their hearts these past weeks. She'd gotten to know them with all their strengths and frailties. And although she still didn't understand their way of life, their generosity touched her deeply. "I will use it often, I'm sure."

"And these, too," Emmie said eagerly, stepping into view and presenting Glory with a fine pair of leather riding boots. "I've never used them. I'm not one for horses. But maybe on the ranch, you'll have occasion to use them."

Glory wiped a stray tear from her eye. "Yes, I'm sure I'll make good use of them. Thank you. Thank you all."

She rose up to embrace Emmie, hugging her tight. "You helped save my life. I'll never forget that."

"We'll never forget you, either," Emmie said, then glanced at all the women in the room. "Will we?"

Embraces followed, along with words of hope and encouragement from all the girls. Even Mattie came up to give her a hug, the embrace a bit awkward from the shy girl, but nonetheless meaningful. "I'll bring up a basket of food to take with you. It'll get you through the first few days on the ranch."

"Oh, thank you, Mattie."

Shortly after their meal, Glory set out her gifts on the bed in the room she'd come to think of as her own, a melancholy feeling washing over her. She'd been so anxious to leave here when she'd first arrived, loathing Rainbow House and all it stood for, but now, Glory's mind muddied up with so many conflicting thoughts. Her heart ached for Merry and she hoped she'd find peace and solace when she returned to her hometown. And she worried for the others. Would disappointment and discouragement finally eat at them as well, causing them strife and heartache?

Glory also worried about her own plight. Helping Merry recover had taken her mind off her own dilemma for days, but now she faced the disheartening possibility that Steven's plan might fail. What if she was discovered at his ranch? And what would become of Steven, for helping her? She'd not considered that possibility until this very moment. Steven would be arrested as well, for hiding her from the law.

At the sound of a knock at her door she jumped, startled from her own reverie.

"It's Lorene Harding, Gloria Mae. I'd like to speak with you."

Glory inhaled deeply and strode to the door, recalling Steven's arguments for taking her to his ranch. Lorene had thought it the safest place for her.

Glory scoffed at that notion. No matter what the woman said to the contrary, she knew that Lorene Harding didn't want her here. Glory had been a thorn in her side, an unwanted guest and a constant reminder of a life lost so unnecessarily in an argument that should never have taken place.

She wondered if Lorene felt any guilt regarding her father's death. She wondered if the woman, adored by all the girls here, even had a soul.

Glory opened the door briskly.

Lorene stood with a small basket in one hand and two bolts of material in the other. Glory stared at the fabric, one bolt, a soft blue-patterned silk and the other of flowery broadcloth.

"Hello, Gloria Mae."

"Mrs. Harding." Glory stepped away from the

door to allow the woman entrance, but the woman shook her head, refusing to come in.

"I only came to give you these. I brought this material back from San Francisco for Steven's house, but he tells me you're in need of clothes. There's plenty of material here for both." She handed the bolts over and then gave her the basket. "Sewing implements. I think you'll find everything you need in there."

Glory's heart sang with joy. She loved to sew and now she'd have material enough to make a dress or two and keep busy sewing up curtains and whatever else the house might need.

"Thank you. I'll make good use of it."

Lorene nodded, seemingly pleased that Glory had accepted her offer without an argument. Clearly the woman understood how she felt about her. And for just a scant second, Glory thought to refuse, but she couldn't very well do that, when the material was intended for Steven's house.

Lorene searched her face, roving over her, almost in an assessing way. "You've healed well here, but you'll be safer at my son's ranch."

Glory nodded, then remembered the Bible Lorene had given her days ago. "Oh, I have to return this to you." She set the material down then grabbed the Bible from the tabletop and handed it to her. "The marker is quite lovely."

Lorene opened the Bible and lifted the marker out, caressing the lace tenderly, her finger tracing over the one red embroidered rose. "Yes, it is. It was a gift from someone dear to me."

Glory wouldn't announce that her father had one just like it. She couldn't quite bring up the subject of her father around Lorene, not trusting what harsh words might come out of her mouth.

"Would you like to keep the Bible?" Lorene asked.

The gesture touched her deeply, but surprised her even more. "N-no, thank you. Carmen brought me one from church."

"Carmen, in church?" Lorene smiled then reached out to touch her cheek. Glory would have flinched but for the warm look in the woman's eyes. "You're a sweet child, Gloria Mae. Trust Steven to keep you safe."

And then Lorene was gone.

Glory closed the door, dumbfounded. She had only a few hours left at Rainbow House. She should be joyous.

Yet she felt almost as she had when her father had been killed.

Lost.

Chapter Eleven

The wagon lurched. Glory felt every bump in the road, every uneven jolt that jostled her body. She'd been ushered into the back of Steven's buckboard wagon and hidden beneath a layer of supplies. Nothing much could make the ride pleasant—she'd been tossed in like a sack of grain, covered with a scratchy wool blanket and surrounded by all manner of ranching equipment and food staples. Steven had leaned a bag of sugar next to her shoulders, a sack of flour by her head and he'd even seen fit to cover her backside up with two lightweight wooden boards, that suddenly didn't feel light any longer.

"How're you doing back there?" Steven called out in something of a whisper.

"I can't breathe. I'm being beat up by a sack of potatoes and my backside hurts like the dickens," she whispered back.

Steven chuckled. "Hang on, Glory. We're well out of town. Soon as I make the bend in the road, I'll get you outta there. And then I'll see to your backside," he said, his amusement ringing in her ears.

She grumbled a reply and heard Steven chuckle again.

It seemed like half an eternity before the wagon stopped and she felt the weight of the boards, then the blanket being lifted from her.

"Sorry, couldn't be helped," Steven said, and the scent of fresh air and dry earth pleasured her senses. The dark sky illuminated by hundreds of bright stars lit Steven's face as she peered up. He reached for her hand then lifted her from the wagon.

She stared into his eyes and noted all amusement was gone, replaced by a serious look. He watched her walk away from him as she stretched her legs and rotated her head, working out kinks from her uncomfortable ride. "How much farther?" she asked.

Steven leaned up against the wagon. "Just a ten minute ride from here."

"What do you call your ranch?"

Steven scratched his head and shrugged. "Haven't got a name yet. It's got to be something…I don't know…something meaningful. I've been thinking on it for a time."

"Is it safe for me to be out here in view?"

Only the hoot of an owl off in the distance troubled the solitude of the night. They were miles away from Virginia City, although since being concealed in the wagon, Glory couldn't fathom in which direction they'd traveled.

"We're on my land now."

There was so much pride in Steven's tone, such a satisfied sound of accomplishment, that Glory found herself smiling.

He smiled back.

Then glanced at her lips.

Glory's breath caught in her throat. Images filled her head of Steven's mouth claiming hers, his hands caressing her body and their hearts pounding in rhythm together. Just as she imagined Steven entertaining those very same thoughts, he stepped back and away, shifting his attention to his restless horses.

Fancy snorted, the other horse whinnied, both seemingly eager to reach their destination.

"We'd best get going again."

She moved to the side of the wagon and placed her hands on Steven's shoulders, readying to be lifted aboard. He peered deeply into her eyes and spoke with honesty. "I understand that your life hasn't been easy this past year. And just when you'd made new friends and felt safe at the house, I had to pull you away." He let out a long sigh, taking a moment, it seemed, to gather his thoughts. "I promise to do my best to protect you, Glory. I'm asking you to trust me."

Glory remembered what he'd told her days ago. She offered him a small smile. "But not too much."

He blinked hard, as if recalling his own words. "You can trust me in all regards, Glory. We'll be living out here, pretty much secluded, all alone, but you have my pledge that you'll never have anything to fear from me. And as soon as we find a way to get you out of this mess, you'll be free to do as you please."

Glory couldn't get that thought out of her mind as they approached Steven's house. She didn't fear Steven as much as she feared herself. Feelings rushed in as she glanced at the man sitting by her side on the wagon seat, guiding the horses and taking her away from trouble. She wondered how much longer she'd be able to deny what those wayward feelings meant. She'd admitted time and again she'd hated him, but hatred wasn't an isolated emotion, as she'd once believed. Along with that sentiment came dozens of others to perplex and confound her.

And the thought of being free again was a dream she didn't dare indulge at the moment. There had been so many things she'd wanted to do, but not one held appeal now. Her life was a puzzle and about as muddied up as a streambed after a hard rain.

"We're home," Steven announced, pulling up on the wagon's brake.

Home? Glory hadn't felt at home anywhere but with her father in the house where she'd been raised with love and kindness.

Steven's ranch wasn't her home. It was her refuge, her sanctuary.

It was the outlaw woman's hideout.

Steven helped Glory down from the wagon and glanced at the house they'd be sharing. "I know it isn't much right now. There's still some work to be done. You've got no cupboards for the kitchen and you'll have to watch your step. I haven't gotten around to building the porch along the front of the house yet."

The truth was Steven had been dreaming of a place of his own since he'd worked his first round-up at the age of fifteen. But his plans had never included a woman living here. He supposed he'd never thought of himself as a man to take on a wife, so the place he'd built reflected that. His home wasn't large, just one bedroom, with a decent enough kitchen area and a parlor one might call homey. The house had plank floors and real windows and there was plenty of room to expand, but Steven never believed he'd have the need.

The only woman he'd been smitten with had been Reverend Caldwell's daughter, a girl whom he'd admired from a distance. And now, Steven thought with wry amusement, he'd be living with her and trying his darnedest not to let whims of fancy distract him from his duty to protect her.

Glory put a hand on his arm. Tingles of awareness from her soft touch coursed up and down his body. The solitude of the midnight hour and the soft glow of moonlight on her face only helped to illuminate his desire for her.

"It's a lovely house, Steven. I bet it's even finer-looking in daylight."

Steven smiled at her generous offering. "You must be tired. Let's get you settled and into bed."

Glory hesitated, her eyes wary as if she just realized her living conditions. This wasn't Rainbow House with a multitude of rooms and floors where one could pick and choose. Steven wouldn't be leaving her to her privacy, as he had so often when she lived in town. No, they'd be confined now to close quarters, living in this small ranch house together.

"You'll take the bedroom," Steven announced, attempting to alleviate her fears. "I'll sleep in the parlor."

Glory drew in her lower lip, a move that tended to fascinate him usually, but he halted that way of thinking. He couldn't afford those lusty thoughts. "I'd sleep in the barn if you'd like, but it's far enough away that I wouldn't hear you, if anything happened."

Glory shuddered, her body flinching with a tremor. "What would happen?"

He shrugged, reluctant to frighten Glory with the gloomy possibilities. She was a wanted woman. No telling what might happen if Ned Shaw showed up, looking to avenge his brother's death, or if the sheriff got wind of Glory living here. "Anything could happen. We're pretty far from town."

"Isn't that the point?" Glory asked, her light-blond brows lifting in puzzlement.

"Yeah, that's the point—to hide you away. But there's dangers on a ranch, regardless."

Glory peered out, seeming to note the empty corrals and the ranch pretty much uninhabited. "I don't see any animals. Are there any in the barn? I didn't notice any cattle grazing, either."

Steven had planned to have his ranch running by now. He'd planned on buying stock horses for his ranch and begin breeding, but weeks ago, he'd come upon a lovely young woman who'd nearly perished in a fire. Coming upon Glory had sidetracked all of his plans. There were some animals on the ranch. He'd built a coop just behind the barn and filled it with two dozen squawking chickens. Inside the roofless barn a milk cow named Greta resided. Steven hoped to finish building the roof soon, then Greta would enjoy the company of the livestock he planned on raising.

"This isn't a cattle ranch, Glory. I'm gonna breed horses here. There's a big market for them with all the folks pouring into Virginia City. There's also a need for good cow ponies in the ranches south of here. I figure to have a good-size herd this time next year. Now, about the sleeping quarters—"

"I wouldn't put you out of your own house."

Steven nodded. "Fine, then. Let's both get some rest. The sun'll be up before we know it."

Making sure she stepped up carefully, Steven ushered Glory inside and lit several lanterns. Picking one up, he handed it to her then led her to the bedroom. She glanced around, taking the room in as well as one could in the middle of the night.

"I've got some quilts and other female things in the wagon."

Glory's face registered amusement. Her pretty mouth lifted and she turned to set the lantern down on the dresser. "Female things?"

"Yeah, you know. Mirror, brush and comb, fancy soaps, that sort of thing."

"Oh? And where'd you get them?"

Glory stood inches from him in the dim light, the faint scent of roses drifting up to tease his senses. It would be the first of many temptations he would have to deny, he was certain even with her blond hair disheveled from the wagon ride, and her dress wrinkled beyond repair, she was still the prettiest woman he'd ever laid eyes on. "You promise to accept them?"

"I don't know that I could promise that."

"But they are things you'll need, right?"

"Well, yes. I suppose."

"And I could lie to you and say I'd bought them at the mercantile."

"But you couldn't very well do that without arousing suspicion, could you?"

"No, I couldn't. So, you'll accept them without complaint?"

"Steven, why would I ever complain about such lovely things?"

Steven twisted his mouth. He wouldn't lie to Glory. "Because they're from my mother."

Glory's face fell, her expression more than grim. "Oh."

"She says a woman needs female things around her. She wanted you to have them, Glory."

Glory nodded slowly, but the argument he'd expected didn't come. Instead, Glory's eyes swelled with unshed tears. Steven couldn't take watching sadness, indecision and despair steal over her face. "I'll be back, Glory."

Steven left Glory to her musings, wondering if she'd ever find forgiveness for the losses she'd had to endure. Hell, he didn't know much about the Bible, but he was certain that forgiving past sins was a virtue to be highly regarded.

He walked out to the wagon and lifted the gifts that his mother had sent, wrapping them in a quilt for Glory's bed. All he could do was present them to her and hope she'd come around.

And he'd not speak of it again.

Glory rose early the next morning, her predicament weighing far too heavily to allow her restful sleep. She'd never been good with change, and these sleeping arrangements had disturbed her even more than her rather bleak circumstances at Rainbow House. Her life was in as much disarray as her mussed-up hair and wrinkled clothes.

Those two things she could do something about. She'd smoothed out her dress last night and laid it across the dressing table. A glimmer of sunlight streamed into the window, brightening the room considerably. Glory peered at her herself in a tall mirror propped against the wall and immediately grimaced at the reflection staring back at her. "Mercy," she whispered, then reached for the pearl-handled brush that Steven's mother had given her.

She sat on the bed and stared at the brush in her lap, her mind spinning with labored thoughts that were far too taxing for the dawning hours. "Mercy," she repeated.

What difference did it make if she accepted these things from Lorene Harding? She'd already been eating the woman's food, living under her roof at Rainbow House and taking a host of other things offered. Would using these lovely, much-needed articles change her opinion of the woman? Would she love her father one iota less because of it? Surely she couldn't be that big a fool to think so.

Glory removed the pins from her hair, letting the tangled mess fall down past her shoulders. She lifted the hairbrush and began the ritual of brushing through until the knots were untangled and her hair glistened once again.

She braided her hair and let it hang long, a much easier style for the ranch, one that wouldn't have her readjusting pins and fallen tresses all day long.

She donned the blue silk gown again, hoping that sometime today she'd have time to sew a new dress, one more fitting and far less revealing for her own sensibilities.

Once dressed, Glory set out to make breakfast. She strode to the kitchen by way of the parlor and gasped, seeing Steven fast asleep on the horsehair sofa. His clothes shed, he lay there naked, but for the drawers he wore. She glanced away quickly, but not before noticing so many revealing things about him, like the peaceful look on his face, making him appear boyish. Yet in direct contrast, his burnished skin layered with a thin coating of spiral hairs upon a strong and powerful chest spoke only of his masculine appeal.

Glory swallowed, recalling the tempting ways he'd touched her while they were trapped in that abandoned mineshaft. She'd always remember the tender-sweet words he'd spoken and the way he had of making her seem a cherished prize. Glory would never forget those sensations. She'd never once been treated in such a kind, yet pleasingly shocking way by a man.

That Steven could charm her, she was certain. But she was just as sure that he could never be the man for her. No, not Lorene Harding's son. She could never give her heart to him. To do so would be the greatest disgrace to her father…and to herself.

Glory entered the kitchen and smiled with relief. It appeared Steven had a fully stocked kitchen, with supplies stacked up on the counter, along with a few dishes and cooking utensils. Glory could finally do something constructive with her time. At Rainbow House, she had to nearly beg Mattie to allow her to help out with even the tiniest chores. Glory had hated feeling useless there. Only after days and a good deal of persistence on her part, had Mattie finally relented in allowing her something worthwhile to do.

Glory took out a large bowl, poured flour then added eggs and milk. She began stirring up the biscuit batter, all the while thinking about her shy friend Mattie and the other girls at Rainbow House. She wondered how Merry was faring, and hoped that she would truly leave Rainbow House to return to her folks' farm. For Merry, it would be the best thing.

And Glory now realized, perhaps for the others,

staying on was best for them. Funny, how she'd judged them so harshly, not fully understanding their plight. Glory would never condone their way of life, but she understood them all much better now.

Glory lit the cast-iron stove and set her biscuits to cooking. She found a sack of coffee and proceeded to fill a pot with water. Once done, she cracked eggs into a skillet and added a few strips of pork rind for flavor. She also added herbs that she'd found, pinching off a few tiny leaves and mashing them up into the mix.

"Something smells awfully good."

Steven's voice startled her. She turned to find him leaning against the doorway, smiling at her. "Morning."

"G good m-morning." She busied herself with the meal, ignoring Steven's smile, the lean of his body and the way he'd only half dressed, his pants and shirt not yet buttoned up. Heavens, he appeared handsome with mussed-up hair and that sleepy-eyed look.

Why was it a woman couldn't do the same? If a woman came out looking like that, one would think she'd fallen off a wagon into a cow-chip pile. "Will eggs and biscuits do?"

Steven entered the kitchen. "Honey, your cooking's got to be better than anything I could whip up. Whatever you want to do is fine with me."

She nodded, feeling his overwhelming presence in the room. He stood close by, watching her.

She ignored him.

"I reached for my gun when I heard noises out here," he said.

She whirled around to face him. "Should I have wakened you?"

He chuckled and his dark eyes gleamed. "You did. Only once I realized it was you making a ruckus out here, I didn't mind. I sort of liked waking up, having you here."

"Steven," Glory said, putting warning in her tone. He'd promised last night she'd have nothing to fear. "Don't say those things."

"You don't want the truth?" he asked, reaching for two plates from the counter.

"I—I, no. Not that kind of truth. My truth is far different. I'm wanted for murder, Steven. I don't know what will become of my life."

"You still don't remember anything?" he asked, setting the plates on the table, but keeping a vigil on her face, his expression now somber.

"No, I can't recall. I close my eyes at night and pray for something, anything to come to me. But nothing does."

"Maybe, now that you're out here, away from town and all the bad memories, maybe something will come to you."

"I hope so."

Steven scratched his chest. Her gaze fastened to that area, where his fingers pulled taut the hairs, making them curl up. Glory found it hard to tear her eyes away. A lump formed in her throat when he caught her staring.

"You should button your shirt, Steven," she announced boldly. Mercy, how did she ever find her tongue enough to say such a thing?

He glanced down at his unfastened shirt and something profound seemed to dawn in his knowing eyes. "Seems to me, I got myself in a haystack of trouble for asking the same of you."

"Oh," Glory gasped, her hand covering her chest.

He grinned, an all-out wide opening of his mouth that befuddled her mind. "You do like me, Glory."

Mortified, Glory closed her eyes and whirled around. "No, I don't Steven. I don't like you one bit."

Steven didn't relent. "Some truths are harder to bear, Glory. You don't want to, but you *do* like me."

Glory piled his dish with food and set it in front of him. "Think what you want, Steven. Only I know what's in my heart."

He glanced at the food and took up his fork. "Your head says you hate me, but your heart, now that's a different matter."

Glory took her plate and sat down to face him. She'd not allow Steven to win his point. They had to live here together, for however long, and the rules had to be set down. "You promised last night that I'd have nothing to fear from you. Was that the truth or a lie?"

"I don't lie."

"You've lied many times, Steven. To the sheriff. To people in town. You've lied to shelter me."

"That's different. I won't lie to you."

"Fine then, no more talk of such matters."

Glory was about to take a bite of her eggs when Steven stated quite bluntly, "The truth is you won't ever have anything to fear from me, but that doesn't mean I don't want you, Glory. It doesn't mean I don't crave your body next to mine at night. That's one truth that I'll have to bear. And it won't be easy, so maybe it'd be better for you to hang on to your hate, honey. It'd be better for us both."

Chapter Twelve

Glory spent the day inside the house, happy to have a plan in mind to keep from thinking about Steven's declaration this morning. No matter what he claimed, Glory had to hold firm to her resolve. Steven Harding had been brutally honest. She supposed she should be grateful that he'd warned her outright, but his warning did nothing to quell her burgeoning curiosity.

It doesn't mean I don't crave your body next to mine at night.

A shudder ran through her. She recalled those bold words and the look in his eyes when he spoke them to her.

Steven made her feel things she thought she'd never feel again. He made her wonder if there could be more between a man and a woman than what Glory had come to know with Boone. Something inside told her Steven was a much different man than Boone. Sadly, she realized, she could never truly find out exactly what those differences were. She couldn't and wouldn't explore her feelings for Steven.

Glory kept busy and tried to forget her plight for the time being, pouring her concentration into something far more productive. She made curtains for the kitchen using the blue patterned material that Lorene Harding had given her. It had taken her only half the day to fashion them to fit over the window. There were no curtain rods in Steven's ranch house, so she'd tacked the material up and made ties that could be pulled back and hooked to allow sunlight in. Standing back to gaze at her creation, she decided she liked the afternoon light coming in from the west window.

The rest of the day, she worked on a dress for herself. Finally, she'd have a practical dress to wear that covered her decently from neck to ankles.

Lorene had thought of everything, from a variety of sewing needles and matching threads to buttons and yards of thin lace. Lorene had even included a copy of *Harper's Bazaar* that showed patterns that Glory could reproduce and enlarge to fit her size.

Glory hummed a happy tune while cutting out the pattern and afterward she took each and every stitch to heart, making sure they were tidy and even. She had always prided herself on her sewing talents. Today, her mood couldn't be more lighthearted, so when Steven walked into the parlor, she smiled up at him with a big grin.

"What's got you in such a happy mood?" he asked, removing his hat from his head.

"I think I'm just happy to be doing something." She continued to make one straight, even stitch after another, keeping focused on the shoulder seams of her newest creation.

"I saw the curtains you made for the kitchen."

She looked up from her stitching, wondering if Steven liked them. She couldn't tell from his tone.

"Pretty. I never thought I'd...that is, I never thought the room could look so nice."

"They do brighten the kitchen, don't they?"

He nodded slowly, then ran a hand through his hair. It was early in the day. She hadn't expected him for dinner until nearly sundown and from the perplexed look on his face, he hadn't planned to be here so early, either. "You know how to shoot a gun, Glory?"

Shocked, she peered at him intently. His question was the last thing she'd expected to hear. She hadn't been raised to uphold violence of any sort. What kind of fool notion spun around in Steven's head this time? "No, Steven. I don't know how to shoot a gun."

"Well, it's time you learned."

"I don't want to learn."

"Doesn't matter what you want."

Glory blinked back her surprise. What was Steven telling her? Was he ready to cast her out on her own? Or was it something even more urgent? Perhaps he'd heard that she'd been discovered here. Perhaps her days of freedom were numbered. "I've lived nearly nineteen years of my life without knowing about guns. I don't plan to change that now."

Steven smirked, wry amusement lifting his upper lip up crookedly. "Nineteen whole years?"

"Well, almost nineteen, coming next winter."

"Glory, don't fight me on this. I've been giving it some thought. It's necessary."

"Why, Steven? Why is it necessary?"

"Because I've got to leave you alone tomorrow for most of the day."

"You've been gone all day today and I've done quite well."

He shook his head. "I've been here, watching and working. But tomorrow I've got to pick up my horses miles from here and I can't very well take you with me."

"You're getting your horses tomorrow?"

"They were due to be delivered here, but I can't chance that, so I thought to intercept them at the Stadler place. I know for a fact that they'll deliver to the southern ranches first, before coming up here. I figure I can ride hard and get to old man Stadler's ranch by noon. There'll be no need for anyone to come up here, then."

"How many horses are you getting?"

"Half a dozen. I'll add more later on. But for now, it's a start."

Glory continued making her stitches. "Won't it look a bit suspicious for you to intercept your horses?"

He shrugged. "I'll make up an excuse, like I had business that took me right by Stadler's place and I was anxious to see my new stock. Won't be a problem as long as I shove the cash in their hands. Money has a way of quieting people's questions."

Glory let out a long weary sigh. None of this could be helped, she supposed. "I'm sorry to be such a disruption in your life."

And Glory meant it. Out of his sense of duty, Steven had set his life aside in order to help her. As soon as she could, she'd leave him to work his land, allowing him no more distractions, no more worries.

Steven stared into her eyes. "Glory, if you don't want to be a disruption, then let me show you how to handle a gun. I'll sleep better tonight."

"And I won't sleep at all."

"Sure you will. The gun I'll give you won't even make a dent under your pillow."

"My pillow?" she nearly shrieked. She set down her sewing to regard him. From the determined look on his face, Glory knew he wasn't jesting.

"Meet me outside when you've finished up what you're doing."

"But dinner…"

"Will wait. We're losing daylight, Glory."

Steven waited for Glory out back behind the house. When she finally appeared out the back door, a sour look contorted her face. Steven ignored the look, this being too dang important for both of them.

"Are you sure this—"

"It's got to be done, Glory," Steven insisted. "Here, get used to holding this." He set a Remington .44 caliber army pistol in her hand. "It's small enough to hold easily and not all that heavy."

Glory peered at the gun as though it was plagued with disease. She took in a full breath, making her chest push out the lace on her gown. His gaze automatically riveted to the soft swells of her breasts. Damn, he'd sure be glad once she made herself that "proper" dress that she'd been hankering to do. Steven had more willpower than most men, he figured, but Glory sure pushed him to his limit at times.

"It won't bite, Glory," he said abruptly.

Glory blinked her eyes closed. "It reminds me of what happened to my father."

Steven covered his hand over hers, the cold gunmetal a dark contrast to Glory's warm and delicate fingers. He spoke softly now. "Guns can save lives, too, honey. I'm hoping you'll never have call to know that. I'm hoping you'll never have to use it—''

Her eyes flashed open. ''I can't imagine using this on anyone,'' she breathed out passionately.

They stared at each other for long moments and the truth hit Steven hard, like a blow right between the eyes. He knew now, deep down in his gut, right then and there that Gloria Mae Shaw had not taken a knife to her husband. He knew right then and there that she could never have killed Boone Shaw, not even to defend herself. No, she'd never have hacked up a body with such deliberate and cold intent. Never.

The truth was in her eyes, on her face and in a heart that beat so damn sweetly that Steven had to turn away, the revelation of her innocence causing havoc to his mind.

If she were innocent, he'd have to prove it.

Glory deserved her freedom. She deserved a new start on life. She was young and beautiful. She could have all the things a young woman wanted—a happy home and family.

Steven had an obligation to her. But he had to remain focused on keeping her safe. He took her hand and guided her down a path that went well beyond the ranch house. They walked over a shallow streambed, finding dry spots to step in as the water trickled by. Steven picked up several small granite rocks and once they'd finally reached the clearing he'd remembered, he set those rocks atop a big boulder, Glory's target. Hell, he'd be happy if the woman learned enough to aim the gun straight, and hitting a target would be something short of a miracle.

''Okay,'' he said, taking several steps back from the makeshift target. ''Ready?''

A small smile lifted her mouth, but there was no joy in her eyes. "As much as I'll ever be, Steven."

"It's okay, Glory. You'll probably never have to use it, but if it comes down to you or them, I surely hope you'll use what you learn today."

Glory didn't respond. She'd resigned herself to this, he assumed, but she certainly didn't like it.

He stepped behind her, trying like hell to ignore the scent of wild roses, the press of her backside against his groin and the silky strands of her braid tickling his chin. "Lift the gun and aim it toward the small rocks."

She did as she was told, pointing the gun.

"Keep your hand steady, your arm straight. That's it. Okay now, squeeze the trigger."

Glory's body flinched. She shuddered and turned to him, her eyes locking with his.

"There're no bullets in the gun, Glory."

She relaxed, her knees nearly buckling. She turned back around and aimed the gun. Bravely, she squeezed the trigger.

"That's good. Probably would've hit that shrub, way over there," he said, pointing to the brush ten feet off the target.

Glory whirled around and he grinned. "Just kiddin'. You did real good."

Glory smiled now, loosening up. "Really?"

"Really, you've got good form."

"Maybe because I'm aiming at rocks. I don't know if I'd ever be able to point a gun at a person."

"I'm hoping you won't have to."

"I'm *praying* I won't have to."

"That's good, too. Try it a few more times, then I'll show you how to load the gun with ammunition.

You need to get the feel of shooting with bullets. It's a whole different sensation.''

"Hmm, I can imagine.''

Steven smiled and helped her point and aim the gun, giving her directions, finding that Glory was a good pupil. She was quick and smart and learned easily, even when she didn't particularly like the subject.

"You've got to respect the gun, that's most important. Respect, not fear it. Fear will only get you hurt.''

Glory slumped her shoulders when their first lesson was over. "You don't expect me to sleep with this, do you?''

He nodded. "Under your pillow.''

"Why? When you're in the house, only steps away?''

He chuckled and glanced away briefly. "Ah, Glory.'' Then peering into her innocent eyes, he captured her attention. "Exactly.''

A rosy blush crept up her cheek. "Oh.''

Steven had promised her she had nothing to fear from him, but his teasing hadn't gone as expected. She'd taken him at his word, then and now. Hell, at times, Glory simply caused a ruckus in his mind, but she was too damn beautiful for his own good. And maybe part of what he'd said was true. Maybe she did need protecting from him. He'd never take her forcefully, but loving Glory meant seducing her. And there were times when Steven thought that taking her to his bed and making tender love to her would be worth the risk to both of their souls. "Just teasing, Glory. I'm trying to put a smile on that sour puss of yours.''

She tapped her foot like a disgruntled schoolmarm

and the look she cast him was no less intimidating, making him surely glad he hadn't loaded the gun she toted. "Steven Harding, you're unmerciful."

"I know," he said without apology. "I just want you to understand how important this is. You might need to protect yourself. Knowing how to shoot will give you confidence. You won't feel as vulnerable if you're faced with tough decisions."

She peered at the gun in her hand. "You mean like whether or not I should shoot?"

"You might have to make a quick decision. Feeling confident with the gun will go a long way in saving yourself."

She directed her gaze at him squarely. "I understand that in my head. I just don't know if when the time comes, I can do it."

"I think you can."

She smiled sadly. "Because you believe I killed Boone."

Steven frowned, feeling a tug at all the strings that tied up his heart. It would be better for her think that, of course. If she believed he thought her capable of murder, it would be just one more wedge to distance her, but Steven couldn't lie to her, not even if it meant her softening to him. Not even if it meant he'd have to muster every shred of willpower he had, to keep that distance in place and permanent. "I know you didn't kill Boone, Glory. I know it in my gut. But I also believe you're a survivor and strong enough to do what's necessary when the time comes. I guess you could say I have faith in you."

Eyes downcast, Glory spoke quietly, the gun she held pulling her arm down to her side. "You have faith, when I seem to question all of mine." When she looked up, her eyes were wide, almost desperate and searching his. "Sometimes I don't know who I am any more."

Steven resisted every urge he had to take her into his arms and comfort her. With boots planted, he inhaled, unable to reveal to her that he knew exactly who she was. She was a wonderfully strong and brave woman. She was young, intelligent and so pretty it nearly hurt to look at her.

She'd been dealt a losing hand one year ago, first with the loss of her father and then in a marriage that should never have taken place. She'd lost all of her belongings, her house had burned to the ground, she'd been left for dead, then been brought to the one place she'd never wanted to step foot in, Rainbow House. Yet, she'd survived it all courageously. She hadn't fallen apart as others might have. She hadn't wept long sorrowful tears. In fact, she'd had enough gumption left yet to give the "ladies" at the house a bad time of it. Then when she'd been needed, she'd set aside her own code of morality to save Merry.

Steven admired her even more now than ever before. But he couldn't tell her, for revealing all would surely seal his fate. If he spoke of these things, she'd know that she'd become much more than an obligation to him. She'd become something that he wouldn't dare name. He'd find her husband's killer and then set her free.

It was the only way.

"You're Gloria Mae Shaw, the same woman you've always been, except that right at the moment, you're going to learn how to shoot an Army revolver using real bullets. Ready?"

She nodded slowly, none too eager for her second bout of lessons.

Steven kept his focus. No more lingering thoughts of making love to Glory. No more admissions to all of her endearing qualities. He began his next set of instructions, "Okay, the revolver holds five bullets in the chamber. This is how you load it…"

Glory answered the knock to her door in the first few minutes before dawn erupted with color on the horizon. Half asleep, she peered at Steven.

"Morning," he said cheerfully, then grinned at her tousled hair and wrinkled robe criss-crossed haphazardly over her chest.

She grunted some sort of reply, still trying to adjust her focus.

"I'm heading out. Just wanted to remind you to stay put inside the house all day. Don't go out and if you see someone approach, don't hesitate—"

"To get the gun. I know, Steven," she said quite grumpily.

"You know how to use it now and I expect you to be on your guard."

She nodded.

"Did you put it under your pillow last night, like we talked about?"

Glory shifted her attention, concentrating on the lantern hanging on the hallway wall, just over Steven's shoulder.

Steven's breath whooshed out noisily. "Okay then, where did you hide the gun?"

Glory began waking in stages, and once fully aware of Steven's badgering, she hoisted her chin and became indignant. Mercy, the man deserved it, waking her from much-needed sleep. Truth be told, she hadn't had many restful nights since the day her father had died. "It's in a safe enough place."

"Glory."

When she didn't respond to the warning in his voice, he stepped inside the room. "Where is it?"

She watched him shuffle around the room, tossing her covers, lifting a table, peeking behind her underclothes set on a peg on the wall.

"I don't have time for this, dammit."

"Don't swear, Steven. It's tucked away inside a drawer in the armoire." She pointed across the room to a heavy dark walnut piece decorated with an inlaid gilded pattern, the finest piece of furniture in the whole house.

Steven strode over and opened all the drawers, finding at last the Army revolver he'd given her yesterday. "It's too far away to do you much good. You won't have time to go searching when you need it. Look, if you don't want it under your pillow, then keep it here," he said, lifting her mattress. "At least it'll be close enough when you sleep."

Glory nodded. "All right."

He glanced at her with assessing eyes, another speech seemingly on his lips. He kept that speech to himself, thankfully, and nodded back. "I'll be home as soon as possible, hopefully before sundown."

"With your horses?"

"If all goes well, I'll have those corrals filled by nightfall."

Glory's bravado suddenly failed her. All of Steven's warnings, all of his preparations hit her fully now. For the first time since Boone's death, she'd be truly alone. It was just for one day, she reminded herself, and to her knowledge no one knew where she was hiding out except for Lorene and the girls at Rainbow House. "I'll be fine," she said, keeping the shudder of fear hidden from him. "Have a safe trip."

Steven stared into her eyes, then his gaze drifted to her lips and a yearning she'd only just come to recognize in him surfaced completely. He wanted to kiss her goodbye.

Mercy, Glory wanted that, too.

But she blamed her bout of sentiment on his constant reminders of the dangers that could befall her. She wanted him only for reassurance, nothing more. A kiss to comfort.

When he leaned in with a dark gleam in his eyes, Glory braced herself for the onslaught of Steven's passion.

His lips brushed her forehead.

The kiss was over before it had begun.

With a jingle of spurs and a flash of his duster, Steven was gone.

Glory watched him from the front window as he mounted Fancy and headed south. She made sure the door was bolted good and tight and at that moment decided that she couldn't go back to bed, there was far too much to do. She wanted to finish fashioning the dress she'd started yesterday. The blue sapphire silk that she'd worn to death had to go. The way the gown displayed her female frame so openly caused her great discomfort.

But first Glory had to make curtains for the bedroom. She couldn't fathom sleeping another night with no covering to the windows. As she'd dressed this morning she realized that she'd be fully exposed to anyone who might amble by in the daylight. She hadn't given it much thought while Steven was on the property, but it was far different with him gone from sight.

Glory worked until noon on broadcloth curtains with the smallest flowery print in shades of pinks and blues, happy to have completed them before meal-time. With the curtains up in the bedroom now, keeping her privacy intact, Glory set about making a quick meal in the kitchen. She lifted the egg basket only to find it empty. "Darn it."

Glory had her heart set on an easy meal of grilled eggs. She'd wanted desperately to finish her new dress before the end of the day. She glanced out the window, noting that the henhouse just beyond the barn couldn't be more than fifty feet away from the house. Without a soul in sight, Glory debated for half a minute about venturing outside before she hoisted the egg basket and strode out the front door. She'd be back within minutes, she reasoned, and no one would be the wiser.

Glory made quick work of retrieving the eggs from the cackling hens and stomped off the hay that had littered her boots as she made her return to the house. She was halfway through the yard when a moving flash caught her attention. On instinct, she turned in that direction. Her breath caught instantly as she noted a rider coming forth in a wagon from far off in the distance where the land had become flat and visible for miles after a rather long arduous bend in the road. "Mercy!"

With the egg basket balancing precariously in one hand, Glory raced to the house and once inside bolted the door shut realizing that she was completely exposed. The parlor windows were large and inviting, allowing any element, be it man or beast to peer inside. She'd wished she'd had the forethought to cover those windows as well.

Heart pounding like a wielding hammer, Glory squeezed her eyes shut. What should she do.

The image of cold metal popped into her mind and as much as she hated to admit it, relief swamped her as she strode with purpose to retrieve the gun from her mattress. Steven had said she shouldn't have fear, only respect for the weapon, and right now, Glory had nothing but the utmost respect for the Army revolver whose pearl handle felt like ice in her hand.

She debated about staying put in the bedroom, but a curious need to see who rode up to Steven's ranch had her moving quickly to the front window. She crouched down low and peered out, her face barely peeking out from the low window frame. The wagon continued to amble down the road, only now Glory could make the image out more clearly. And it wasn't a wagon at all, but a buggy with one sole rider at the reins.

She let out her breath and straightened to full height, straining her eyes to make out the passenger. Only once she was absolutely certain, did she drop the gun and unbolt the door, letting out a loud whoop. "Merry!"

Glory began waving, relief and joy erupting into giddy laughter as she witnessed Buddy, the apricot pooch jump down from the wagon and race toward her on his short speedy legs.

"Oh, what a treat!" She scooped Buddy up into her arms the moment he reached her and snuggled her face into his curly fur. It wasn't but a minute more when Merry's buggy pulled up, her eyes bright, her face flushed under the noontime sun.

"It's good to see you, Glory!" Merry set the brake on the buggy and bounded down from her seat with all the exuberance of an eager young child.

"And I'm glad to see you doing so well! Gosh, Merry, you look wonderful."

Merry grinned. "I feel pretty wonderful."

Glory set the pup down and embraced Merry with warmth. This unexpected visit, today of all days, was truly welcome. Glory hadn't realized how much she'd missed female companionship of late. Growing up in Virginia City, where the male population greatly outweighed the female, Glory hadn't made too many lasting friendships. Oftentimes, what families had come didn't stay long if the mines or fields hadn't paid out and those few girls she'd come to know as friends had moved on with their families, most likely searching for the next big gold strike.

Glory had found solace in time spent with her father and in his teachings. It wasn't until she'd come to Rainbow House and gotten to know some of the women there that she realized how much she missed the camaraderie that went on between womenfolk.

"I have news to tell," Merry said with a smile, "and a favor to ask."

"Well, surely." Glory grasped her hand. "Come inside, please. Steven's gone to pick up his horses, so it's just the two of us. I hope you'll share your news with me over Mattie's peach pie. She sent along some provisions to make sure I don't starve Steven to death."

Merry chuckled. "That sounds like Mattie. I think I'm going to miss her cooking most of all."

"Watch your step. As you can see, Steven hasn't built the porch yet, but it's an easy climb up into the house. Come on, Buddy." The pup raced past them and with a big jump, landed onto the entrance of the house.

Glory ushered them inside the kitchen then set out plates and poured lemonade into two big Mason jars. She sliced the pie and served it with a dollop of cream. "Here you go."

"Thank you." Merry took a bite and glanced around the kitchen, her eyes seeming to take it all in.

"It's not finished yet," Glory explained, feeling a bit proprietary of Steven's house, though she truly had no right to feel that way at all. "Steven's going to build cabinets and there's more to do, but it's—"

"Nice, real nice, Glory. I like the curtains."

"I made them yesterday."

"Steven's got to be pleased…having you here and all, making his house a home."

Glory swallowed and glanced away. "It's…awkward. I don't really belong here. I don't really belong at Rainbow House. I don't know where I fit in. Steven sees me as an obligation and living with that, knowing what he might face if I'm discovered here, that's the worst of all."

"Steven knows the consequences, Glory. That tells you something about him, doesn't it?"

Glory stared at Merry for a moment. "He's dutiful, that much I know."

"And honorable. Lorene saw to that. Surely you don't blame Steven for anything that happened in the past."

Glory thought on that, realizing that she didn't hold Steven personally responsible for what had happened

to her father. She'd be a fool to think so since Steven
hadn't had a choice in his life, being the son of a
well-to-do whorehouse madam, any more than she'd
had, being the daughter of a preacher. "No, I don't
blame Steven," she said honestly, but she'd also realized she'd been far less generous with forgiveness.
It's where her faith truly tested her and Glory knew
without a doubt that she'd failed in that regard. "But
it doesn't change anything. Nothing at all."

Merry's eyebrows lifted with her smile. "Doesn't
it?"

Glory shook her head at her friend's probing questions. She should be irritated at the things Merry
brought to light, yet Glory found her company enjoy-
able. There wasn't any use dwelling on things she
couldn't very well change and that meant any kind of
relationship with Steven Harding being completely
out of the question. "No, Merry. If things were different, maybe…"

"You'd fall in love with Steven?"

Inwardly, Glory gasped with shock, the thought of
loving another man—Steven—was too perplexing to
contemplate. She ignored the shudder of anxiety that
coursed through her. She spoke softly and as directly
as she could, "I thought I loved Boone. That was a
mistake. Perhaps I don't know what love really is."

Merry smiled, but with sympathy and understanding in her eyes. "I thought I loved someone, too, but
whether you truly do or simply think you do, the pain
is the same, I imagine."

Glory peered up into a set of eyes that were wiser
and more perceptive than Merry's young years.
"When did you get so insightful?"

"Since you saved my life, I believe. I've been doing a lot of thinking lately. I'm leaving town day after tomorrow, so I came to say goodbye.''

"Oh, Merry. Everyone's going to miss you terribly, but you're doing the right thing.''

"I know. I wired my folks to let them know I'm coming. Got a wire back just yesterday afternoon and they're happy to have me come.''

Glory reached over the table to take hold of her hand. She squeezed with gentle pressure. ''Of course they're happy, Merry. You're their daughter.''

"It won't be easy,'' she said, her voice strained. ''But I'm determined.''

"That's good. My father used to say an easy task isn't really a task at all. He'd say, the harder the trial the bigger the reward. I think he meant that in all ways, not just dealing with the Lord.''

"Yes,'' Merry said softly, ''I think he was right.''

"Father was…often right,'' Glory said, speaking with great sentiment. ''I'm glad you came out to say goodbye, Merry, but I know Steven will regret not seeing you.''

Eyes twinkling, Merry jested, ''Well, I'll leave it to you to give him a big farewell hug for me.''

Glory smiled. ''You know I'll do no such thing, but I will say goodbye for you.''

Merry's mood sobered as she lifted Buddy onto her lap. The pup licked at her hand, a subtle command to stroke his head, which Merry obliged without pause. ''I have other news. Ned Shaw came calling last night.''

Just the mention of Ned's name brought a measure of fear and foreboding. Glory hadn't been especially close to Boone's brother, but she knew he blamed her for Boone's death. He'd been the one so sure of her guilt, making all manner of accusations. Glory still had no memory of that fateful night when Boone died, the night her world had been shaken to the very core, so she couldn't defend her actions, couldn't deny any of his accusations.

"And he spoke of me?" she asked, holding her breath.

Merry hesitated. With eyes downcast, she nodded. When she finally lifted her head, her expression spoke of sorrowful regret. "Yes, he spoke of you."

Glory swallowed, almost fearful of asking. "W-what did he say?"

"He said, uh, that you'd been a terrible wife to Boone. He said that his brother shouldn't have died by your hand and that you'd run off, getting away with murder."

Glory sat perfectly still, unable to take a true breath of air. "Dear Lord."

"Glory, he was just spouting off," Merry offered in consolation. "He'd come in looking dapper, wearing a fancy new suit, and flashed enough cash around for everyone to see. Ruby made sure to keep his whiskey glass full and his tongue wagging. He'd gone on about his rich strike."

Puzzled, Glory asked, "His rich strike?"

Merry nodded. "It seems his claim is very prosperous. He's pulling hundreds of dollars' worth of ore out every day."

"But I remember nothing of the sort. Ned had fallen on hard times. He had debts. Boone said his brother had always been foolish at the gambling tables. Weeks before Boone died, Ned had come to the house, asking for money but we had no cash to loan him. Ned had been just as distraught as Boone, discouraged that his claim had all but played out. Neither one of their claims were worth the time they'd put into them. Although, Boone hadn't been working his claim for some time. He'd pretty much given up. I thought Ned had as well.''

Merry shrugged. ''Do you think that he would have come by the money another way?''

''I don't know,'' Glory said, deep in thought. She peered into Merry's questioning eyes. ''It doesn't seem likely.''

''It's a puzzle, then,'' Merry said, stroking Buddy's curly fur. ''You'll tell Steven what I had to report? He said he wanted to know every word that came out of Ned's mouth.''

''I'll be sure to tell him.'' Although, Glory didn't see how this information, baffling as it seemed, would help in any way.

An hour later, Glory stood in the parlor, arms outstretched as Merry pinned the bodice of her new dress. ''Isn't it a big snug?'' Glory wiggled about realizing there was hardly room to breathe.

''It fits your form perfectly, Glory. Would you rather it fit like a sack?''

''Of course not, but a bit more breathing room, please.''

''All right, I'll let it out some. It's really quite pretty on you. I bet Steven will like it.''

Glory made an unladylike snort, a trait she'd picked up from Carmen. ''It's not as fancy as Emmie's gown. And it's surely more suitable for a...for me. I doubt he'll care one way or the other.''

Merry stopped working to gaze up at her. ''Steven will notice and he'll care, even though you've buttoned yourself up to your neck with material.''

"It's a proper dress, Merry."

"Yes, I agree. Proper, but there's still no hiding behind it. You're covered up, but your form is just as exposed as before. A woman can't hide her body from a man, if he's at all interested. Men can see beyond all that."

Glory lifted her brows but she didn't voice her question. It was painfully obvious that Merry knew a good deal more about men than Glory, but she didn't want or need any instruction on what entices a man. She wasn't living with Steven for that purpose, yet the thought had crossed her mind whether he would like her new dress or not.

Glory squeezed her eyes closed, admonishing herself for worrying over Steven's reaction to her attire when he arrived home later. Mercy, she had more important things to think about. A heavy cloud of doubt hung over her head at the prospect of being discovered and arrested for a brutal crime she didn't know whether or not she'd committed.

Merry smiled warmly as she continued pinning material, working on the hem now. After a time, she muttered, "You just wait and see."

Glory wouldn't have long to wait since Steven had promised to come back before sundown. The hours had flown by. Having Merry here had not only been a great distraction, but a pleasant surprise as well. They worked together on the dress until it was finished, Glory happy to listen to Merry chatter on and on about her folks, her home and her hopes for the future.

When it came time for Merry to leave, Glory walked her outside. Midafternoon sunshine beat down on them in the yard. Merry turned to her with a smile. ''I'll miss you.''

''Oh, Merry. I'll miss you, too. And thank you again for helping with the dress.'' Glory had put it on the instant the dress was finished, determined to give Emmie back her gown once she'd washed it.

As she stared at Merry, a deep sense of peace settled in her belly. Glory knew in her heart that Merry's homecoming might be a bit difficult in the beginning, but she had no doubt that Merry would be welcomed with loving arms. She wanted to offer to write to her, but Glory had no future to speak of, no way of knowing where she'd be or how she'd fare. She'd been clinging precariously to the present, without much regard for the future.

''I was glad to help. After all you've done for me, it's the least I can do. And even as I say that, I still have to ask a favor of you.''

''Anything, Merry. I'll help you in any way I can.''

Merry hugged her tight, a joyous, jubilant embrace that sparked Glory's curiosity. What on earth could she possibly agree to do to make this girl so happy?

''You'll take Buddy, then? You'll keep him for me?''

Chapter Thirteen

Glory glanced at the pup that had fallen asleep at her feet on the kitchen floor in utter disbelief that Merry had given him up. The young girl's reasons seemed sound enough. She didn't want any reminders of her hurtful past and although it wasn't at all Buddy's fault, the memories would be still be there to haunt her every day and night. Merry had made her decision days ago to give him up, even before Glory had moved out to the ranch with Steven. And the ranch seemed far more fitting for a rambunctious little dog, where he could run wild and free, rather than to be cooped up indoors most of the day at Rainbow House.

Merry hadn't changed her pet's name after all, deciding to leave that up to Glory, if she was so inclined. Glory had been too stunned at the notion of keeping the dog, and what Steven might have to say about it, to worry about what to call Buddy. Buddy was a fine name. Wouldn't the animal become confused if she'd changed his name now, when the poor pup had a new home to contend with as well?

"Oh, I don't know about this," Glory muttered out

loud. The pup lifted his head upon hearing her voice, then lazily plopped it back down to rest on his front paws and close his eyes once again.

Glory stirred beef stew over the stove, tossing peeled carrots and string beans into the pot. She had potatoes boiling as well and hot coffee brewing. Glancing out the window, she looked for signs of Steven's return. Glory had managed to keep herself busy with chores and Merry's visit, but now bright orange pools lowered on the horizon as the sun faded rapidly, a constant reminder that Glory was once again alone.

After Merry's departure earlier in the day, Glory had replaced the gun under her mattress, thinking she'd been fast to reach for it when she'd spotted that buggy coming toward the house. But she'd been grateful for having it, feeling far less helpless and vulnerable. As it turned out, she'd had a pleasant afternoon with a new friend, instead of fearing for her life and having to defend herself.

The carrots had just about softened in the pot when Glory heard the distant sound of thundering hooves. Buddy began barking and raced to the front window. Glory followed him and peered out. Steven had arrived, just as he'd promised, before the sun had fully set, bringing with him a string of horses. Glory didn't know much about livestock, but the small herd he guided into the corrals seemed a fine-looking lot.

Joy washed over her, a tingling that started at her crown then followed its way down her arms, chest and torso until her entire body was enveloped with stunning sensation.

"He's home."

Buddy lost interest immediately and walked away from the window, but Glory continued to smile, happy to see Steven home safely. Happy that he'd succeeded in bringing his horses in. On impulse, she flung the door wide, ready with a heartfelt greeting, but indecision warred in her head. She couldn't call to him. She couldn't race into his arms. This was not a happy homecoming for a man who shared a life with his woman.

For just the briefest moment in time, Glory had forgotten the real reason she lived here. She'd forgotten who Steven was. With just one look at his handsome face, she'd forgotten everything she'd vowed to remember.

Glory closed the door slowly, but she couldn't quite quell the rapid beating of her heart, the untold truth that would never come to light. She couldn't quite forget the thrill she'd experienced in that one moment when Steven had come home.

Glory returned to her kitchen duties, setting out plates on the table, readying for the meal. Within just seconds of his arrival, the back door burst open and she turned to find Steven standing there, looking slightly rumpled with dust layering his clothes. As his gaze flowed over her, she noticed the deep lines of fatigue at the corners of his eyes. He stared at her with intensity, assessing her from top to bottom, then darted a glance at the stove, peering next at the table she'd set for their meal.

"Everything all right?" he asked, finally.

She had a good deal to tell him, but later, after he'd cleaned up and had something to eat. "Everything is fine."

He nodded. "I'll be right back."

Glory glanced through parted curtains and watched Steven discard his dusty shirt, remove his undershirt and wash up in the water barrel outside. Water dripped from his hair onto his chest, spreading out into droplets that coursed the breadth of his upper body and finding camouflage in the spiky hairs that covered his bronzed skin.

Glory drew oxygen deep into her lungs.

It wasn't as though she hadn't seen a bare-chested man before. On occasion, she'd seen Boone that way, but in her mind there was no comparison. Steven's shoulders were broader, his arms more firmly defined with muscle and his chest more powerful. Glory knew she should turn away and ignore the sensations rippling through her, but she hadn't the will to do so.

She continued to watch him cleanse his body, wiping his face with his shirt, then rub his skin over and over, drying himself. Then, without warning, he turned toward the window and caught sight of her watching him. Their eyes met and he froze, the hand holding onto his shirt stilled in midair. The only movement she noted in that brief moment was the slightest parting of his lips, the faintest hint of a smile emerging.

She jumped back from the window. Heart pounding, her hand flew to her chest. "Dear Lord."

Mortified, Glory wished the ground beneath her feet would part in two and swallow her up. She had trouble breathing, panic and embarrassment warring within her. Rapid heat swamped straight through her, bringing heat to her throat and cheeks. She ran her hands down her face, searching for an excuse, a reason to explain to Steven why she'd been spying. But there was no explanation she could offer. Steven would know the why of it, no matter what sort of reason she could manage. She decided to leave it be and pretend it didn't happen.

Yes, that's what she had to do. A true gentleman wouldn't bring up the matter. This would be testimony to Steven Harding's true nature.

By the time Steven entered the kitchen smelling fresh and clean and wearing a different shirt, Glory's nerves were raw. She fidgeted while setting out the meal, unable to look him in the eyes. She poured coffee into mugs, portioned out the stew, sliced up the potatoes, all without glancing once at Steven.

She served up his dish in a hurry and turned away, but his hand reached out for hers, managing only to grasp her wrist. He held on gently. "Glory?"

"Hmm?"

She blinked and stared down at the food.

"Why is Buddy here?"

She nearly died with relief. "Oh, uh, Merry came out for a visit today. She asked a favor of me, us…I mean, you. She asked if Buddy could stay on at the ranch."

The pup had been resting by the warm stove and Glory had almost forgotten he was there. Apparently it was the only thing on Steven's mind at the moment. "I didn't have the heart to refuse. She's leaving Virginia City soon and thought it best to leave him behind. I know I had no right—"

"You had every right." He spoke so surely, with such resolve that Glory ventured a look at him.

"Merry is a friend to both of us. If keeping Buddy will help her, then it's settled."

Glory nodded and took her seat. "Thank you. She said to say goodbye."

"You did a good thing for her."

She shook her head. "No, the decision was hers to make."

Steven took a bite of his food and chewed thoughtfully. "You helped her heal, Glory. The healing was mostly on the inside. You gave her courage and hope for a better life."

Glory wouldn't comment. Steven had just about admitted that entertaining men at Rainbow House was *no* life for a woman. Glory wished she could make the others see that. She wished she'd been able to convince them all to leave prostitution behind in favor of something more respectable, but who was she to pass judgment when her own life was in such shambles? Small wonder why the women hadn't taken heed of her advice.

And Steven, too, would never make that admission. To do so would be to admonish his mother and the only way of life he'd known while growing up.

"Did everything go all right with the horses?"

Steven lifted his head and grinned. "Better than I'd hoped. Two of the mares will foal come summer and Black Cloud will do his best with the other mares to, uh…" Steven cleared his throat and Glory blushed from the images flashing in her head.

"Black Cloud is the stallion?" Glory asked, once she found her voice again.

Steven nodded. "He's a beauty. I'll show him to you later on. Now, tell me all about Merry's visit."

Glory braced herself, an uncanny feeling settling in her stomach knowing she'd have to tell Steven about Ned's visit to Rainbow House. She knew Steven would have questions. Glory did, too. The two brothers hadn't been that close, yet Ned seemed to take

Boone's death to heart. He'd blamed her for his brother's death.

Glory couldn't shake the feeling that Ned would love nothing more than to see her hanging from a rope.

After dinner, Steven stepped out of the house to check on the horses. The night air refreshed, and a cooling spring breeze lifted his hair from his collar and ruffled his shirtsleeves. He leaned on the corral fence unable to wind down just yet. Excitement stirred in his belly at the prospect of finally seeing his plans come to light. He had a ranch house very nearly built, a corral full of horses, a barn full up with hay and chickens in the henhouse. Hell, he even had a dog now.

But he realized it wasn't enough.

Something had been missing.

And it hadn't taken long for him to recognize what that hollow emptiness meant.

He'd found out the moment he'd rushed through his kitchen door today, seeing Glory bent over the stove, stirring up his meal. Damn, he'd half expected her to run into his arms with a warm welcome home. He'd stared at her, in her newly sewn dress—a dress that matched the curtains in his kitchen—as if to say she belonged right there, as part of his home.

For a quick second, Steven had believed it so. Warmth swelled in his chest until, like a blissful dream you'd never want to end, he'd finally woken up.

He banished the fool notion from his head and blamed his bout of melancholy on fatigue. He'd raced home as quickly as the string of horses he'd led would allow, a burgeoning need to see Glory driving him hard. It had been a fruitful day, but Steven hadn't truly enjoyed his success until he'd walked through the door today to find Glory safe and sound at home. He'd worried over her all day, wondering if anything might occur at the ranch while he was gone. Luckily, Glory had shared a pleasant day with a friend.

And they'd both gained one curly-haired apricot pup.

But a nagging thought plagued him lately. If Glory hadn't taken that knife to her husband, and Steven was certain she hadn't, then someone else had killed Boone Shaw. What of Glory and the injuries she'd suffered under her husband's brutal hand? Had someone killed Boone in an effort to protect her from that attack? Or had someone wanted both of them dead?

None of it made much sense.

But Steven vowed to delve into the matter, especially since the latest bit of news about Ned Shaw's visit to Rainbow House left him with more doubts and questions.

"So that's Black Cloud?"

Glory's soft voice gave him a start. He'd been too deep in thought to notice her approach. She stood beside him at the corral fence, staring at the stallion.

Steven swept a quick look around the premises, wary of having Glory outside in the open, though he knew that most likely nobody would ride out to his place after sundown.

"That's Black Cloud," he said. "He's just about the finest piece of horseflesh in the territory. I paid a hefty price for him, but he's well worth it. He'll sire his share of great quarter horses."

"And you'll breed these horses to sell?"

Steven nodded. "There's big demand for good cow ponies. This breed of horse has the stamina and endurance for working a herd. They're fast and agile. With the gold and silver strikes in the area, and more people flowing into the cities, the need for beef is high. The cattle ranches are growing in size, too, and a good quarter horse is worth a lot to a ranch. I plan on buying another dozen or so, getting a few more stallions. By this time next year, I hope to have all the corrals filled. Maybe I'll have to build another barn." Steven smiled at the prospect.

He turned his back on the stallion to lean against the corral fence, his shoulders braced on a railing. "You did all right today, Glory."

She laughed bitterly. "I panicked and went for the gun the minute I saw someone coming my way."

"That's what you should have done. You didn't know it was Merry coming for a visit."

Glory shuddered, her trembling clearly visible. "I don't know if I'd ever have the courage to use the gun, but I felt less vulnerable for having it." She let go a long troubled sigh. "This is all so unbelievable. A few years ago, all I wanted was a nice home and a family. I wanted children, many of them," she whispered into the night, as though the notion was far from her reach. "Now, I'm hiding from the law and reaching for guns. Everything in my life has changed, and I can't do a thing about it."

Steven scrubbed his jaw, his fingers riding over the rough stubble of a two-day beard. "I know it seems that way now."

It was small consolation to a woman whose entire life had been twisted into a tight knot of desperation.

"I don't know what's to become of me. And you,

Steven. It isn't fair of me to jeopardize all of this," she said, gesturing out with a sweep of her hand. "Your ranch, your dreams, everything you've worked so hard for. If we get caught, you'll go to jail, too."

Unshed tears filled her eyes, but she spoke with such firm resolve, Steven's gut clenched. "Nobody's going to jail, Glory."

He put as much resolve in his tone as she had, but he had nothing to back up his statement, no way of reassuring her. She remembered nothing of that night. She might believe she killed Boone, but Steven no longer thought that to be the case.

"You can't say that, Steven. You don't know what will happen in the future."

"I have a pretty good idea. You're gonna have those children you want one day, Glory. You'll see. And all of this will seem like a bad dream."

Glory shook her head, a frown marring the perfection of her face. "That doesn't seem possible now. I mean, the children. And as for the bad dream, I'm afraid I'm already living it. But I don't have to include you in my hardship."

"What does that mean?" Steven didn't like her tone and he experienced something close to fear as he noted the firm, stubborn set of her chin.

"I can't live with this any longer. Your obligation to me is over. You've done your part. You saved my life and I thank you from the bottom of my heart, but I can't stay here forever. I can't allow you to sacrifice everything for me. Tomorrow, I'm going back to Virginia City. I'm going to turn myself in."

Boldly and with purpose, she strode toward the house, leaving Steven to stare after her. She'd shocked him. Steven couldn't let her go. He couldn't imagine Glory being tossed into jail, or worse, being strung up for a crime she didn't commit.

I can't stay here forever.

Yet, that's exactly what he wanted. He realized it now. He wanted to come home after a trying day and find her there, just like he had today, blending in so beautifully with all of his dreams.

He wanted to take her into his arms and comfort her, making her forget all the bad things in her life. He wanted to make love to her, until their bones ached and their hearts sung. He wanted Glory, without a doubt.

The realization dawned without much surprise. He'd been fighting it for weeks now, his head battling his heart. From the first moment he'd witnessed the brutality laid upon her the night he found her surrounded by flames, the minute he'd looked at her bruised face, her body beaten so badly he could barely stand it, Steven had been done for.

Without his knowing it, she'd taken his heart that night.

There may be no future for the two of them, no hope for anything lasting, but he wouldn't allow Glory to make another mistake. It would be on his conscience, because all of her troubles had begun when she'd lost her father and secondly, because he'd vowed to protect her.

He caught up to her in three long strides. Reaching out, he gripped her upper arm and turned her to face him. "I can't let you do it, Glory. You're not going back to Virginia City."

She closed her eyes. "I have to, Steven."

The plea in her voice tore him up inside.

"No, not yet. You said that you can't stay here

forever. Honey, it's only been a few days. Is this place so horrible that you'd rather rot in jail?''

Glory's eyes flashed with surprise. ''No, of course not. This is a beautiful ranch, Steven. But you deserve to be free of me so that you can work here, without fear of repercussion from the law. Don't you see, that's why I can't—''

''Yes, you can.'' Steven tightened his hold on her. ''I'm a grown man, Glory. I know what I'm doing, what I'm risking. But you've got to trust me and trust yourself. Give it time. You might remember something. And while you're waiting for that to happen, you're safe here. I promise.''

A small smile played at her lips. ''Steven, that's an impossible promise to make.''

He smiled back, seeing her lips curving up as a good sign. ''I never make a promise I can't keep. Trust me, Glory.''

She swallowed, and contemplated for a long moment. Then finally she nodded. ''I'll stay a little longer, Steven.''

''It's settled.''

Glory walked slowly toward the house. As she stepped up onto the threshold, he called to her, ''And Glory.''

She turned to look at him.

''You look real pretty in your new dress.''

''He's kinda ornery for such a small dog,'' Steven said, as he tried to retrieve his red bandana from Buddy's clenched teeth. The pup thought it a game and after a time, Steven saw it that way, too. Though tired from the long day, Steven thought to indulge the pup and his antics before turning in. He squatted on the parlor floor and played the tug-along game with the animal.

"He's playful, Steven. He's still a puppy." Glory had already taken a shine to the dog, defending him like a mother hen.

The dog growled, a low and deep rumble from his throat that wouldn't spark an iota of fear in even the weakest of God's creatures.

"Oh, isn't he the sweetest thing?" Glory asked, coming to sit on the parlor floor next to Steven. She stroked the dog's head lightly and for one instant, Buddy stopped to enjoy the attention lavished upon him before turning his attention back to yanking on the kerchief with all his slight might.

Steven tugged harder, but the curly-haired pup only wiggled his bottom and dug his paws into the floor. "He's stubborn, that's for sure."

"He's male," Glory said dryly.

Steven stopped yanking to look at her.

The sweetest smile graced her face. She sat close to him, the faint scent of roses wafting up, distracting him from his cause. Damn, he was surely glad he'd convinced her not to turn herself in tomorrow or anytime soon. He'd bought some time, but soon he'd have to figure out the puzzle of Boone's death. As long as Glory stayed with him on the ranch, she'd be safe. He'd see to it.

She seemed more relaxed now that they'd settled the matter, the indecision and wariness all but gone from her expression. Having Buddy here helped, the pup an entertaining diversion from her troubles. "He's ornery, stubborn and sweet?"

Blue eyes twinkling, she responded, "Like I said, he's male."

Steven grinned and dropped the bandana, giving up the game with the dog. He was finding Glory's game far more interesting. "I suppose you know some men like that?"

Glory shook her head. "Not some men, only one." She stood and straightened wrinkles in her dress, averting her gaze.

Steven stood, too, waiting for her to look at him.

When she finally did, what he noted in her clear blue eyes made his heart skip. "Are you speaking about me?"

"Maybe," she whispered.

"Maybe? So you think I'm sweet?"

He meant it as a jest, but Glory peered at him with sincerity, a look that Steven couldn't mistake. "Yes, you've done so much for me."

"Glory, I..." What could he say? He couldn't very well admit what he felt for her. Hell, her life was complicated enough right now. And he knew what she felt for him was gratitude, nothing more. "Nobody's ever called me sweet."

"No? What about the women you've been with?"

Steven hadn't expected such a bold question from her. No, sir, not such a bold question at all. "Now, that's not a subject I like to encourage."

"Have there been so many?"

Steven swallowed hard. "Glory."

"You say you're just friendly with the girls at Rainbow House."

"That's the truth."

"So, are you saying you've never—"

"Never."

"But you seem to know, I mean to say, you seemed so experienced when you kissed me. I thought—"

Kissing Glory had come as naturally as breathing. She was a woman made for passion, although her sense of morality and perhaps the horrible way she'd been treated by her husband had her questioning and doubting herself. She knew nothing of the pleasures that can occur between a man and woman. "Glory, I didn't say there haven't been women, just not the ones you know at Rainbow House."

"Oh," she said, understanding dawning in her bright eyes. This sure wasn't a topic Steven wanted to discuss with her.

He scratched his head. "What's this all about, anyway?"

Glory hesitated and he witnessed great indecision in her expression. Then, taking a deep breath, she explained, "It was something Ned said. He told everyone I'd been a terrible wife to Boone. I began thinking that maybe it was true. I was young and inexperienced. There'd been a whole lot I didn't know. I kept the house clean, put decent meals on the table every day and listened when he spoke. I'd been good at that, but maybe, not good enough...in other ways."

Anger surged forth, taking hold so strongly that Steven had to mentally bank the emotion before he could bring himself to speak. "You're good enough, Glory. Any man who doesn't think so is a fool. You've got nothing to worry about in that regard."

Glory didn't appear convinced. The woman didn't know how beautiful she was, both inside and out, how making love to her should be a thing to cherish, to treasure. He couldn't fathom her lacking in that way. He'd had a small taste of her passion and it was unforgettable. Yet, he was certain nothing he could say right now would change her mind.

"One day, you'll know it for a fact, Glory. Now, it's getting late. It's time we both turned in. I'll walk you to your room."

"No need," she said quietly. "Good night, Steven."

He watched her walk away, then settled himself down on the sofa. Judging by the way his bones ached it wouldn't be long before he fell asleep. He closed his eyes and relished the silence.

Minutes later, high-pitched whimpering disturbed his peace. He rose to search for the pleading sound, finding Buddy scratching behind Glory's door. The dog looked up with eager eyes. Steven knew he'd been tossed aside, in favor of someone far more appealing. "Smart dog."

He lifted Buddy and knocked on her door.

Glory answered the knock instantly. "Oh, I was just about to get him," she offered. "After I finished undressing."

Lantern light cast a teasing glow over her body. Her nightgown covered her well, but Steven couldn't miss the curves and hollows underneath, silhouetted by the dimming light. Her hair cascaded down her back flowing freely, wild and loose. Steven's willpower ebbed somewhat, but he clung to the remaining shreds.

He handed the dog over. "Seems he prefers your bed."

Glory scooped the pup into her arms and cuddled him close to her chest. The dog's head fit snugly between the slopes of her breasts. She kissed the pooch lovingly. "He can sleep with me."

Steven rocked back on his heels. "Well, heck, if

that's all it takes, I'll be scratching at your door tomorrow night.''

Glory's face flamed, then she looked him squarely in the eyes, her chin up. She spoke softly, but with conviction. "Sweet, stubborn...and ornery."

A chuckle escaped. Glory could always make him laugh. "See you in the morning, Glory."

He settled back down on the sofa with a deep sigh of resignation. Glory made his tired body come alive. He banished all of the enticing images flashing in head. Wouldn't do him any good to hope or to wonder.

But he knew one thing with absolute certainty.

He'd never had cause to envy an animal in his entire life, but that curly-haired mutt was one lucky dog.

Chapter Fourteen

*T*here was blood everywhere. Red pools like stream-
ing rivers cut the ground in two. Shouts and screams
rattled in her head. "Don't kill him," a voice called
out. "Don't, please." And the face of a stranger appeared, a coldblooded murderer. He held a knife in
one hand and a gun in another, but a moment later
he was gone, melting into the crimson ground until
he became the very blood he'd caused. For miles, all
she could see was the thick red liquid. It layered the
earth, climbing over shrubs, up trees and fanning out
to spread its wrath on everything bright and clean
and pure.

And then the fires came, the flames whipping about
like wielding swords eager to slice the sky in half.
The bright color of heat mingled with the blood.
There was no separating it now, no way around it.
She was engulfed in flames and blood. Black smoke
choked the air like the devil of death.

"No!" a voice cried. "Don't kill him."

Smoke layered the air like a thick blanket. She
couldn't see anymore, the flames too bright, the blood
too red, the smoke burning her eyelids.

She screamed and screamed, the stranger's face appearing once again, then disappearing, and others came as well, to laugh, their scorn evident in their evil smiles.

And then her father appeared, his face so calm, so at peace. "It's all right, my child. Have no fear. There is always light, even when darkness consumes you." Then he was gone.

"No, Father, don't leave me. Don't go, please," she cried.

She felt herself being lifted, as if floating up, cushioned in the safety of familiar arms.

"Glory, shh, honey. It's all right now."

She opened her eyes as beads of perspiration trickled from her forehead. Her heart pounded hard and fast as she gazed into Steven's concerned eyes. He sat on the bed next to her, cradling her as one would a child, and great relief flooded her senses. The nightmare was over.

"Steven."

"I'm here, Glory. You had a bad dream."

Thoughts rushed in as she became fully aware of where she was and whose arms held her so tenderly. "I, uh, it was awful."

"Tell me," he asked, "I want to know."

"I've never dreamed of that night before. It's the first time that I recalled anything."

"That's good, honey. What did you remember?"

"I saw the flames and the blood. I saw faces, Steven. Many faces but nothing makes much sense. I can't seem to puzzle it out. It seemed so real, so clear, but now the memory is fading. I'm losing it."

"It's all right, Glory. That's how dreams are sometimes. But it's a good sign. It means that your memory might return soon."

Glory trembled, a shaking she couldn't control. The dream had seemed so real. It had been harsh and wicked. If the reality of what happened that night was as true then Glory wasn't sure she wanted to recall anything more.

"Tell me, who did you see in your dream?"

"Strangers mostly, and some faces I recognized, but I can't be sure, because it's all kind of fuzzy now."

"You cried out for your father."

"Yes, he was there. He came to me just before," Glory stopped, realizing the significance in what she would now admit. "He came to me just as you lifted me up. He came to save me."

But it had been Steven who had saved her both then and now. It had been Steven to rescue her from this bad dream.

"Can you remember if Ned or Boone were in your dream?"

"I think so, but I can't be sure." She seemed to recall familiar faces, but they'd all frightened her, except of course, her father's face. That had been the only consolation in her dream. "Why do you ask?"

"I wonder if all the talk of Ned Shaw today stirred up your memory."

"It's possible. I just don't know."

Steven tightened his hold on her. "You're trembling. Try to calm down, honey." He lowered his voice, whispering softly, "I'm not going to let anything happen to you."

Glory peered into Steven's eyes. His concern touched her in ways she'd never been touched before.

Other than her father, no one had ever been so protective. No one had ever made her feel this safe, when in truth she had no reason to believe it so. She wanted to ask him why he cared so much, but she knew the reason. He'd said it once already. He felt responsible for her. She was his obligation. For tonight, as her trembling ebbed and her heart slowed, it was enough.

Steven lowered her down onto the bed. "Can you sleep?"

"I don't know."

"Want to try?"

Glory held on to Steven with no thoughts of letting him go. He came down onto the side of the bed next to her, his hold on her comforting. Glory feared sleep now. She feared reentering that nightmarish world again. Steven would be her savior tonight. She cradled her head onto his chest and snuggled in. "Yes, I want to try."

And when Steven wrapped her into his arms good and tight, Glory took her first calm breath.

She knew her demons wouldn't reappear tonight.

Steven woke slowly, the delicate scent of roses curving his lips up into a smile. He opened his eyes and his smile widened. During the night Glory had turned onto her side and now he found himself behind her, her body tucked provocatively against his. His hand rested on her torso, his fingers spread out, just under the swell of her breast.

His body grew tight instantly.

He squinted against the pain in his groin, trying to ignore the sharp pang of desire that seized him with gripping intensity. He wanted her with such yearning that he could barely breathe. He knew the smart thing to do would be to get up and put some distance between the two of them, but he couldn't quite manage that. He couldn't bring himself to give up the sense of peace that settled in his gut as he woke with Glory by his side, regardless of the pain that being so near her caused.

There wasn't much he could do but relish the time he had with her. Tangled in the sheets, with hair flowing freely now, blond waves covering his pillow, she made the prettiest picture, one that would stay with him long after Glory was gone.

Steven held on to the moment as long as he could and just as he lifted up to rise, Glory stirred. She shifted, made a little pleasured moan then turned his way. She wound up in his arms, faces close, bodies even closer.

She blinked, then cast him the sweetest of smiles. "You stayed."

"And you slept. Peacefully, I hope."

She inhaled deeply and gave him a slow nod. "Yes, peacefully. Thank you."

"For?"

"For not making me ask."

"Anytime."

He reached out to touch her soft cheek, tracing a fingertip down her face until he met with one corner of her mouth. She parted her lips slightly, an innocent enough move that sparked his internal fire. "You're pretty in the morning light."

She glanced at his lips for a long moment, then sighed. "This is highly improper," she remarked, as if just coming to realize she'd slept with him last night.

"It was innocent enough, Glory. A friend helped comfort another. There's nothing wrong in that."

Glory contemplated, her brows knitting together. "Are we...friends?"

She was much more to him, but for now, perhaps always, he'd have her think it so. "Well now, that's up to you."

She'd spent most of her time at Rainbow House hating him, or so she'd said. Steven wondered what emotions played havoc with her mind. He wondered how she truly felt about him. And he also wondered if she'd ever see him differently, as the man that he'd become, regardless of his upbringing.

Glory stared at him, her expression unreadable.

Steven used that time to rise, moving away from her enticing body and tempting mouth. He'd be her friend for as long as she needed him, but lying beside her had him thinking more than friendly thoughts. She'd blush down to her toes if she knew the path his mind had taken.

He bent to cover her to her chin with the sheet. "While you're thinking on it, I'll go check the horses. Go back to sleep if you'd like."

Buddy, who'd been lying at the foot of the bed, took advantage of Steven's leaving. The dog scooted forward and found the curve of Glory's body then settled in. Without thinking, it seemed, her hand went to the dog's fluffy head and she began to pet him.

"I'll make breakfast," she offered immediately.

Steven knew that although she needed more rest, she'd felt it her duty to cook for him. He shook his head. "No. You rest up some more. You didn't get much sleep last night. I'm not all that hungry, anyway."

Casting him a tentative look, she asked, "Are you sure?"

"I'm sure. I'll see you later."

She yawned and stretched out. Sleek as a cat, her arms rose above her head and once she settled down into the bed again, she nestled with Buddy. "I'll make something special for supper."

He nodded, wishing he could climb back in bed with her and hold her the way he had last night. *She* was the only "something special" he wanted. "You've got yourself a deal, honey."

Glory closed her eyes and nodded slowly, drifting back to sleep before Steven had walked out of the room.

Glory burned supper. The special meal she'd promised Steven hadn't turned out special at all. She'd ruined the pork that he'd brought back with him yesterday from the ranch where he'd bought his horses. Overcooked and tasting just this side of old leather, Steven had managed to chew and chew and chew until Glory thought his teeth would fall out. But he'd made no comment, even when her potato pudding had turned out watery and tasteless. The only thing edible from the meal was the leftover peach pie that Mattie had sent along. Glory denied herself a piece, losing her appetite all over again when she noted Steven's steadfast expression.

He'd taken his punishment without qualm or complaint.

Tears stung her eyes so she turned away to wash the dishes. She poured water into the dry sink and took up a washcloth.

She stilled when Steven came up behind her. "Need some help?"

She shook her head, praying her tears wouldn't flow, hoping he wouldn't see her devastation over something so insignificant as a ruined meal. But Glory *was* devastated, for many reasons, the most prevalent being the state of her life at the moment. Coping with everything that had happened in the last year hadn't been easy, but she'd survived, barely, until ruining one silly meal had brought it all to a head.

Doubts crept in. Steven had convinced her to stay with him here, but wouldn't everyone be better off if she turned herself in?

Steven held out hope that she'd remember something soon. The nightmare she'd had last night weighed heavily on her mind. Was she on the verge of getting her memory back, or was that nightmare more a result of all the talk Merry had brought to her about Ned and his misgivings?

She'd been distracted while cooking up the meal. It had been the cause of its imminent destruction, but her distraction had gone further than her nightmare. Her mind had wandered off, daydreaming about waking up with Steven beside her. He'd stayed throughout the night, without pause, without her having to ask and when she awoke, she'd been happy to have him there.

Were they only friends? Or something more?

"Glory?" Steven's question had gone unanswered.

"I've m-managed to spoil your dinner," she said in a shaky voice, "the least I can do is clean up the kitchen."

"It wasn't that bad."

She whirled around to face him. "It was horrible. You nearly choked every time you took a swallow!"

Steven chuckled, a light coming into his dark eyes. "Okay, so it wasn't exactly—"

When he hesitated, Glory pursued his replay. "Exactly what?"

"Edible."

"There! You see. It *was* horrible."

Tears dripped from her eyes. She hated to appear weak and ridiculous, but she couldn't put a halt to her emotions. She couldn't stop the onslaught of her feelings. She'd bottled them up too long and now, all she felt inside came barreling forth.

"Glory, what's wrong? And don't tell me ruining one meal's got you so disturbed."

She threw her hands up in despair. "It's…everything."

She turned abruptly and took up the washcloth, her tears flowing down freely. She scrubbed a pan with all of her might. Steven stood behind her and she fully expected him to sigh with exasperation, the way Boone always had whenever she'd been distraught.

But Steven had simply removed the washcloth from her hand and wrapped an arm around her waist. "Lean back, Glory. Lean on me."

She sobbed. "S-seems I'm always…l-leaning on you." But she rested back against him anyway and laid her head on his shoulder.

He was strong and powerful and so sure of everything. Being in his arms helped her connect with that. He helped strengthen her, pulling her out of her dark despair.

"You have every right to be frustrated and frightened. You have every right to hate what's happened to you. You go ahead and cry if that's what you need to do right now. But remember this. You're not alone. I'm here.''

She nodded slowly, letting his words calm her, letting his strength sustain her. She wasn't alone. She had Steven. And he had her gratitude.

He tightened his hold on her. ''I know what you need—to get out of here for a time. And my new mares need exercising. We can take a ride later on when the sun fully sets. Would you like that?''

She smiled and turned to him. She knew she must look a sight with a tear-streaked face and puffy eyes, but she didn't care at the moment. ''I'd love that, Steven.''

Glory rode a bay mare named Nutmeg, her cinnamon-brown coat glowing beautifully in the moonlight. The sleek female horse took her lead from Black Cloud. Steven had insisted on riding the stallion, claiming the horse had been restless tonight and needed the exercise. They rode into the back pasture on Steven's land, making sure to keep to the cover of darkness. Glory wore her midnight-black cape, her head covered with the hood.

She wasn't an expert horsewoman, so Steven had chosen the most gentle of horses. The lady-broke mare had intelligence, knowing with just a slight move or tug on the reins what Glory wanted of her, making her night ride more pleasurable.

The ride was exactly what she needed. Doubts washed away and her head cleared of all pensive thoughts as they rode at a gallop, giving the horses a much-needed workout. Exhilarated from the refreshing air, the agile horse and the man beside her, Glory didn't want the ride to end.

When they returned to the ranch, Steven unsaddled Black Cloud first. The horse snickered and pranced, sidestepping and pulling at the lead rein Steven held in his hand. Black Cloud snorted and Steven tried to soothe him. "Whoa, there, boy. Calm down."

"What's wrong with him?" Glory asked.

Steven opened the corral gate with a quick shove and pulled on the horse's rein, until the reluctant stallion finally entered the corral. "He's not cooperating. Seems he needs a lady tonight." Steven took off the bridle, then stroked the horse's snout, whispering to him.

Nutmeg pranced over to the corral gate and whinnied, showing interest in the stallion.

"They've been dancing around each other all night. Better dismount, Glory."

Steven closed the corral gate and walked over to help her down, reaching for her waist. He smiled when her feet hit the ground. "Looks like Nutmeg is going to be bunking in Black Cloud's corral tonight. And with any luck, I'll have another foal before long."

Glory smiled back, feeling more alive and free than she'd had in weeks. "Is that all it takes?" she breathed out.

Steven's smile widened. With a finger he shoved his hat a bit higher on his forehead. "Well now, it's a mite more complicated than that." He stared into her eyes for a moment piercing her with a beckoning look, one filled with many possibilities.

A minute later, Steven freed Nutmeg of her saddle and bridle and led her into Black Cloud's pen. Closing the gate, Steven leaned against the fence, peering at his two new acquisitions.

Glory sidled up beside him. She wasn't ready to say good night or go back into the confines of the house, the moonlit ride had sparked all of her senses. She stretched her arms along the corral fence, bracketing her boots up on the lowest rail, lifting her a good ten inches from the ground. From that point, she gazed at the two horses, seeing them as a part of Steven's future.

Steven noted her position and came to stand behind her, his body pressed close, with his hands wrapped loosely around her waist, bracing her from falling.

"He's a bit of a devil, tonight."

"I can see that," Glory said, keeping her gaze trained on the horses teasing and tempting each other. They played a game of chasing, confronting, then chasing again, all around the corral pen, their snorts of lust and desire not to be missed.

"It's been said all true thoroughbreds can be traced back to three horses. Their line is that pure. They were brought to Europe almost two hundred years ago. They don't come any faster or finer." Steven spoke with pride, sharing his knowledge. "The quarter horses are fastest in the quarter mile, that's how they came by their name."

Glory continued to stare at Black Cloud. He skirted the perimeter of the corral, pursuing his female. The mare led him on a merry chase.

"He's got only one thing on his mind," Steven offered in a slow lazy drawl.

Glory dug her teeth into her bottom lip. Steven's warm breath in her ear caused a commotion to her insides.

"Stallions get a bit crazed around a female. They're meant to breed, and Black Cloud's been restless all day. What he wants is right in front of him. He has only to take it."

Steven tightened his arm about her waist.

"What about her, does she get..." Glory took a swallow, embarrassed at what she was about to ask. "Does she want the same thing?"

"See how she's prancing around him? She's spreading her scent and Black Cloud...can't stay away."

Steven's voice, low and husky in her ear, caused goose pimples to rise along her arm. She shuddered, a slight little tremble that rocked her whole body.

"Are you cold?" Steven asked, the granite wall of his chest bracing her from the back. He wrapped her cape tighter around her, but it was the heat of his powerful arms holding her, that made her, hot...and tingly.

Glory didn't grant him a reply. She couldn't speak. Not now. She watched Black Cloud circle his mate, snorting, his sleek body primed and ready. The mare watched him intently, rooted to the spot. Glory couldn't move, either.

She felt her defenses crumble, being in Steven's arms, allowing him to hold her, together, watching this mating ritual. She knew she should turn and leave but her gaze fixed on the horses, mesmerized, and her heart pumped double time.

"You know what they're going to do now, Glory?" Steven asked softly.

"Yes," she admitted. She knew about mating, but her own experiences hadn't been pleasurable. They had only caused her anguish and sorrow. She swallowed down, feeling Steven's solid body up against her, his hot breath inflaming her senses.

Steven's lips caressed her temple. "Do you want to go inside?"

"No," she answered with honesty. She didn't want to be anywhere but here, in Steven's arms.

Steven nuzzled her neck, but Glory only felt his hot hard manhood pressing against her from behind.

"Now," he said devilishly, "Black Cloud gets what he's waited so long for." Steven inched his fingers up, leaving her waist to probe the sensitive skin under her breasts. She'd given him free access to her throat and he planted tiny kisses there, moistening her neck with his tongue. Shivers of delight spiraled up her spine and she ached for him to touch more of her.

"So damn sweet," he whispered, kissing her chin, the path of her jawline, her temple.

Glory heard the mare whinny, and she glanced over. Black Cloud had mounted his mate, his ebony coat gleaming like black onyx. The mare struggled, but the male continued his pursuit until finally they had joined.

"Is he hurting her?" she asked, voicing her concern in a raspy whisper.

"No, sweetheart. It's natural, the way God intended."

"It doesn't look natural." And Glory knew the falsity of her words. It was the Lord's way. Procreation. Yet Glory had to turn away, unable to watch any longer, unable to see the mare dominated by the stallion.

Memories flooded in, of Boone, and the way he'd taken her roughly, with no regard to her feelings, her own wants and desires. There had been nothing natural in their joining, nothing pleasurable. Glory had thought to be a dutiful wife she must endure the act of lovemaking without complaint. She'd never known a moment of delight or joy, yet she'd never thought it a woman's right.

"Glory," Steven said, the anger in his voice tempered with restraint. "Did Boone hurt you?"

Glory squeezed her eyes closed. She couldn't discuss this with Steven. She couldn't bring herself to answer his probing question. What good would it do to bring to light her failures and disappointments? She couldn't change anything. It would be better to put it out of her mind. Much, much better.

"I don't want to talk about it," she whispered, and judging from Steven's long labored sigh, she knew he'd heard the answer with her unspoken words.

Glory moved away from Steven, jumping down from the fence, confused by her own desires, unable to banish the memories of being with a careless, inconsiderate man. She headed for the house.

"It doesn't have to be that way, Glory."

Steven's firm resolution put a halt to her steps. She peered at the ground, wondering if she misunderstood.

Steven came up behind her. He didn't touch her, but only whispered so softly that the words nearly drifted away in the night air. "Making love can be tender and gentle. Something to cherish."

She shook her head, because she'd never known lovemaking to be that way. She'd never had any comparisons, any way to trust in what Steven declared. Nothing in her life had turned out as she'd hoped. She'd lost almost everything of importance, but most of all, she'd lost her ability to trust. Her faith had been all but shattered.

Steven came to stand in front of her, his dark eyes filled with understanding. He reached out to caress her cheek, his finger gently stroking her skin. "You should know that kind of tenderness."

Glory looked into Steven's eyes, searching his face for the truth. This man, who had saved her life and then shown her nothing but compassion and patience, was the last man on earth she should have dealings with. He'd been the enemy in her mind for so long and yet he'd become so much more to her. Steven Harding had become her savior—a devilishly handsome man who'd protected her, ready to give up his own safety for the sake of hers. "I hated you, Steven," she said quietly, with regret and reproach.

Steven's lips curled up. "I know." He bent his head and brushed his mouth over hers lightly. The kiss had been quick and soft. "But I don't believe you hate me now."

Heat flamed her face. Mercy, she didn't know what she felt for Steven Harding. She wanted to blame and resent him. She'd lashed out at him, accused him, been a thorn in his side whenever she could, foolishly believing her actions would ease her pain in some small way.

He wrapped his arms around her waist, holding her carefully, like one would a delicate budding rose. "I want you, Glory. I have for a long time."

She heard the soft whinny of the mare and the stallion's snort as their hooves beat at the ground. Steven's words when he'd spoken of Black Cloud, echoed in her head. "And if I agree, you'll take what you've waited so long for?"

His eyes bored into her and he shook his head. ''No, sweetheart. I'll give to you and you'll give to me and we'll take whatever pleasure there is together.''

Glory's heart lurched. If only that were true. If only she could believe him. Indecision waged a battle in her head.

''Let me show you, Glory,'' Steven offered, his voice silky with persuasion. He kissed her again, just as gently as before, his lips a combination of teasing torture and sweet regard. ''Let me show you the tender side of loving.''

Chapter Fifteen

Steven cursed under his breath when a fiery ash swirled up to burn his hand. He poked a stick into the fire in the parlor's hearth and flames ignited, brightening the darkened room, lending a measure of warmth. The night air had chilled considerably, bringing a draft into the house. For Glory's sake, he'd built the fire.

He didn't need the extra heat. His body still hadn't cooled from his exchange with Glory earlier. He'd offered her all that he could, all that he had to give, but it hadn't been enough.

Glory still didn't trust him. She'd been scarred by the brutality of a man who should have protected and loved her, but until this night Steven hadn't realized to what grave extent. He'd witnessed fear and misgiving, her emotions evident on her face and in the light that had vanished from her eyes. Steven hadn't pressed her, hadn't tried to seduce her to his will.

That's not the way he wanted Glory. The decision was solely hers to make and he'd told her that very thing. While his body ached painfully and his heart nearly crumbled, he had stood firm. "I won't press you," he'd told her, "but I'll be here if you change your mind."

Glory had gone to sleep a short time ago. He knew the exact moment when she'd lowered the lantern and climbed into bed. She creaked the door open once, giving Steven a smidgen of hope, but it was only to invite Buddy inside.

Steven had worries about Glory and his own fears came to light. Had Glory's uncertainty tonight been tied directly to him? Did she still see him as the enemy? He held no hope of a future with her. She'd never compromise her belief that a life with him meant a deep and perhaps lasting betrayal to her father. But he'd wanted to give her one night. He'd wanted to make tender, sweet, slow love to her. He wanted to help erase that part of her memory that held her hostage to help her heal.

And selfishly, he admitted, he wanted to experience the joy and beauty of their joining, at least once.

Steven straightened, lifting up from the hearth, too perplexed to sleep, his body still wrought with desire.

He sat down on the sofa, stretched out his legs and contemplated Boone Shaw's death. He had to clear Glory's name. He had to prove her innocence. He owed Glory that much, then she'd be free.

It was the only way either of them would find any peace.

Through the kitchen window Glory watched Steven up on the ladder, hammering in long planks on the roof of the barn. The morning sun beat down with ferocity, bronzing his face to a golden hue, with little regard to the hat perched atop his head. She stifled a gasp when his hammer missed its mark, pounding his hand instead. He'd let out a loud curse and his expression, even from this distance, appeared more than grim.

He'd been keeping busy these last three days, building kitchen cabinets, completing the barn, grooming his horses, and for the most part, ignoring her.

He rose early, often refusing breakfast and grabbing only a biscuit or two to take with him outside. He worked from dawn to dusk, it seemed, and by the time he came in for supper, he'd been too tuckered out from exertion to pay her any mind.

They'd spoken little since that night with the horses, but whenever Steven did address her, he'd been friendly and kind. Glory wondered if she'd overstayed her welcome. She wondered if he wanted her gone from the ranch. Nothing in his manner pointed to it, but Glory's gut told her Steven had something on his mind.

So when he entered the kitchen later that morning, surprise registered. She couldn't quite keep her expression steady. "Oh. Hello."

Grabbing a cloth, she wiped cherry stains off her hands. She'd woken up determined to put a smile on Steven's face today, hoping that cherry cobbler, made from dried cherries she'd found in the newly-dug-out root cellar, would see to that.

When he noted her creation, he cocked his head and cast her half a smile. "I love cherry cobbler."

"It'll be ready by supper."

"I hope to be back by then."

"Are you leaving?" Glory asked, tamping down her alarm. He hadn't made mention of going anywhere, but then, he hadn't been confiding in her lately.

"I have to make a trip into town. Is there anything you need?"

"Oh." Glory darted glances around the room. Steven had the kitchen well stocked. She couldn't think of one thing that she needed. "No, not this time. Will you be stopping by Rainbow House?"

"Wasn't planning on it. But if you need something from there, I can—"

"No, it's not necessary," she said, shrugging one shoulder. "I wondered if there was news of Merry…and the other girls."

"I'll let you know if I hear of anything."

"Are you picking up suppl—?" Glory began, then noticed his bruised hand. "Oh!" She stepped closer and reached out to lift his hand carefully. "You're injured."

Steven glanced at their joined hands. "Stupid of me. Takes a fool to hammer his own hand."

Glory stood there, with his hand in hers. This was the closest she'd been to him in days. She felt his perusal, his dark eyes roving over her, and tingles of awareness shot straight through her. His breath touched her cheeks as he continued to gaze at her. Glory's senses awakened fully. Her heart pounded furiously in her chest. "It needs tending. Let me wash it and wrap it with a cloth."

She made a move toward the water pitcher on the table, but Steven reached out with his other hand, stopping her. "No need. I'll be fine."

"But the hand is bruised so badly, it's turning color. It must be painful. You won't be able to hang on to the reins without it being wrapped."

Steven sighed. "If you insist."

"I insist," Glory said, glad the stubborn man had given in. She led him over to the dry sink and poured from the pitcher, washing the hand gently. She took up a clean cloth and wound it around his hand with utmost care. "You know, you're not such a good patient."

He grunted. "I've never had anyone..." he began, then cleared his throat. "I've never needed to be any sort of patient."

Glory looked up from beneath her lashes. "It's the least I can do. Heaven knows, you've tended me enough times. I can't even begin to repay you."

Steven pulled his hand from hers and when she glanced up, his eyes flashed with anger. "I don't want your gratitude, Glory."

Glory opened her mouth to speak. No words came out.

"I have to go," he said, quietly. "You keep that gun handy."

"I will." But Steven didn't hear her reply. He'd already departed out the back door.

The wagon lurched, chugging up Six-Mile Canyon. It was an arduous road that led to Virginia City, the elevation a challenge even for a strong team of horses. But the vista more than made up for the tedious ride. Steven always loved the way the town nearly reached up to touch the white puff clouds, the sky seemingly more blue from up here. And the city itself, as he peered out from his vantage point, bustled with life, each long street slightly more elevated than the next, creating a town tiered in steps.

Once he reached the heart of town, he left his

horses and wagon at the livery, taking off on foot. And although there were only four churches of various denominations in Virginia City, there were more than six dozen saloons and gaming houses in the area. Steven hoped he'd get lucky today. He'd investigate the biggest and the best, hoping to catch sight of Ned Shaw. He didn't know the man personally, but he'd seen him around town enough to recognize him. Steven had a gut feeling that Ned Shaw held answers to many questions. This time around Steven wanted to listen to what he had to say.

He found him two hours and ten saloons later, in a small but extravagant Irish pub next to the Young America Fire Company. Steven ordered a drink and stood in the corner of the bar, hat riding low on his forehead as he pretended disinterest. Ned sat at a poker table, with his back to him, puffing on a cigar.

The Rainbow girls hadn't exaggerated. Ned Shaw cut a fine figure, wearing a tailored suit, polished boots and a bowler hat that most likely cost more than a ranch hand's weekly salary.

"You lose again, Shaw," one of his opponents gloated as he raked in cash from the table. "Good thing you've got yourself a rich claim. Good thing for me, that is."

Shaw took a puff on his cigar. "Don't count me out just yet. Deal the cards," he demanded, "the day is long from over."

"Sure thing. I'm willing to take your money."

An old miner seated next to Shaw, holding a pair of queens, commented dryly, "Don't know why you ain't pullin' that ore outta your stake right now, instead a sittin' here all day. Hell, in my day, ain't nothin' woulda stopped me from workin' my claim, no matter that none panned out worth a darn. *Borrascas* they were, every dang one.''

Ned turned to the older man. ''That ain't any of your business, old man.''

The miner spit a wad of tobacco onto floor. ''Maybe not, but even a sourdough knows you can't leave your claim for too long. Someone might just get a jump on you. And nothin' the law can say about it. It being legal and all.''

''I know the law, Judd. Now are you finished giving me the schoolmarm lesson?''

''Ah hell, I'm done, Ned. It'd be a dang shame to see you lose your claim.''

''That ain't gonna happen.''

''Are you folks in or out? Last I checked, we was playing poker,'' the fourth player said with impatience.

''I'm in,'' Ned said.

''Me, too,'' Judd replied, ''I got nothin' but time.''

The game broke up thirty minutes later. Steven hightailed it out of the saloon before Shaw could get a look at him. Steven hadn't gotten what he'd expected out of listening to Shaw. He'd only made one reference to Glory, calling her that bitch his brother married and how he hoped she was dead. Steven's jaw clenched then, but he held back, realizing listening in would be more productive than pulling Shaw up by his collar and slamming a fist in his face.

But he had gotten something worthwhile from this trip. He banked on a hunch and had one more stop to make, to the Claims Office before he could return home to Glory.

Steven pushed through the kitchen door, eager to see Glory cooking up a meal, wearing that dress that matched his curtains and smiling up at him when he entered. To his disappointment, she wasn't there.

"Glory?" he called out.

The house seemed to embrace the silence, where not a clatter, a creaking, not even a tiny sound could be heard.

"Glory!" he shouted again, rushing through the empty parlor, opening her bedroom door, checking the root cellar, then striding out the front door to the barn and then the chicken coop.

There was no sign of her or the dog anywhere on the ranch.

Glory and Buddy were missing.

Steven controlled his panic, though his heart raced with dread. He searched the grounds once again, and only after long minutes of probing, did he find Buddy's pawprints alongside of what could be Glory's footprints. God, he hoped so.

He followed them out past the back of the house until the earth became a low-growing meadow, grazing land for his horses.

There the trail ended.

Steven followed his instincts and headed north toward a cropping of trees far off in the distance, glancing around all the while, hoping to catch sight of her in the fields somewhere.

He wouldn't allow negative thoughts to swallow him up. He wouldn't even consider something bad happening to Glory. He couldn't fathom the loss, so he continued on in hope of finding her.

Minutes later, Steven found her. Anger surged forth. He banked his temper the best he could, wondering what on earth had gotten into the woman. She and Buddy were splashing around in a small creek, the sun beaming down on her bared skin as she scooped water and poured it onto her hair. She wore only a chemise, the gossamer fabric clinging to her wet skin.

Steven leaned back against one of the trees, arms folded, one booted foot crossed over the other. Slightly hidden by the shadows, he watched in wonder, his anger slipping considerably in favor of something far more dangerous. His body tightened with need, the raw sensation he'd been living with lately, barely contained. Like a starving man awaiting his last meal, Steven couldn't tear his gaze away. All of the hunger he'd controlled for so long slowly and methodically destroyed his willpower.

Buddy paddled as fast as his short feet would allow. Glory's laughter echoed against the trees, a sweet throaty sound of delight. She picked Buddy up and washed him, pouring water on the squirmy dog and rubbing his fur clean, before setting him adrift again.

Buddy could hold his own, Steven thought with a wry smile. The pup maneuvered his way to the far bank and shook vigorously, spraying darts of water all around.

Again Glory chuckled, then resumed her own bath, sliding down the thin sleeves of her chemise to use her rose soap on her shoulders. Steven would swear the scent drifted by, teasing his senses.

The water was only waist-high, so Glory bent and scooped again and again, washing her shoulders, her throat, and lower yet, allowing Steven a view so damn alluring, he nearly choked on his own breath.

Then Buddy barked with tail wagging and eyes

peering directly his way. Steven had been caught. Damn the dog.

"What is it, Buddy?" Glory asked, before she looked in the same direction as the dog's gaze.

"Oh!"

She tried to cover her breasts, criss-crossing her arms over her chest.

Steven swiftly removed his boots, his socks, then his shirt. He entered the water heading straight toward Glory.

"Steven?"

He continued, splashing his way through the slow flowing water.

"Steven," she breathed out. "What—"

He came within inches of her and gazed with leisure, noting how the last shred of blazing sunlight made her moist skin glow. "Damn, you gave me a scare. I couldn't find you."

"Buddy ran off."

"And you chased him?"

She nodded, still covering her body with crossed arms.

Steven glanced at a rock on the bank. "You just happened to have a blanket and soap with you?"

"No, don't be silly. I never knew this creek existed, but Buddy found it. And then I went back to the ranch to get the bathing supplies. The water looked so inviting, so I came back here. And...well, I had Buddy with me the whole time."

"Your new protector?"

They both glanced at the pup that had lain down on the dry earth, lazily soaking up sunshine.

"I had the gun, too," she offered.

Steven's brows arched.

"It's under my dress on the rock."

Steven didn't bother looking in that direction; he had everything he wanted right in front of him.

Glory peered up at him with wide eyes. "Are you angry?"

"I was. You weren't supposed to leave the ranch. When I couldn't find you…let's just say I'm not willing to go through that ever again. I figure that after putting me through such torment, you owe me."

Glory's brows knitted together. "What do I owe you?"

Steven grinned. "A bath."

Steven unfastened his gun belt and tossed it onto the bank. When he began stripping out of his pants, Glory whirled around, shocked, by his bold move and by the flutters of desire invading her stomach. "W-what are you doing?"

"Can't have my bath with my pants on," he stated, then continued in a softer tone, "but I'm leaving my underdrawers on."

Glory heard his pants land onto the bank somewhere. She shivered. "You expect me to give you a bath?"

"You owe me, remember?"

When Glory didn't move, Steven reached around to pull her back against him, holding her gently. He spoke in a quiet, velvety tone. "I'm only asking for a bath, sweetheart. I promise."

Glory turned in his arms to face him. "You promise?"

Steven nodded, a slight bobbing of his head. "I told you already, I'll never take anything you're not willing to give," he said evenly, then added with a grim smile, "Even if it kills me."

Glory couldn't hold back her own smile. The thought of touching Steven, soaping his skin, running her fingers through his hair, was far too tempting to resist. "I do owe you, for making you worry."

"Yes, you do," he said, his smile no longer grim.

"And you won't mind smelling like roses?"

"A whole garden of roses wouldn't bother me."

Steven turned around, giving her his back. "Wash me, Glory."

He'd known it would be easier if she didn't have to face him. He'd been right. She stroked the soap over his back, her palm splaying over the broad contours, his undeniable strength. She moved slowly then more deliberately and then when she'd gotten the courage, she asked him to kneel.

He obeyed her command without qualm, allowing her to pour water over his head. She washed his hair, running her fingers through the thick dark strands, noting how the hair at the base of his neck curled up, adorably, like a child's, or a very appealing man's. Deep yearning threatened to unnerve her. Glory fought the feeling, continuing on until it was time for Steven to stand and turn to her.

She asked him shyly, "Do you want me to finish?"

Steven lifted up, like a mythical god rising from the water. He turned to face her. "I'd want you *never* to finish."

Glory took in a sharp breath.

Mercy.

Steven smiled, but his eyes shone with heat, appearing hotter than the Nevada sunshine. He grasped her hand that held the soap and laid it on his chest. "Don't stop, sweetheart."

Tentatively at first, Glory ran the soap over his chest, building up a little lather and working it in. Her fingers traveled over him, the hairs on his chest prickly, the muscles underneath powerful. Glory moved slowly, with care and longing. When her fingertips grazed the area below his navel, Steven sucked in a breath.

She looked down. A mistake. His manhood stood erect against the material of his underdrawers.

Bravely, Glory lifted her head to peer into his eyes. He shrugged, his lips lifting in a crooked half smile. "You're the only woman I've wanted like this, Glory."

Shame didn't come, and neither did fear. Glory's heart pounded wildly and she ventured to ask, "Like what?"

Steven glanced away for a moment, as if deciding how to answer. Then his eyes met hers with honesty. "Sometimes when I look at you, I can't breathe. It's like you're the water of my life. If I don't take a drink, I'll die."

In that moment, it seemed Steven had reached down deep into her soul and touched a chord in her that had never been touched before. It was as though he knew her heart, taking it in his palm and cherishing it with lovely words and tender emotion.

In the past, Glory had compared Steven to her late husband, Boone. She knew that comparison to be unfair now. She'd worried about trusting a man again, worried that Steven was just another charmer, someone who'd take from her everything she had, then abandon her, leaving her alone, an empty unloved shell of a woman. She'd fought hard against that, thinking Steven would hurt her in the same way Boone had.

But as she looked into his gleaming eyes, she witnessed sincerity and compassion. She saw a man who would treat her with tenderness, as he'd promised. She saw a man who would give to her and only take what she chose to offer.

Glory wanted him. She wanted to know that kind of gentle, sweet loving he had pledged. She wanted to place herself in his hands, and for once, reacquaint herself with the faith and trust she'd lost. She wanted Steven, for as long as they could be together. She didn't know her future. She only knew her past, and many parts of that still didn't fit, but she did have the present. She had a man standing before her, baring his body and soul to her.

Perhaps she did owe him this. She certainly owed it to herself. She extended her arm and reached behind his neck, smiling and bringing his head down to hers. "I'm thirsty, too, Steven," she said, brushing her lips against his. She kissed him again, this time more soundly, applying pressure to his mouth eliciting from him a deep groan of pleasure.

"You are?" he asked, planting soft exquisite kisses along the rim of her lips.

"Yes," she said, then whispered in his ear, "I want to lie with you and give you that drink. We'll drink together and maybe die a little as well."

Glory had never been so brazen, but she'd spoken from her heart, the words flowing out with pent up passion.

"Ah, Glory," Steven said, with a plea in his voice. "Sweet, sweet Glory."

Steven swept her up into his arms and carried her to the bank of the creek. He set her down and unfolded the blanket she'd brought, spreading it out between two trees. He led her over to that spot and brought her down with him.

"Here?" she asked, seeming the fool, but needing to know his intentions.

"I'd never make it back to the house now, sweetheart." His groan was enough of an answer. "Don't worry, Glory. The sun's setting and nobody knows this area."

"I'm not worried," she said, gazing up into his handsome face. She stroked his cheek and he turned his head to kiss the inside of her palm. "Not worried at all," she breathed out.

Steven ran his hands up and down her arms. Moisture still clung to her skin in small beads that pooled in provocative places. Blond waves flowed down her back, wet and untamed, the hair dampening the blanket she lay upon. Her chemise pressed against her body in wrinkles and folds that stirred his blood. They faced each other, eyes meeting, hearts hammering and bodies brushing. "No one will ever hurt you again, Glory."

She sighed into his mouth when he took a deep soulful kiss. He caressed her shoulders, stroking her softly with each touch a new exploration. Then with care, he slipped the sleeves of her chemise down altogether, lowering the material to expose her breasts.

"I'm dying a little right now," he rasped out.

Tenderly, he cupped her, running his fingers over one beckoning bud, creating tingles of heat that made her ache with need. He kissed her again and again while his fingers worked magic caressing her breast and flicking the tip with the utmost precision. The ache inside grew stronger.

He dipped his head and moistened her nipple with his tongue. A jolt shot straight through her. She squirmed, her body requiring something...something more.

"Hold on, sweetheart," he said urgently.

Glory heard a bird chirp, Buddy whimper in his sleep and the air around her smelled delicately of roses. Her senses heightened, feeling everything two-fold.

The sun gradually made its descent, most likely putting a chill in the air, but Glory didn't feel cold. Incredible heat swept through her and she was lost, caught up only in the spiraling sensations Steven created.

To her surprise, Steven laid back and she heard his breath whoosh out. "We have to slow down, honey," he said.

Glory didn't understand. She didn't have enough experience, and she didn't want to think about the rough way Boone had always taken her. "Why?"

Steven turned to her, his eyes twinkling, but she noted a hint of pain as well. He took her hand, planting a sweet kiss on her knuckles. "Because I vowed to make this good for you, that's why."

"You are, Steven. You're making it perfect," she said.

He groaned, a deep growl emanating from his throat. "Just give me a minute, okay?"

Glory nodded. "Can I do anything?"

Steven closed his eyes. "Pray for me, honey."

"What?" Glory certainly misunderstood.

"Never mind." He reached up and pulled her

down on top of him. Her slender body spread out over his broad one. Immediately, she felt his manhood, the erection that bore into her through the thin fabric of her chemise.

"Mercy."

"I agree." Steven grunted when she wiggled her body to get more comfortable. "There's no hope for it. I'll be as gentle as I know how to be, but it's got to happen soon."

He rolled her onto her back and kissed her deeply, parting her lips to stroke her tongue. She whimpered, a sound not unlike Buddy's, a sound she'd never made before.

"You're really killing me, Glory," Steven said, kissing her again and again, his hands probing her body, caressing her softly, gliding over her breasts, her torso, leaving no part of her gently and lovingly untouched. And then he cupped her between the legs, his hand covering her female mound. The sensation startled her. She grew moist instantly. "Oh, Steven. Oh, please," she called out.

"Just a little longer, sweetheart. Just a little longer," he repeated, reassuring her.

She didn't know this sensation, this burst of pleasure-pain. And when he slid his finger inside gently, slowly sliding back and forth, tiny explosions erupted, causing her to moan with unguarded delight. "Oh, yes."

Steven brought his mouth down to suckle her breast as he continued to stroke her. Glory's body flamed. Her heart raced madly. She called to Steven again and again, each moment sheer torment and pure joy.

Steven lifted her chemise, and pulled off his drawers. He rose above her, meeting her eyes. "I won't hurt you."

She believed him.

With her heart and her soul, she trusted him not to cause her pain.

"I know."

He entered her and she saw his restraint, the pleasure he held back for her as he filled her.

"Ah, Glory," he said, his voice shaky. "Move with me, sweetheart. Let's drink together."

He thrust into her slowly, carefully, pacing his movements. Glory closed her eyes, relishing the feel of him inside her. There was no pain. There was no shame. Steven fit her perfectly. She gazed into his eyes as she moved with him.

He smiled briefly, but there was so much more in his expression. He concentrated on bringing her pleasure, on bringing her to the pinnacle, on giving her all that he had.

Glory gave back. She lifted up and together they moved as one, his thrusts coming stronger, with more demand. Glory was ready for him, for his power and strength to consume her. She wanted to witness the pleasure she could bring to him.

"Glory, Glory," he called out, taking her higher.

She heard his thrilling plea.

"I'm here, Steven," she managed as he brought her to the edge.

"Stay with me, sweetheart," he rasped out in the moments just before they spiraled out of control.

Glory's heart thumped, her blood pounded, her body exploded as Steven thrust one last time. They met each other at the crest, then slowly both descended downward.

Steven lay on his back once again, taking her with him. He kissed her forehead, her cheek and her lips. "Damn, Glory. That was incredible."

Glory sighed in his arms. She'd never experienced such tenderness and restraint before. She'd never known how beautiful the joining of two bodies could be. Steven had shown her. He made her feel cherished, giving her something she would never forget. "Oh, Steven, I never knew."

Steven snorted, but it almost came out as a chuckle. "You may not believe this, but I never knew, either."

Glory lifted up to stare at him, surprised at his revelation and not sure how to take it. "How can I believe that? You've been with women."

"Not that many, Glory. And not the women from Rainbow House, but women who'd sell their bodies."

Glory squeaked out a silly notion. "Are you comparing me with them?"

"Sweetheart, there's no comparison. There never could be. What we shared...well, it's special. I never knew it could be like that."

Glory knew a hefty dose of satisfaction and pride. That Steven hadn't experienced anything like their lovemaking before meant a great deal. The wonder of their joining surprised her, now even more so.

She laid her head on Steven's shoulder, tucked safely in the arms of her gentle savior.

The man who'd once been her enemy.

Chapter Sixteen

"Steven, you've got cherry cobbler on your chin."

"Kiss it off me, sweetheart," Steven said, coming to sit on Glory's bed. After they'd returned to the house, he made sure Glory got some rest, insisting he wasn't hungry for supper.

He had an appetite, though…for Glory. She was the only one who could ease his hunger tonight.

She lifted up to lick the cobbler off his face and then kiss him. Steven's heart pumped hard and fast. He kissed her back soundly then looked her over. "Did you rest?"

She answered with a slow nod and a sweet smile. "I did."

"That's good. I brought you cherry cobbler. It's supper."

She chuckled. "It's hardly supper, Steven."

"It's all I need. Are you very hungry?"

She shook her head. "No, not really. Cobbler is fine."

Steven took up the plate he'd set on the bedside table. He broke off a piece and fed it to her.

She grinned, eyes twinkling, and swallowed down

the food. "Not a bad cherry cobbler," she commended herself. "Mattie's recipe."

"Remind me to thank Mattie," Steven said, offering her another piece and deliberately allowing a few chunks to fall onto her chest.

He kissed her lips then lowered his mouth to lick the cherry morsels from the material of her dress. "Whoops, wouldn't want to stain this new dress of yours," he said, lowering her down upon the bed. He unfastened a button, then another and another, until Glory's breasts nearly popped out.

"Steven," she whispered, unable to mask the sexy urgency in her voice. "What are you doing?"

Steven smeared a bit of cherry juice just above her nipples and stroked his tongue over, licking it off. "Mmmm, having dessert."

"Ohhh," she sighed, the tips of her breasts extending like twin peaks.

He couldn't contain his smile. His lips lifted up crookedly. "Want some more?"

"Oh, yes," she answered, her blue eyes growing to their darkest hue.

Steven removed his shirt, tossing it without care. He lay down next to her and handed her the plate. She rose above him slightly, feeding him a piece. He chewed and swallowed, then Glory bent down to lick off the remnants from his mouth.

She didn't know how enticing she looked, leaning over him, her dress parted down the middle, almost falling from her shoulders. She destroyed his willpower. He had no self-control left. He kissed her desperately, his lips claiming hers with soul-searing potency. He drove his tongue into her mouth, tasting the sweet cherry, filling his nostrils with the pungent aroma of roses.

And when she spread a line of cobbler across his chest then bent to lick from his chest, a deep guttural groan escaped. His manhood strained against the confines of his pants. He groaned again, uncomfortable with need, the agony of desire threatening to do him in.

"Are you all right?" Glory asked, lifting up to peer into his eyes.

He could only be honest with her. His brain couldn't begin to conjure a lie in his state anyway. "Once I'm inside you, I'll be fine, sweetheart."

Through the dim lantern light Steven witnessed Glory's deep rosy-hued blush. Yet, as she looked into his eyes, her hands went to his pants. Steven sucked in a breath and helped her remove them.

Then to his fascination, Glory undid the remaining buttons on her dress. She discarded it easily, exposing herself fully to him. Stunned by her beauty, Steven simply stared.

Then after a moment, he braced her hips, helping her mount him. "I'll take only what you have to give, Glory."

Glory understood and she began to ride him, slowly, her body undulating, each movement giving to him all that she had to offer. She made a startling picture, one that he'd forge into his memory forever, as her body swayed, her breasts bounced slightly and her hair cascaded down her back. Steven knew, from the look on her face and the bold way she moved that he'd given her something she'd never had before.

He'd given her control.

She stayed with him for long captivating minutes

until Steven could barely contain his own lust, then finally, she shuddered wildly, a fiery fall that enveloped him and he too gained release.

She fell onto the bed next to him, wordless.

He wrapped an arm around her, planting tiny kisses along her throat as he held on to her tight. He'd sleep with her tonight, maybe he'd make love to her once more, but by morning's light, he'd have to see about proving her innocence. She deserved to be free of this prison. She deserved to make her own choices in life. Steven had good instincts. He believed he knew how he could help her now.

He only hoped that he had the courage to let her go.

As she slept in his arms, Steven thought back to the bath she'd given him, then of the silly game they'd played with her fruit concoction. He spoke into her hair, softly, knowing she slept, "You've ruined me for cherry cobbler."

And he knew that once Glory was gone, he'd never be able to take a bite of his favorite dessert again.

Glory bustled about the kitchen, brewing coffee, making biscuits and frying eggs. She'd gotten up just as the dawn welcomed the day, but Steven had already left their bed. She'd been disappointed at first, feeling abandoned, needing the security of his arms and body around her, but then she realized that today was just like any other.

Steven had work to do. He had a ranch to run. He had a life, separate and apart from hers. She had no claim on him despite the wonderful way they'd spent the evening and midnight hours making love. She had no future to call her own, not that she'd hoped for one with Steven.

She'd held on to her bitter hostility for so long that she didn't know her own mind any longer, much less know what was in her heart. She'd made one too many mistakes in the past, and it had almost cost her her life. No, she couldn't possibly hope for any kind of a future with Steven Harding.

She couldn't call him the enemy and he was certainly more than a friend, but Glory had no way to name their relationship. She had no way to define what she and Steven meant to each other.

He'd shown her a tenderness she didn't know existed. He'd made her feel cherished and treasured. He told her with unspoken words and subtle moves that a man could be gentle and still be deemed virile and strong. He'd proven that compassion when mixed with male sensuality could be a beautiful thing.

Glory smiled, remembering the different and inventive ways Steven had made her feel wonderful last night. The glow of her thoughts must have been apparent on her face, because Steven walked into the kitchen and smiled with knowing, intelligent eyes.

"Daydreaming?" he asked.

Glory turned toward the fry-pan and lifted a shoulder. "Maybe."

He came to stand behind her and whispered near her ear, "You were thinking about last night."

She didn't comment.

"You were thinking about me."

The refusal was on her lips, but Steven didn't allow it. He spun her around and kissed her deeply, drinking from her lips. "Can't say as I blame you. I can barely concentrate on my work, thinking about you."

Glory slipped out of his embrace, pretending to keep busy cooking up the eggs. She had such mixed, confused feelings about Steven and her predicament. His nearness only added to her perplexity and when he kissed her, all good sense seemed to vanish. Glory had to find a way to muddle through the distressing thoughts threatening to undermine her composure.

"Eggs are ready," she said, ignoring Steven's stare. Though her back was turned from him, she knew sure as the sun rose up this morning that Steven's dark eyes bore a hole straight through her.

He let out a long lingering sigh and took up a plate, filling it with biscuits and eggs. Glory brought the coffeepot over and filled his mug.

She waited for him to sit down at the table, before taking a seat. When she thought he'd pursue the subject of their lovemaking, he surprised her, throwing her completely off guard.

"I need to know about Ned Shaw's claim."

Glory blinked and took a moment to formulate her answer, unsure what Steven had on his mind. "As I told you once before, it hadn't worked out as he hoped. His claim was as fruitless as Boone's. Ned ran up tremendous gambling debts and came to Boone for help."

"Was he angry that Boone didn't give him money?"

Glory searched her mind, thinking back. "He was at first, but Boone assured him we didn't have any money to lend. It was the truth. He'd barely gotten enough specks out of his claim to keep us fed. And as the weeks went by, Boone mined his claim less and less, feeling utterly hopeless."

"But Boone hadn't finished mining his claim. According to the claims office, each parcel is three hundred feet long including all the land and offshoots east and west of it. That's a lot for one man to mine, especially if his heart isn't in it."

"Boone never said. I just assumed that to be true, because he'd pretty much given up."

"Did you know that Boone's claim was in your name, too?"

Glory nodded. "When we first married, I had some money. Boone used it to buy equipment and he said we'd be equal partners. Later, I realized it was just another way for Boone to charm me."

Steven grunted, his eyes flashing anger. "Right out of your money."

"I made a mistake with Boone," Glory said unable to keep the indignation out of her tone. "I shouldn't have married him. I shouldn't have let him charm me. I know that now." She squared him a look and spoke as plainly as she knew how. "I don't plan on making any more mistakes."

Steven's chair squeaked against the floor when he stood abruptly. "Last night wasn't a mistake, Glory."

Glory stood then too and spoke from her heart. "Maybe not for you," she said quietly.

A tick worked at Steven's jaw. His gaze pierced her with heat. "Not for you either, dammit. It wasn't a sin. You have nothing to be sorry for, Glory."

"I'm not sorry, Steven." Goodness, she'd never be sorry for the thrilling yet tender way Steven had taken her last night. She'd never be sorry to have experienced such sweet loving.

"Then what's eating at you?"

"I gave myself to you willingly last night and I

take full responsibility, but because of that...I might be with child.''

His expression softened as if he pictured a little babe in his mind. ''That wouldn't be a mistake, Glory. It'd be a gift.''

''No, a child out of wedlock wouldn't be a gift at all.''

''Out of *wedlock?*'' He appeared surprised, his eyes widening as though she'd said something unfathomable. ''Hell, we'd get married.''

Glory shook her head, though pleasing thoughts of living here with Steven filtered into her mind with grudging clarity. She could almost envision it, but there were too many forces working against them. ''That *would* be a mistake.''

Steven's jaw tightened and a flash of color lit his dark eyes. ''Because of who I am?'' he asked, his voice edgy, impatient. ''You wouldn't want to give your child my name?''

Glory thought on that for only a second. ''No, Steven, I might have believed that once, but that's not the real reason. It's because of who *I* am.''

''Hell, Glory. What's that mean?''

Glory tried to put into words how she'd been feeling. She finally came to understand what had been missing in her life. ''I've made one mistake after another. Even before my father died, I think I went along with everything that everyone else wanted, without giving much thought to what was really important to me.''

''You made a valiant effort to shut down the brothels.''

Glory waved that off. ''I tried and at the time, I thought my efforts might have some impact. I was a fool to think it. I have a better understanding now of how things are. I'll never condone the whorehouses, Steven. I couldn't possibly, but I better understand the need for them to exist.''

''And the girls?''

''Yes, I see them a little differently now.''

''And my mother?''

Glory closed her eyes. She hadn't the faith Jonathan Caldwell had. She hadn't the forgiveness. It was as if the circumstances of her father's death held her hostage. She was a prisoner to images of her father's bloody body lying on the cold ground in the center of town. And her captor—those thoughts wouldn't let her go.

She gazed into Steven's eyes, hoping to make him understand. ''I have little forgiveness in my heart, Steven.''

He studied her for a moment.

''I'm sorry.''

He pursed his lips, drew in a breath and finally asked, ''So what do you want, Glory?''

She noted his need to truly understand, although his expression wasn't too accommodating.

''I almost ruined my life once. I need time. I need to think things through better. I can't make any more bad decisions.''

She couldn't jump into a marriage with another man, not unless she was absolutely certain it was the right thing to do. Her life had almost been destroyed once already. And Steven, well, he was Lorene Harding's son, after all. She didn't know how, if or when she'd ever get past that.

Glory looked into Steven's somber face, his eyes dark and foreboding. She knew she had unintentionally hurt him. She'd never wanted that. He'd been wonderful to her, taking her in, nursing her back to health and sheltering her the best way he knew how. Searching deep into her heart, she knew Steven had become an important part of her life. She had strong, urgent feelings for him. The sight of him entering the kitchen just moments ago had made her flutter in the most pleasing way.

Had she fallen in love with him?

How could she be sure? She had thought she loved Boone once. She wondered if what she felt for Steven had more to do with the gratitude she felt toward him than any true and permanent stirrings of the heart.

She offered him an explanation, perhaps a consolation, something they both could understand. "I'm a fugitive, most likely going to prison or worse one day, so there's no point discussing any of this."

Steven jammed his hat on his head. He stared at her for a long time, his stance rigid. "You're not going to prison. I'm going to see to that today. You just sit tight, keep the gun close and I'll try to get back before midnight."

Alarm registered quickly. Steven's leaving sparked fear in her heart. "Where are you going?"

With a sharp, determined, almost cold glint in his eyes, he responded, "I'm planning to prove your innocence. I've got a good idea what happened to Boone. You'll have your freedom soon enough."

He strode fiercely toward the kitchen door, then stopped, lowered his head and turned. He came right up to her, kissed her long and deep on the lips and gazed into her eyes. "You'll be free to leave here and start your life over."

Dumbfounded, Glory watched him leave, his spurs jingling as loudly as her befuddled mind.

Steven sat hidden behind a small cluster of rocks, watching and waiting, noting half a dozen miners working their claims along the rushing streambed that welcomed runoff from Mount Davidson. This unpredictable waterway had been the source of many placer miners' wealth, whether by method of panning or use of the wooden rocking sluice to locate the buried ore and, in Boone's case, the cause of his early demise.

As the sunlight began to fade many of the prospectors took up their equipment, ready to call it a day. Interestingly enough, as the hours passed, Steven noted there'd been no sign of Ned Shaw. He'd checked earlier at Ned's claim, located half a mile north, and now he surveyed the strip of land that Boone Shaw owned.

This might have been another of the days Ned Shaw spent gambling, which Steven surmised would make his waiting here a complete waste of time. But Steven's gut told him to hold on, or had it been his heart doing the talking?

He'd bared his soul to Glory this morning, only to have her meet him with a stunned expression. He'd offered her marriage should she be with child and she'd neatly refused, declaring it would only compound another mistake.

None of it would have been a mistake in his estimation. But Glory clearly didn't see it that way. He knew that he had to clear Glory's name, for both of their sakes. She needed her freedom. She needed to resume her life or rather, make a new life for herself, one that surely didn't include him.

He had his ranch. He had the prospect of a good future. Up until the night he'd spotted her lying nearly dead, engulfed in flames, he'd never wanted anything more. Glory had given him a taste of what life might be like, sharing a home and chores, working together then falling into bed, holding onto each other through the night. He'd shown her tenderness, she'd shown him passion. But it hadn't been real. They'd simply been biding time, until Glory had to leave.

A roving reflection off the water brought his head up. He peered out, over the rocks and heard a sound off in the distance. Straining his eyes to catch a glimpse, he witnessed lantern light and what appeared to be a man, working the claim—Boone Shaw's claim. He couldn't make out the man's features, but Steven knew without a doubt the man was Ned Shaw.

All the pieces of the puzzle fit now.

Boone hadn't been working his claim effectively, too despondent and impatient to see it through, but his brother must have secretly found the gold they'd both coveted. Boone's stake held riches that far outweighed anything he might have imagined, but he'd been lazy and too discouraged to find what had been nearly right under his nose. Ned must have seen this as his one and only chance for wealth, but he had to deal with the problem of getting rid of Boone and Glory in order to gain the riches.

He'd set Glory up as the murderess, planting a knife in her hands and hoping that the fire would muddle up whatever evidence he'd left behind.

He hadn't counted on Glory surviving the fire, but he'd seen to it that she'd been considered a suspect, blaming her for Boone's death, removing himself from suspicion altogether. According to the girls at

Rainbow House, Ned had surely painted himself the grieving brother.

While at the claims office, Steven had learned that once a miner abandoned his claim, the stake would be up for grabs within weeks. It was all legal and binding. But Ned couldn't afford to wait. He had heavy gambling debts that needed paying straight-away. He'd been desperate and once he'd found Boone's claim to be a rich one, he'd had to work secretly through the night to extract the ore. He'd been counting on the fact that Boone made it known his claim was a *borrasca,* a failure. Wouldn't be likely any miners would jump his claim in the near future, giving Ned a chance to mine out all the ore.

Steven dipped his head and sat back, contemplating.

He'd caught Ned in the act, but unless he got the sheriff out here to witness Ned's deceit, it would be one man's word against another's. He hated to leave the scene, but he had no other choice.

Steven rose slowly, drew his gun and bent down, making his way through the dry brush. He headed toward where he'd reined in Black Cloud. The horse snorted, a loud gush of air that echoed in the quiet canyon. "Shhh, boy," Steven whispered, coming upon his nervous steed.

The stallion pranced, clearly agitated, stomping his hooves into the ground and Steven recoiled, thinking he should have brought Fancy instead, loyalty winning out against speed.

But that was the last notion he'd had, before a thump on his head obliterated all thoughts.

Chapter Seventeen

Steven's head ached like the devil. The cutting pain pounded his scalp like a hatchet. He opened his eyes slowly, wincing at the thin ray of light that beckoned his attention. With narrowed eyes, he glanced around. He was tied up with his hands bound behind his back and his ankles tied together. He found himself leaning askew against the wall of an abandoned mine as if he'd been tossed down that way. The cold dank interior didn't rattle him, nor did the fact that his hands and feet were bound. But the rats, wandering around like chickens with their heads chopped off, now that was a different matter. Skittish rats and creaks and moans from within a mine meant trouble. Cave-in trouble.

"Won't be long now."

He heard the voice from around a bend in the hollowed-out mineshaft. Then Ned Shaw came out of the shadows holding a lantern.

Steven glared at him. "What won't be long?" Although Steven sort of figured out already what Shaw had in mind.

"I've triggered the mine." Shaw grinned, his eyes

dark with anticipation. "Little fuses that won't make much noise, but enough to collapse these walls. No one will ever find you."

Shaw crouched down to Steven's level and narrowed him a look. "You've had her all along, haven't you?"

Steven turned his head, unwilling to give Shaw any information.

"Won't do any good to deny it. You must've found her that night. It's the only thing that makes sense. You'd have no call to come nosing around here otherwise. She would have died in the fire, and everyone would have blamed her for Boone's death. I made it look good, beating her like that, making it appear that she'd been defending herself."

Steven whipped his head around. "You! You did that to her?"

Shaw grimaced, shaking his head. "Didn't want to. Sorta wanted her for myself, but she put up a fight. The lady refused to cooperate. What choice did I have?"

Steven spit out his words. "You damn bastard. You killed your brother and beat a defenseless woman." He struggled with the ties behind his back, willing his hands to come free so that he could crush Ned Shaw into pulp.

Shaw let his accusation go unanswered. When he lifted up to full height, he scratched his head. "What I couldn't figure is why she never came forth? She could've pointed her finger at me and been done with it."

Steven pursed his lips, refusing to shed any light on the situation. If only Glory's memory had returned before this, she'd have recalled everything and Shaw would have been arrested. He'd taken a chance sticking around, but he was a gambler, after all and greed had a way of making a man do foolish things.

"Never mind. I'll find her. As soon as I light this here spitter."

Steven noted the short fuse Shaw held in his hand and figured Shaw had the front of the tunnel rigged with black powder. He played with the rope binding his hands. He had to find a way out of here before Shaw could get to Glory.

An instant of panic set in. He froze in fear that he wouldn't be able to help her. She'd be at Shaw's mercy. And the last time that happened, he'd almost killed her.

"Gloria Mae," Shaw began with a sickening smirk, "must've gotten your gut all twisted up for you to risk your neck like this. And now you're about to die. But don't worry, I'll do my best to console her."

Steven watched him walk toward the bend in the mine until he was out of sight. He struggled with the ties now, sending up a prayer to heaven to help him get free. He had to get to the ranch before Shaw did. He had to save Glory.

But first, he had to survive the blast.

Cold dread seeped in. Glory wrapped the red shawl Ruby had given her even tighter around her nightgown, hoping that Steven would return home soon. Buddy lay curled up next to her on the sofa as orangegold flames blazed from the fireplace, but neither helped quell the chill in her heart.

She'd pushed Steven away this morning with harsh words. Unintentionally, she'd hurt him. Confused by myriad emotions whirling around, she'd spoken as truthfully to him as she knew how. In her mind, he was still a Harding, but in her heart, he was the man who'd taught her so many things about patience and tenderness.

Glory feared that she loved him.

She feared what her heart seemed to know, but her mind wouldn't allow. After her marriage to Boone, she often wondered if she was capable of true love. Would she recognize it at all once she'd met the right man? She'd been wounded and perhaps the scars ran too deep to overcome. Maybe all she felt for Steven was undying gratitude for saving her life, protecting and sheltering her.

She wished he'd come home.

She missed him.

And prayed for his safety.

She didn't know what he had in mind for tonight. He'd been too angry to share his thoughts with her. He'd raced off the ranch riding Black Cloud, like a man determined to get far away as fast as he could.

A grim shudder coursed down her body. She stroked Buddy's head, more to comfort herself than the pup. She needed the connection, to feel something warm and alive to assure her that everything would turn out all right.

It was after midnight. Steven had promised to be home by now. She'd waited up, unable to sleep.

And then she heard him. Black Cloud's hooves beat a hasty rhythm as they approached the house. Joy and great relief flooded her senses. She couldn't abide anything happening to Steven on her account. She couldn't imagine him being hurt or injured.

She offered up a quick prayer for Steven's safe

return. "Thank you, Lord," she whispered aloud, her voice carrying in the quiet room, causing Buddy to lift his head. He peered at her, his big brown eyes in askance.

"Steven's home," she said, joyfully. She believed the dog understood.

Glory rose quickly from the sofa, eager to see Steven. She'd throw her arms around his neck, pull his head down and press a kiss to his lips, letting the consequences be what they may.

Glory thrust the front door open, her smile wide and unguarded.

She came face-to-face with Ned Shaw.

In that instant she recalled everything that happened to her the night of Boone's death. She shoved the door hard, trying to shut out Shaw, but he was too fast. He jammed his palm against the door to stop it from closing, thrusting his body through the opening. "Now Gloria Mae…is that any way to greet your brother-in-law?"

Glory's mind flashed images, sharp, fleeting, unbearable memories of that fateful night. The pieces all came together and everything that had once clouded her mind became vividly clear. Ned Shaw had been the one. He'd come to the house and deliberately picked a fight with Boone.

Glory had no time to enjoy the welcoming relief that she hadn't been the one to stab Boone to death. She had no time to enjoy her newfound innocence.

Her mind conjured up the details of that night. She recalled her screams, her shock and fear when she'd seen Ned holding a knife on Boone.

"Get back in the house," Ned had said, tossing her a glance, his voice rough and somber.

Glory had stood in the doorway frozen with fright.

Boone had taken that instant to lunge at Ned, probably never quite believing his brother would really use the knife. A fight ensued and Glory had found herself mixed up in it. She'd tried to help Boone, but Ned had taken a quick swipe at her, throwing her down to the ground and knocking her out.

When she'd woken up, couldn't have been more than a few seconds later, she was surrounded in blood. Boone's blood. She had screamed at the sight of his lifeless body next to hers. She had screamed at the injustice. She couldn't stop. The sound of her screams was so shocking, even to her ears, that she no longer heard them.

Ned had hoisted her up. He had put a hand over her mouth and dragged her inside the house. She recalled now how badly her face had hurt from the blow she'd taken. "Shut up," he'd said, "and I might let you live."

That's when Ned had made his proposition to her. He told her all about the riches his brother had been too lazy to mine, all of the riches that they could share. He told her, in no uncertain terms, he wanted her, and all the while Glory had resisted, shaking her head, backing away, unable to believe any of this nightmare was really happening.

She had made a dash out the front door, screaming for help. It was late at night and they had no neighbors close by. Ned had caught up to her, furious at her escape attempt. He began calling her horrible names. She'd never seen a man with such fury in his eyes. And now she remembered how he'd slapped her, again and again, until her legs would no longer hold her, until her body could no longer withstand the pain.

It was all she remembered until she'd woken up in a strange bed, with a strange man tending her wounds.

Her mind snapped back to the present. She shoved the front door harder, but it was far too late. Ned had succeeded in wedging his way in. The next thing she knew, he stood in front of her with the door shut behind him. Trapped, her heart raced, but this time Glory knew better than to try to overpower or outrun him. She had to outsmart him and it would take every ounce of courage she possessed tempered with restraint and wisdom to stay alive.

"What do you want?" she asked, tamping down her revulsion. Ned Shaw had become the devil in her mind. She couldn't look him in the eyes without seeing thick bright blood.

Ned took a long leisurely look at her, taking in the hair that had come loose from her braid, the thin white nightgown she wore, covered by Ruby's audacious red shawl. His penetrating gaze unnerved her, but she stood her ground, unwilling to show any fear.

"You've changed," he said, and she didn't miss the note of suspicion in his tone. "Still a beauty, but something's different about you."

Glory turned her back on him and walked toward the fireplace. She couldn't believe she acted so casually with a coldblooded killer, but this was her only chance for escape. She knew firsthand the pain Ned could inflict if angered. She hated him with every breath she took, but she didn't dare show that hatred.

"Yes, I've changed," she said. "Losing a father and a husband will do that to a woman."

Ned approached her, coming within inches of her

face. She bolstered her courage while trying to ignore her terror at having him so near.

"You didn't love Boone."

His accusation numbed her. No, she knew that she hadn't loved Boone. She'd always known that in her heart, but never so clearly as right now. "He was my husband."

"He was lazy and stupid," Ned snarled. "He didn't deserve you."

He didn't deserve to die at the hands of his brother, Glory thought grimly, but she kept her expression mild.

Ned narrowed his eyes. "Tell me, when you opened the door just then, there was more than shock on your face. There was recognition. I saw it in your eyes."

Glory glanced out the window briefly. She couldn't help wondering where Steven was but she didn't dare alert Shaw that he might be showing up soon.

"I had amnesia. I couldn't remember anything."

"Until you saw me, right?"

She closed her eyes, warding off the images that caused her anguish. "Yes. When I saw you standing there, it triggered my memory. I remember everything now."

She glared at him now, unable to hide her disdain and disgust. "You murdered Boone and wanted everyone to believe I'd killed him."

"It was a good plan," he said smugly.

"And then what?"

"And then I file on your claim. I get legal rights to the strike I found."

A shiver ran down her spine and the chill stayed with her. Glory backed away from him slowly, making her steps seem normal when every instinct she possessed told her to run. Shaw had reason to want her dead. She glanced out the window once more, hoping for a sign of Steven.

"He's not coming."

"W-what?" She whirled around to face him completely. Deadly intent was written on Shaw's face. He glared at her and she witnessed the truth in his eyes.

"Harding. He'd dead by now."

"No!" Glory's hand flew to her chest. She felt as if all of her blood drained from her body. "He's not dead."

She refused to believe it.

"He's not coming to save you, Gloria Mae."

Glory lowered herself down onto the sofa slowly, as if she were floating in some strange dream. She'd never known such pain. Even Ned's beating hadn't left her with this much hurt. Tears spilled down her cheeks. She put her face in her hands and cried silently. Buddy curled up against her, his little body acting as a shield, a cushion to the dreadful pain she experienced.

"Very touching," Ned said with no remorse, giving her little time to grieve. "But now that he's out of the way, I have to decide what to do with you. You see, you're the one person who knows the truth about me. I should probably kill you."

He scratched his head lightly as if pondering something as mundane as what he should eat first, the peas or carrots on his plate. Glory glanced at the weapon holstered on his right hip. He had yet to draw his gun. She posed no threat to him in his mind, and up until this point Glory wouldn't have thought so, either.

But as she shoved aside the agonizing truth about

Steven's death, she began formulating a plan. For Steven, because of the many times he'd protected her. For the shelter he'd given her and the kindness and tenderness she'd only known with him, Glory decided to fight for her life. She decided to avenge Steven's death or die trying.

It was worth a try, she mused, because Ned Shaw wasn't a compassionate man. He wouldn't grant her mercy. He wouldn't allow her to live, unless he had something to gain from it.

She recalled the night Boone died, summoning up images of Ned's hands on her, trying at first to seduce her, trying to bend her to his will. Glory had fought him off, repulsed by his actions, disgusted by his intentions. She'd angered him with her blatant rejection. His vile temper emerged and she'd almost died at his hands.

Tonight, she'd have to become a different woman. With the lessons she'd learned from the Rainbow girls, Glory would play the most serious game of her life, hoping to come out the winner.

Glory banked her tears. With resolution, she stood and purposely allowed the crimson shawl to fall from her shoulders. She pressed the material around her body, allowing the shawl to slowly drape down, caressing her curves.

Ned's eyes flashed immediately. She'd sparked his interest. But he wasn't a fool and Glory had to play this perfectly, or she'd become another of his victims. "You don't want to kill me."

His mouth twisted and Glory knew a moment of trepidation. "Why not?"

"Because I remember what you really wanted the night you...the night Boone died."

"Yeah? And what did I want?" he asked, narrowing his eyes.

Glory took a step toward him. Heart pounding hard, she ran her hand down her throat and then farther until her fingertips caressed the swell of her breast. She smiled, hoping to appear seductive. Judging by Ned's intense gaze, she might have succeeded. In a breathy whisper, she answered, "Me."

Suddenly and without warning, Ned grabbed her arms, pulling her to him. She tamped down her fear, denying him a struggle and hoping to convince him that this is what she wanted. "You didn't want that then, why should I believe you now?"

Lust made his eyes gleam. He stared at her with wary impatience. His hot breath on her face repulsed her.

"I—I—" she began, praying for inspiration. Then, as if she'd been struck by divine guidance, a thought emerged instantly and she knew exactly how to reach him. A greedy man might understand another's greed. "I've got nothing. And no one. My father is gone. Boone is dead. The man who'd sheltered me is also g-gone." How she hated saying those words. "I've no money, no home. I lived with your brother in poverty. It's time I took something for myself. We would be rich. We'd have everything."

Glory gazed into Ned's eyes and nodded. "We could have it all," she whispered. "You and me."

She smiled once again.

He released her arms and stepped back, assessing her. Desire warred with disbelief. Glory saw his indecision, and worried that he didn't believe her.

She let the shawl drop entirely from her body and began unbuttoning her nightgown. Two buttons at the very top came undone. It was all she'd allow for now. She ran her tongue along the edges of her mouth with slow and calculated deliberation.

Ned arched his brows.

Glory played the part of a temptress the best way she knew how. She'd had a lesson a while back from Julia that she'd never forgotten.

"You willing to prove it to me?" he asked, his voice taking on a raspy whisper.

Glory swallowed, drawing air into her lungs in increments. With more boldness than she believed she possessed, she turned her back on him and walked slowly toward the bedroom. "Why don't you come in here and find out?"

She heard the scrape of Ned's footsteps on the floor behind her. He followed her into the bedroom. Glory stopped when she reached the right side of the bed by the night table. She turned to him and smiled.

Ned stood on the other side of the bed, a far enough distance away for Glory's sensibilities. She couldn't bear for him to touch her again.

Dark, hungry eyes roved over her body. Glory suppressed a shudder. "If this is a trick, I'll kill you with my bare hands," he warned with a low voice seemingly laced with more desire than suspicion.

Glory undid the rest of the buttons on her nightgown. Slowly, she shifted the material off her shoulders. "This is no trick."

She let the nightgown fall from her body, exposing the thin cotton chemise she wore underneath. Ned's sharp intake of breath told her she held his full attention…and she had him off-guard. She wished he would remove his gun belt, but to ask would only arouse his suspicion.

"You gonna stand there all day, or get into this bed?" He rubbed at his groin, his manhood apparent, pressing against his trousers.

Perspiration rose up on her body, although not from heat but stark cold fear. Glory managed a coy smile. "We're going to have a long night in this bed," she said, then glanced at the Bible on the nightstand. "Oh dear." She showed Ned the Bible Carmen had given her. "This part of my life is over now. Just let me tuck this away."

She reached down to hide the Bible under the mattress and in one swift move, came up with her gun. She pointed the army revolver straight at Ned's heart.

Chapter Eighteen

Grim determination kept Steven alive. He managed to unbind his hands in the seconds before the mine collapse, allowing him a means to get farther away from the blast. It wasn't ingenuity on his part that freed his hands, but more Shaw's smug certainty that Steven wouldn't survive. His wrists hadn't been bound tight enough to begin with and he'd worked feverishly at them whenever Shaw wasn't looking.

Steven barely escaped the explosion that brought down the walls of the mine. He'd made a dash toward the interior of the mine once he'd freed his legs of their bindings. The explosion had thrown him at least the length of his body, but he rose from the ground, unscathed for the most part.

Now, as he stood in the tunnel, darkness engulfed him. He coughed violently, his lungs filling with the soot enveloping the air. Layers of dust floated down, covering his clothes like winter's first snow. Steven caught his breath momentarily and then another wave of heavy coughing erupted.

Shaw may have been right. Maybe he'd never survive this. He didn't see how he could find his way out of the rubble, but sheer doggedness on his part wouldn't let him give up hope.

Once the dust settled and his coughing ebbed, he worked his way with arms stretched out, walking as a blind man would, toward the front of the mine. A glimmer appeared, the tiniest ray of moonlight acted as a beacon as his eyes made their quick adjustments.

The plug of rock that shored up the face of the mine wasn't complete. Steven sent up a prayer of thanks. "Hallelujah." And he thought of Glory and the faith she was certain she had lost. If she could see this, the slightest crevice opening to the right side, perhaps only a mouse could manage, her faith would be renewed instantly. Steven saw the light reaching in from the other side. He'd have to work swiftly, but with utmost care so as not to disturb the pattern of tiered rock that fit together like a large intricate puzzle, to create space enough for him to slither through.

He worked carefully as he calculated which rock to pull and when. It seemed a dauntingly slow task, when his mind and heart raced to get home to Glory. Not soon enough, the gap had been dug and Steven hoisted himself up, snaking his way through to the other side.

Fresh crisp air nearly choked Steven's lungs. But after a time, his breathing regulated again and he headed out on foot toward town. As much as he'd like to reach the ranch, he would never make it on foot. Again, he cursed his bad decision to favor Black Cloud tonight. Fancy would've been the wiser choice. She wouldn't have spooked so easily, alerting Shaw to his whereabouts. And she might very well have been waiting outside the mine for him, once he managed his escape.

Steven walked fast, the climb up the hill to the city arduous, but he didn't allow the steep incline to slow his steps. When a wagon pulled up, he hopped on, grateful to the drunken miner making his way back to town. Didn't take but a moment to convince the miner to turn over the reins. Steven commandeered the wagon and drove the team hard and fast. They made it to C Street quickly and Steven jumped down, a swift thank you on his lips.

Once Steven entered Rainbow House, he barked rapid orders in succession, bringing the women out from their rooms to greet him in the main parlor.

"Marcus, saddle up a horse for me and bring me a rifle. Mother and Ruby, alert the sheriff that Boone Shaw's killer is at my ranch. He's after Glory and I'm heading out to stop him. Emmie and Carmen, bring any medical supplies you have to the ranch tonight."

"Steven," Lorene's eyes went wide. "You look worse than death. What's happened? And who needs doctoring?"

"Ned Shaw tried to kill me and now he's after Glory. And if I have my say, Shaw's going to need doctoring if he lays one hand on her. There's no time to explain."

Marcus returned shortly, his ruddy face flushed, his forehead sweating. He handed him the Winchester. "Take my horse. She's saddled up and ready, she is."

"You go with him, Marcus," Lorene demanded.

"Aye, ma'am. That I will. But it'll take me a while to get a horse from the livery at this hour."

Steven nodded. "I can't wait. I've got to go."

"Be careful, son," Lorene said to him.

Steven couldn't stop long enough to assure his

mother that he'd be all right. He had enough trouble assuring himself that he'd make it to the ranch in time to save Glory. The hell of it was, too much time had passed already. Shaw might already have reached the ranch…and Glory.

Emmie and Carmen had gathered the supplies. "We'll take the buggy and be there as soon as we can."

Steven left them all to their tasks and rode off into the night, praying he wasn't too late. He'd already had his share of lucky breaks today. Could he possibly hold out for one more?

Steven rode his horse hard, his nerves raw. Each time he reached a landmark, the sugar pines just outside of town, a meadow of poppies yet to bloom or every bend in the road he'd banked in his memory, he became more alert, more anxious. Minutes seemed to stretch into hours and finally, he reached his property.

Steven thought to sneak up on his ranch house, but decided he didn't have the luxury of time. Instead, he pushed forward and reined in his horse once he'd reached the front of his house.

He dismounted and lifted the rifle, certain that Shaw had already found Glory. Black Cloud was tethered outside and had been ridden hard.

Hidden by darkness, Steven peered into the parlor window, seeing only shadows dancing across the walls. Someone was in the bedroom. His mind shut down, refusing distressing thoughts to filter in. He entered the house carefully by the front door, noting that Buddy, the watchdog, slept on the sofa. His luck was holding. If the dog started yapping, he'd lose the element of surprise. Moving through the shadows he managed to make his way farther inside the room.

And then he saw Glory.

With her back to him, there was no mistaking that she was half-naked, wearing nothing more than a slip of material.

And he heard Shaw's menacing voice telling Glory to get on the bed.

Steven didn't hesitate. He couldn't imagine Shaw touching Glory, not even for a second. He burst through the opened doorway, rifle drawn and ready to fire. "You move and you're a dead man."

Steven didn't know who had been the most shocked. Shaw's jaw dropped just as his hands lifted up in surrender. Glory's face beamed with both surprise and amazement. And Steven, well, he couldn't believe Glory held Shaw at gunpoint. The woman pointed the army revolver at her assailant with vigilance and only when he'd come bursting into the room had her hand wavered from the target slightly.

Steven kept his rifle trained on Shaw, but walked over to stand beside Glory, making a quick assessment of her well-being out of the corner of his eye. "You okay, Glory?"

"Oh, Steven," she breathed, "he told me you were dead."

"He tried his damnedest. I'm not that easy to kill, I suppose."

"Thank the Lord for that," Glory said, casting him a shaky smile.

"There's enough gold and silver in that claim for all of us," Shaw declared.

Steven focused his full attention on Shaw. "Not enough in the entire Comstock Lode as far as I'm concerned. You're going to jail. The sheriff is on his way. Get a rope, Glory. I'll tie him up while he writes out a confession.''

''I'm not confessing to nothing.''

''I'm an eyewitness to Boone's death,'' Glory said. ''And I remember now how you tried to kill me.''

Steven knew then that Glory's memory had returned. The horror he'd tried to shelter her from had come back. He'd seen it by the stark look on her face, the trembling of her body.

''Get that rope, Glory. Confession or not, he's going away for a long time.''

Within minutes, Shaw had been tied up, Glory had gotten dressed and the sheriff had arrived with Marcus.

''He's all yours, Roy,'' Steven said, leading the sheriff into the bedroom. ''He killed Boone Shaw, and after beating Glory, left her to die in that fire, framing her for the murder. He tried his hand at killing me tonight, too.''

Sheriff Brimley nodded, taking his prisoner out. Marcus heaved Shaw up onto a horse, belly down. But Brimley left his prisoner with Marcus to return to the house.

''I'd like a word with you, privately.''

Steven glanced at Glory. She nodded, letting him know she was all right. He hated leaving her for a second, but knew that soon, he'd have to give her up for a lifetime.

''Out by the barn,'' Steven said and the two strode in that direction.

''I know what this is about, Roy,'' Steven said as he stopped up short of the barn door.

Roy Brimley took his hat off to scratch his head. "You had her all along, didn't you?"

"Yep."

"Even though you knew she was wanted for questioning. Now, that's a real obstruction of justice, Steven. Don't know as to how I can overlook it."

"Arrest me if you will, but I'd do it all the same if I had to."

Roy's graying brows lifted. "That so?"

Steven nodded. "She was beaten so badly at first, then she couldn't recall anything. Ned had it rigged to make it look like she killed her husband. What kind of chance would she have had if I turned her in? She appeared guilty…even to me. But Roy, if you'd seen the brutality she suffered, you'd have done the same thing. Turns out, Ned was the one who'd beaten her. She's as innocent as a young foal."

Roy's mouth twisted. "I have a duty to see justice done."

"This is justice. The killer's been caught and an innocent woman has been set free."

"You duped me."

"Not intentionally. I was protecting Glory, is all."

The sheriff narrowed his eyes. "Hmmm. You going to marry her?"

Steven's heart lurched. If only things had been different between them. But Glory had a new life to live. Making a fresh start was what she seemed to want. He'd gotten the clear message that she thought marrying him would be a mistake. "I believe the lady has other plans."

Sheriff Brimley jammed his hat back on his head. "You did a good thing for her, even though you should have trusted in the law. And I suppose losing a woman like Gloria Mae is punishment enough." There was nothing but regret in his tone. "I'm letting you go, but I'm not happy about it. Not one bit."

Steven gave the sheriff a slow nod, his admiration for the lawman growing. "I appreciate it."

Steven's luck was holding. Glory was safe, they were both alive and he wouldn't be arrested for hiding her. He bid farewell to the sheriff, thanked Marcus for his help and watched the wagon make its way down the road, carting Ned Shaw off to jail.

Steven entered the house, took one look at a clearly shaken Glory and immediately took her into his arms. He held her tight, breathing in her scent, nuzzling his face in her silky hair. "It's over now, sweetheart."

"I can't believe I'm really free."

"Believe it," Steven said, keeping regret from his tone. Glory had stayed with him only a short time because she'd been hiding out from both Shaw and the law. The danger had passed. He had no claim on her any longer. That realization ate at him fiercely.

"Thank you, Steven. For all you've done for me." She stepped back for a moment to look him over. Her light-blue gaze traveled over the length of him and once satisfied that aside from a few cuts and bruises, Steven had escaped the ordeal unscathed, Glory whispered softly, "You almost died tonight, because of me. I'll never be able to repay you."

"There's no—"

The door burst open just then and Carmen and Emmie appeared. They rushed into the house to greet them.

"You're all right," Emmie said, her voice jubilant. "We ran into the sheriff on the road. He told us how

Glory caught Shaw, pointed a gun right at the scoundrel's heart.''

Glory embraced her friends. "Oh, it's good to see you!''

"We did not know what to think,'' Carmen began, after they'd all hugged sufficiently, "when Steven showed up at Rainbow House. We feared the worst. Thank God, He heard my prayers. You are both safe.''

"Yes, yes. We are both safe,'' Glory agreed, tears of joy spilling down her face. "Steven saved my life.''

Steven smiled, though his gut was in turmoil. He knew his time with Glory was limited. "Glory had everything under control. She held on, capturing Shaw all on her own.''

"I did, didn't I?'' She asked, as though just making that realization. "He told me he'd killed Steven.''

A look of pain marred her face. She cast him the smallest of smiles. "I'm so glad you're alive, Steven. My life wouldn't be worth much if I'd caused your death.'' She peered at the girls again. "That's when I came up with the plan. I, um, had to get Ned into the bedroom.''

"You mean you coaxed him into the bedroom?'' Emmie asked, her eyes taking on a bright light.

"Perhaps she has learned something from the Rainbow girls after all, no?''

Carmen's comment put a scowl on Steven's face. The reason for Glory's state of undress had become clear. She'd been the one to initiate the false seduction.

Glory glanced at him with trepidation. "Um, yes.

I—that's where the gun was hidden. Under the mattress.''

"You shouldn't have taken such a chance," Steven admonished, his hands balling up into two fists. Glory had gone to extreme means to catch Shaw, but if he had gotten even the slightest jump on her, her fate would have been much different.

"I didn't have much choice. But I would have died first, before letting that man touch me."

Steven winced at both the thought of Glory dying and the thought of Shaw... "I would have killed him myself." He spoke softly, but with deadly intent.

Carmen and Emmie glanced at each other and decided at that moment to make a swift departure. "Well, we're glad you're both unharmed. But we have to report back to Lorene. Steven, I'm sure your mother is sick with worry," Emmie said.

Both women hugged Glory once again and he walked them out. "Thank you for coming. Glad we didn't need those medical supplies."

"*Si,* we are also glad. Glory will stay with you now, no?" Carmen asked.

Steven swallowed down hard. Glory wouldn't need him. She was free and safe to do as she pleased. And the sooner she left, the sooner they'd both be able to get on with their lives. Steven shook his head. "Doubtful, Carmen. I plan on taking her back to Virginia City tomorrow."

Both Carmen and Emmie frowned, but kept silent.

"Tell my mother I'm fine. I'll try to come see her soon."

The women drove off in the buggy and he returned to the house. He was finally alone with Glory.

For their last night together.

* * *

Exhausted, Glory struggled with all that went on tonight. She sat quietly on her bed with Buddy on her lap, contemplating all that she might have lost this evening. Her life, for one. And Steven's. She'd be eternally grateful that Steven had survived the explosion and cave-in that might have killed him. She would never have recovered from his death. Her conscience wouldn't allow it. His loss would have shattered her.

She cared for Steven more than any other man she'd ever known yet, she still didn't know what was in her heart. She struggled constantly with her own lack of trust and faith. She had trouble forgiving. And most of all, she'd never known true freedom. She'd never been on her own before. Being the daughter of a minister had its drawbacks. So much had been expected of her. So much had been thrust upon her as a child and then as a young woman. Glory hadn't really known her own mind. She followed dutifully in her father's footsteps and then tried hard to be a devoted wife. This was her one chance to get it right.

She heard a sound and when she looked up she found Steven standing in the doorway watching her. He leaned against the door and tilted his head. "You ready to head back to Virginia City tomorrow?"

Glory stared into Steven's eyes. He'd shut himself off from her, the look he cast her, unreadable. "Father had a small home near the church. No one lives there now."

She'd been thinking about this for a time. The home had been part of the church grounds and when her father died, another minister had moved in. But to her knowledge, he'd only lasted in Virginia City for six months before moving on to a more sedate town in Colorado. The colorful trappings of Virginia City posed a challenge for many, the town being far different than most. With rowdy miners, dozens of brothels and saloons on every street and a lack of decent women, it took a special kind of clergyman to heed the call. Jonathan Caldwell had been just that kind of man. Ultimately, and unfortunately, that trait had led to his demise.

Steven nodded. "I'll take you back first thing."

Glory stood, bringing Buddy up with her. She clutched him close to her chest. "I can't thank you enough."

"I know, Glory. I know."

Their eyes met and held a long, long moment.

"Your obligation to me is over now," she said softly.

He squeezed his eyes shut as if warding off pain. She felt it, too, this feeling of loss, a hollow ache that refused to pass.

"Steven?" She set Buddy down.

He smiled sadly. "You'd best get some rest. I'll sleep out on the sofa. I'll be close, in case you need me."

"I need you now." Glory had known boldness tonight, pretending to be a temptress to catch a murderer, but this request came straight from her heart, without shame or dishonor. "Stay with me tonight."

Steven stepped into the room and her heart skidded a bit. "You'll regret it in the morning," he cautioned sharply.

She deserved that. She'd hurt him this morning and he couldn't hide the injury. But a compelling, overwhelming need to be held and loved by Steven once more had her throwing all pride aside. She shook her head. "No, I won't. I don't know what my future holds. There are so many uncertainties in my life. But I know I want this, Steven. All we have is tonight."

Steven took in a heavy breath. "I haven't got it in me to deny you, sweetheart."

Glory reached out to take his hand. "Then don't."

Steven denied her nothing. He'd made tender, passionate, urgent love to her during the night and they both experienced the bittersweet cravings of two souls who would soon part. Glory lay in bed, sensing the new day burgeoning on the horizon before even a tiny shred of light could be seen. Time was slipping away. Glory would leave the ranch to live in Virginia City once again.

Steven, whose body pressed against hers, tightened his hold as if he knew what she'd been thinking, even as he slept. She turned to him and he cradled her in his arms, a reflexive move that brought their naked bodies as close as two bodies could possibly get. She breathed in his scent, the strong virile smell of man and earth combined.

He opened his eyes, a small smile playing on his lips. A hot glimmer sparkled in those dark depths, the hungry gleam that spoke a silent ancient language— one that Glory could easily translate.

Steven brought his lips down on hers. Her body flamed with the same desperate urgency she'd experienced during the night. He kissed her deeply time and again, treasuring her mouth, caressing her skin, making every cell come alive. She returned his passion, stroking his body, moving as he moved, in tune with his rhythm and pace.

Dawn would soon spread light into the room. Morning beckoned, reminding her that this would be the last time she would be held in Steven's tight embrace. It would be the last time she would ever know this kind of desire.

They fought the light and battled the budding dawn. But as they reached for the midnight sky, together, with one last final grasp, sunlight broke through the darkness.

The new day had begun.

Chapter Nineteen

"It's a good piece of writing, Gloria Mae," Joe Goodman, publisher and editor of the *Enterprise* said, "but it surprises me some."

Glory hadn't been back in town two full days before her father's friend, a man who had spent many an evening dining with the Reverend and his young daughter in the past, had paid her a visit when she'd moved into the small home by the church. He'd graciously offered her a part-time job writing for his newspaper. She suspected his offer had more to do with his long-standing friendship with Jonathan Caldwell and a need to help, than with Glory's writing ability but regardless of the reason, Glory took the position, happy to have a purpose in life again.

"Why does it surprise you, Mr. Goodman?"

"Well," he began, searching the printed article with eagle-sharp eyes, "even you have to admit, up until this business with Ned Shaw, you'd been trying to shut down the brothels in town. But in this piece, you seem to sympathize with Trudy Tremaine's plight."

"She didn't deserve to die that way, soiled dove

or not. She'd been murdered unmercifully and Sheriff Brimley captured her killer. I reported the facts, as they were.''

''Yes, it's definitely an honest bit of writing. I suppose your stay at Rainbow House changed your mind about some things.'' Mr. Goodman peered down at her through his spectacles.

Glory hadn't revealed much to the outside world about her concealment during the past few weeks, but she had confided in her employer that she'd spent time at the brothel, as a guest. The facts were bound to come out sooner or later, but Steven had persuaded her not to speak of her stay at his ranch to anyone. He'd been protecting her again, trying to save her reputation.

The morning Steven brought her back to town had been a day wrought with many emotions. She had a home, which needed tidying and cleaning, but was certainly suitable for the present time. She had her freedom and the prospect of a decent future, but as she'd turned to say one last final goodbye to the man who had saved her life, Glory had the sinking feeling that she'd made yet another mistake.

Steven hadn't asked her to stay on at the ranch that morning. He'd gotten up early, hitched up the team and spoken little to her as the wagon ambled its way back to town.

And as he stood on her porch steps, granting her a small smile and best wishes for a good life, she felt herself shatter, a little at a time, breaking up into pieces that she feared she would never recapture. She'd never be complete again, those splintered fragments lost forever.

''Yes, I've learned a lot about life lately. And from

what I'd gathered about Trudy, she hadn't done anything to provoke her murder. I wrote a little about her background, the events that brought her to Virginia City and to the life of prostitution."

Mr. Goodman added, "You wanted the readers to see her as a person as well as a victim."

"Exactly. Her killer had been ruthless, bent on hurting someone that night. Unfortunately, it was Trudy."

Goodman nodded. "I suppose certain danger comes with that profession."

Glory had to agree. "Yes, danger comes with prostitution. Mercy, I'll never condone it, but the girls often have little choice. And they certainly don't deserve to die because of their lot in life."

Glory hadn't changed her mind about prostitution, but she had gained certain knowledge recently to make her see that life in a different light. Instead of disdain and aversion, she found herself more sympathetic to the ladies who had come to sell their bodies for a price. She understood them better now, knowing them as real women, with hearts that break, and souls that need redemption. Some of them, she knew as friends.

"Well, here's the next batch of statistics for you." Joe Goodman dropped a pile of papers on her desk. "Welcome to the world of publishing."

Glory peered at the papers, noting new births, deaths, and small blurbs of information on openings and closings of establishments in town. Aside from the article on Trudy, which Mr. Goodman had assigned to her because of her ties with Rainbow House, most of the articles she wrote were mundane, boring snippets that had to be included in the newspaper. As the newest and most inexperienced writer at the *Enterprise,* Glory understood that she wouldn't be given any choice pieces of news to report.

Glory walked home that night, feeling especially glum. She knew in her heart what the problem was—she missed Steven. She missed him with an aching that went far beyond anything she'd ever experienced before. And though she'd denied what she felt for so long, she knew now what was in her heart.

Glory sat down to a lonely meal, wondering if Steven did the same. Was he, too, staring at his food, without much hankering to eat, thinking about her?

It had been nearly a week since she'd seen him. She wondered how long Steven would remain lonely. Would he seek a woman for solace in the coming nights? Did he want to share his life and ranch with someone rather than lead a lonely existence?

That that woman couldn't be her tore her insides up. She hadn't the forgiveness. Her cold heart wouldn't allow her to forget that Steven was Lorene Harding's son. Her soul might burn in hell, but Glory held firm to her beliefs, like a rigid wall that she couldn't break down.

Glory went to bed that night with a heavy heart, hugging Buddy close. The dog that Steven insisted she keep was her only source of comfort, although she had no call to complain.

She had her freedom. She had a nice home and a good job. She even had a few gentlemen callers, whom she'd politely but flatly refused.

The only thing missing was happiness.

The next day Glory stood just beyond the shadows of a pine tree, saying a prayer at her father's grave.

She bent down and brushed dried brown needles from the headstone, speaking softly, knowing that her father heard her every word. She shed tears, the pain of his death still fresh in her heart, and wondered if time would ever heal her wounds.

Standing there, feeling close to him, she thought about the unselfish, caring man who had loved her and loved his God without compromise or condition. She wondered why she wasn't more like him. She wondered about what she lacked inside to keep this pain so raw, the hostility over his death so clear in her mind. "I wish I could forgive, Father."

A tear flowed down her cheek, then another and another. She swiped at them swiftly, loathing self-pity and unwilling to give in to it. "I miss you, Father," she said, before standing to leave the cemetery.

"Hello, Gloria Mae."

Glory turned abruptly to find Lorene Harding bending down to lay a small bouquet of wildflowers on the headstone. Lorene was the last person on earth Glory expected to see here. Shocked and confused, a panicked thought struck. "What are you doing here? Is something wrong with Steven? Did the sheriff change his mind? Is Steven in—"

"Steven's fine," she assured her. "Well, about as fine as you are. And I can see by your concern for my son that I wasn't wrong to come here today."

"Why are you here?" Glory asked with great curiosity.

Lorene's eyes flashed with pain, it seemed, then she smiled sadly and spoke with a softness Glory had never heard from her. "I come here often. I miss Jonathan, too."

"Jonathan? You speak as though you knew him."

Lorene nodded and glanced down at the grave. "I knew him well. He was a dear friend."

More than a little surprised, Glory refused to believe her. She refused to acknowledge that her father had anything untoward to do with Lorene Harding. No, she knew her father. He was a simple man with great faith. She knew him better than anyone. He was not a man to be entertained in the brothels. "You couldn't possibly have known him that way."

Lorene glanced away a moment, drawing in a breath. When she returned her gaze to Glory's, tears misted in her eyes. "No, I didn't know him that way. But there's more to me—to both of us—than you might imagine."

Glory stared at Steven's mother, who wore a stately gown of dark-green silk and a matching hat crowning her head in elegance. She tried to see her as being other than a whorehouse madam, attempting without much success to disengage her perception of the woman Glory had always thought her to be.

"Let's sit, shall we?" Lorene offered, gesturing to a small bench in the shade not far from the gravesite. "It's time we talked."

Numb, Glory walked alongside of Lorene, wondering what Steven's mother possibly had to say to her. A small breeze blew by, cooling the air somewhat, and a choir of birds chirped in harmony as Glory lowered herself down on one side of the wooden seat. Lorene sat also and for a moment, both were silent.

"I want to begin by saying I mean you no harm, but it's time that you knew the truth about Jonathan and me."

Jonathan and me. A lump lodged in Glory's throat.

Just hearing the two names in the same sentence caused her a measure of anguish. "What truth is that?"

With directness, Lorene squared her an honest look. "Your father and I were old friends. Dear friends. At one time, and it seems like an eternity ago, we were in love."

"No!" Glory shook her head, shocked with disbelief.

"Gloria Mae," Lorene said with quiet calm, "I was young once, like you. I had dreams and hopes of a wonderful future. I met your father in Boston when we were both very young. We fell in love, a first love. And we planned on a life together, but then my family hit on hard times and we moved away to live with my grandmother. My folks took me West and we settled on a small homestead in Colorado. The separation was hard for both of us. Jonathan had always planned on being a minister. It was his lifeblood, what he was meant to do. We lost contact and over the years we took different paths in life. We both married someone else."

"But this is all so unbelievable. Father never told me. He never hinted."

"That was because of me. No one was to know. You see, after Steven's father abandoned us, I had to find a way to survive. By then, my folks were gone and I had no other family. I found work in a supper house. Often, I'd work just to bring home food at the end of the day. Seems like we kept traveling farther west, wherever there was a prospect of a better job. I even spent time working in a Chinese laundry in San Francisco, but it wasn't nearly enough to keep Steven fed and put a roof over his head. We lived from day to day, until one day, I figured it wasn't living at all.''

"Your story isn't so different from Julia's or Emmie's." Glory voiced her thoughts aloud. "Or the others."

"The stories are all different, but so very much the same."

"Yes, so it seems," Glory admitted even as her stomach churned. She tried desperately to cling to her own beliefs, what she'd always thought to be the truth. It didn't set well that Lorene Harding could march over here and turn Glory's world upside down.

"It was fate that brought Jonathan and I together in Virginia City. By then, I had Rainbow House and my girls and he had you, of course, a beautiful young daughter. He had a home and his ministry. I made him promise not to let a soul know about our past. Your father was a very noble, honest and respected man, and that's the exact reason I wouldn't let any association with me become known. Our time together, our one chance at happiness, had come and gone. We'd both moved on. We'd both had different lives.''

Lorene leaned forward, coming a bit closer to Glory and reached out to place a hand on her arm. "I don't want to cause you any suffering, Lord knows you've had enough, but I must say that I never stopped loving your father. And I believe that he never stopped loving me."

Glory closed her eyes, her heart speeding faster than a jackrabbit. "My father...he still loved you?"

"Yes, we loved each other as friends. We'd lost our chance at love, but we still clung to that friendship. Sometimes, after his Sunday sermons we would meet, just to see each other and talk. They were secretive meetings, Gloria Mae, but innocent.''

Glory's eyes meet with Lorene's in understanding. She nodded. ''Yes, they would be.''

She sat there in silence, listening once again to the jays twittering and the soft sound of the easy wind blowing by. After a time, Glory peered at Lorene with curiosity. ''Why are you telling me this? Why now?''

Lorene smiled halfheartedly. ''Because I know you blame me for your father's death. And believe me, I blame myself for it as well. I've suffered his death each day. But you must know that Jonathan didn't just wander by that day and get mixed up in a tussle. He knew what he was facing. He knew that man aimed to shoot me. Your father shoved me away and stepped in the path of that bullet. He gave his life to save mine. It was a deliberate act of courage and bravery.''

Glory's heart thudded in her chest. ''Because he loved you.''

''Yes, because he loved me. He thought my life was worth saving. And I would have done the same for him if given the chance.''

A sole tear spilled down Glory's cheek. Wrapped up in emotional turmoil, Glory didn't have words. She sat there stonily, absorbing all that she'd learned today. Everything she'd come to know, everything she'd believed in her life, had changed somehow, in one afternoon.

No, that wasn't entirely true. She'd changed her opinion about the Rainbow girls after coming to know them. She'd lived with them for a time, helped to save one, perhaps, but she cared deeply for them all. Just a short time ago, she'd despised who and what they were and now, she thought of those women as her friends.

Lorene patted her hand once, then stood. ''I thought you should know. I think Jonathan would approve. He never wanted to keep our friendship a secret. I was the one who had insisted.''

Lorene smiled, this time in earnest, bringing light to her eyes and rosy color to her face. ''As far as the 'why now' question, I think you know the answer to that, Gloria Mae. Just search your heart.''

Glory searched her heart all through the evening, finding solace and truth. Peace had finally settled within her as she opened her Bible that night to Luke 6:37 and read a passage aloud, finally allowing the wise words to sink in.

'''Judge not, and ye shall not be judged: condemn not, and ye shall not be condemned: forgive, and ye shall be forgiven.'''

Glory's heart had finally opened up. She'd finally let go her anguish and pain. She knew now that she could move on with life without hostility toward anyone. She wouldn't hold Lorene Harding responsible for her father's death any longer, for to do so would be the ultimate betrayal of him and his great sacrifice. Her father had given his life protecting Lorene. He had loved her, without condemnation. He had not judged her harshly as Glory once had.

She mused that even from his grave, her father still had lessons to teach. And Glory had learned, had her faith restored. Oh, she still missed him terribly and wished the events that had occurred one year ago hadn't happened, but she was free now to pursue her dreams.

By rights, she was a wealthy woman. After clearing up details at the claims office days ago, Glory had hired four down-on-their-luck miners to work her claim. She paid them more than fairly for an honest day's work and the claim continued to produce revenue, a flow of money that Glory had never seen before. She'd never want for anything again, except that she did.

She wanted Steven.

But he hadn't asked her to stay.

Like an injured bird that could fly again, he'd liberated her and set her free.

"I don't want to be free," she muttered as she lowered herself down to sleep that night.

Loneliness surrounded her much like the cloak she'd worn to conceal herself while hiding out. It covered her with despair and tightened around her heart with sorrow. She stretched out and hugged her pillow, hoping to dream of Steven.

Morning dawned too quickly, it seemed. Glory had slept fitfully, tossing and turning, unable to find comfort. And as she knew a great measure of forgiveness now, she feared it had come far too late. What was it Lorene had said yesterday as she spoke of her relationship with her father?

Our time together, our one chance at happiness had come and gone.

Was that true of her and Steven as well? Had their time together come and gone? Had they lost their one chance at happiness?

Glory rose and dressed. She entered the small kitchen area, where she'd often sat with her father on Sunday mornings as they talked about their coming day. He'd test out his sermon on her and she'd give him her youthful advice. On more than one occasion, her father had heeded her ideas and then thanked her once the sermon was over. Melancholy seeped in, a bittersweet reminder of how fragile, how very precious love is.

As she sipped her second cup of coffee, loud knocking at her door startled her, nearly causing her to spill the hot liquid onto her hand. She couldn't fathom who'd be visiting so early in the morning.

Glory walked to the door, peered though the curtained window then thrust the door wide open. Glory faced Carmen, Ruby and Emmie. ''Mercy, this is a surprise!''

''It is a bigger surprise to us. We are up at the very crack of dawn, no?'' Carmen said.

''May we come in?'' Emmie asked politely.

''Oh, of course.'' She ushered them inside. ''Can I get you something to eat? I have coffee and there's plenty of food.''

''No, there's no need. Mattie fixed us a plate earlier,'' Ruby said.

''Well, sit down, then,'' Glory said, gesturing to the sofa. ''I'm so happy to see all of you.''

''We have no time to sit. We have the wagon waiting outside. We're taking you away for the day,'' Ruby announced.

Pleasantly surprised, Glory smiled. She couldn't think of a better way to spend her day. ''You are? Where are we going?''

The ladies glanced at each other, then Emmie piped up, ''On a picnic. We have planned quite a pleasant outing.''

''Oh, that sounds lovely.''

Glory was beside herself with joy. She'd been so

lonely lately, and had only Mr. Goodman and the few who wrote for the *Enterprise* to break up the monotony of the day. Going on a picnic on a Sunday morning with friends seemed absolutely perfect.

"Well, grab a wrap and take the dog," Ruby said, smiling when she spotted the red shawl she'd given Glory draped across a wing chair. "We should get going."

Glory took up the shawl, picked up a lazy Buddy and followed the ladies out the front door. They boarded the wagon, Ruby driving the team with Carmen in the front, Emmie and Glory on the bench just behind. They ambled out of town, heading south, the girls chatting and laughing all the while, enjoying the ride. Ruby praised the article Glory had written about Trudy Tremaine, Carmen recited a few verses from the Bible and Emmie relayed tales of Mattie's latest cooking adventures. Buddy spent his time running from one end of the wagon to the other, barking happily at being included in this adventure.

Glory relished the ride and the conversation. She'd lost track of time, but realized that they'd gone quite far from town, passing up many wonderful picnic spots along the way.

Suddenly, Glory recognized the terrain—the certain bend in the road that led to Steven's ranch. "Mercy," she said, leaning back in her seat. "What are you all planning?"

Giggles erupted and knowing glances, but not one of the women responded to her question.

"Carmen?"

"You will see," she answered.

"Ruby?"

"My, it's beautiful up here," Ruby reflected. "Don't you agree, Emmie?"

Emmie grinned, ignoring Glory's intense stare. "Yes, just lovely."

Within minutes, the wagon pulled to a stop in front of the ranch house. Steven stood on the porch, watching, his dark eyes gleaming. Buddy barked his greeting and jumped down, racing toward the barn, apparently happy to be back at the ranch.

Glory's heart did a giant flip. It had been more than a week since she'd seen Steven, the separation seeming more like an eternity. Buddy wasn't the only one happy to be back here.

Steven shook his head at the girls. "You ladies don't give a man a chance."

He helped each one of them down from the wagon. And when it was Glory's turn, he wrapped his hands around her waist, lifting her with ease, his gaze never wavering. He held her tight, planting her safely on the ground, yet Glory felt weightless as though she were floating. They stared into each others' eyes.

Ruby interrupted the moment. "You can't keep a sweet young gal like Glory waiting too long now, Steven. There's a herd of young men in town wanting to court her."

"That so?" Steven asked, applying slight pressure to her waist, his eyes resting solely on her.

"We heard she had three gentlemen callers already. She turned them down flat."

He smiled and gave a little squeeze before releasing her. He turned, announcing to the women, "I had some work to finish here. I was coming for her *tomorrow*."

"Coming for me?" Glory asked, guarding her heart from too much hope.

"We'll be leaving now," Ruby said with a grin, and the women bounded back onto the wagon without pause. Ruby took up the reins. "We've done our part, now it's up to you. Bye, Glory."

Stunned, Glory gave a small wave to her friends and watched the wagon circle around to make its way off the property, the girls waving back and giggling their goodbyes.

Glory turned to find Steven beside her. "Steven?"

He took her hand and helped her up onto his newly finished veranda. The floorboards beneath her feet squeaked with newness. She'd noticed the work he'd done since she'd been gone. He'd been a busy man, but right now, he seemed intent on busying himself with her.

He flashed her a hot, hungry gaze, but Glory also witnessed something else in his eyes—something she'd never seen in him before, vulnerability. "I wanted to finish the house before coming for you. I wanted to offer you a home—my home. The time I spent here with you was the best in my life. Don't tell me it was a mistake. It couldn't possibly be. Not when living here without you, seems like the biggest blunder of my life."

"Oh, Steven. I realize now I was the one mistaken." Lorene had helped her see that. She'd helped her understand that opportunities don't come along too often in life. Glory wouldn't let this chance for happiness pass her by. "My time with you…was the best in my life, as well. I loved living here."

Steven wrapped her in a tight embrace. The wondrous feel of his arms around her created tingles that shot down to her toes. His gaze softened to a light caress and she trembled when he cast her a beautiful smile. "I loved living here, too...because I love you. You made this place a real home for me, Glory."

He brought his mouth down, claiming her lips. Glory whimpered slightly, the heady familiar touch nearly too much for her.

"We can put the past behind us and start a new life, together, right here. Would you consider being a rancher's wife, sweetheart? Will you marry me?"

Glory had no doubts now. She'd learned so much about life and love from Steven. He'd taught her how a man could be gentle and powerful at the same time. He'd taught her what it meant to share their bodies, their minds and their hearts, without fear and recrimination. He'd taught her so many things. She was anxious to learn more. "Yes, Steven. Yes. I'll be your wife." Glory sent up a prayer of thanks to the Lord. She'd almost lost it all, only to be given a new chance, a future filled with promise.

Yes, she would marry this strong, tender man. She would love him with her whole heart, bear him children and have the life she'd always dreamed about. Her thoughts turned to her father. He would approve. He would be happy about the union. Too bad he and Lorene, whose paths had been so different, hadn't found a way to breach that gap. Too bad they hadn't found a way back to each other. But she and Steven had and she planned to live a happy life with Steven always by her side.

Steven kissed her deeply then took her hand, leading her to a work area by the barn. "I couldn't think up a name for the ranch, until I met you." He smiled and pointed out a new sign, with the wood etched out and halfway painted.

She looked down at the marker that would give claim to the ranch. ''The Triple G?''

Steven nodded, taking her into his arms and speaking the words that he'd be whispering for thousands of nights to come.

''Glory…glory…glory.''

FALL IN LOVE WITH
FOUR HANDSOME HEROES
FROM HARLEQUIN HISTORICALS.

On sale May 2004

THE ENGAGEMENT
by Kate Bridges

Inspector Zack Bullock
North-West Mounted Police officer

HIGH COUNTRY HERO
by Lynna Banning

Cordell Lawson
Bounty hunter, loner

On sale June 2004

THE UNEXPECTED WIFE
by Mary Burton

Matthias Barrington
Widowed ranch owner

THE COURTING OF WIDOW SHAW
by Charlene Sands

Steven Harding
Nevada rancher

Visit us at www.eHarlequin.com

HARLEQUIN HISTORICALS®

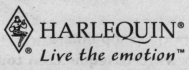

Savor these stirring tales of romance with Harlequin Historicals

On sale May 2004

THE LAST CHAMPION by Deborah Hale

Once betrothed, then torn apart by civil war,
will Dominie de Montford put aside her pride and
seek out Armand Flambard's help to save her estate
from a vicious outlaw baron?

THE DUKE'S MISTRESS by Ann Elizabeth Cree

Years ago Lady Isabelle Milborne had participated in her late
husband's wager, which had ruined Justin, the Duke of Westmore.
And now the duke will stop at nothing to see justice served.

On sale June 2004

THE COUNTESS BRIDE by Terri Brisbin

A young count must marry a highborn lady in order
to inherit his lands. But a poor young woman with a
mysterious past is the only one he truly desires....

A POOR RELATION by Joanna Maitland

Desperate to avoid fortune hunters,
Miss Isabella Winstanley poses as a penniless
chaperone. But will she allow herself to be
ensnared by the dashing Baron Amburley?